CATCH ME, ALPHA

EMILIA ROSE

ISBN: 978-1-954597-08-2

Cover by: The Book Brander

Editing by: Jovana Shirley, Unforeseen Editing, www.unforeseenediting.com

Proofreading by: Zainab M., Heart Full of Reads Editing Services

Beta reading by: Leshae Scheepers, Brittany Pugh, Kayla Lutz

Emilia Rose

emiliarosewriting@gmail.com

To Sean.
Thank you for believing in me.

TRIGGER WARNING

This book contains dark themes, such as memories of sexual
assault and violence. If these are trigger topics for you, I
suggest not reading further.

CHAPTER 1

ARES

"We're all going to die here," Aurora whispered, peering down into the hole we had dug inside her brother's cave. It dropped off into a deeper epicenter cavern with monstrously jagged rocks hanging from the ceiling, torches perched on the walls every few meters, and twenty pathways diverging from the center.

With canary-yellow foam seeping from their mouths, hounds patrolled around an array of at least a hundred dead wolf carcasses and bones directly underneath us. Laid out in rows of ten by thirteen, each fallen wolf had a white orb floating above his or her head.

"We should go," I said to Aurora, grabbing her hand. "Now."

Something about this wasn't sitting right with me.

Aurora hesitated and glanced down into the hole, digging her claws into the dirt. Strands of dirty-brown hair fell into her face, hindering my view of it. The thick stench of blood drifted through the air, making Ruffles scurry away in disgust. Refusing to stay here much longer, I yanked on Aurora's arm.

But she didn't move.

"Mom," she whispered, voice on the verge of cracking.

Among the fallen wolves underground, Aurora's mother—the woman I'd torn to pieces and the woman Aurora had buried mere days ago—laid in the center with her throat ripped out, her eyes glazed over, and her skin a discolored gray.

"Calm down," I whispered into her ear. I placed a hand over her trembling lips to muffle her cries, yet Aurora started heaving uncontrollably. "They're going to hear you."

"What ... are they ... doing to her?" she asked me, her tears catching on my index finger.

I swallowed hard and watched the white orbs pulse above each wolf's chest. If I had known what they were doing down here, I wouldn't have come, because this looked like some dark magic shit that I wanted no part in.

The asshole who had killed my mother walked into the cavern with dragon tattoos etched into the side of his head, fresh scars covering his body, and dead eyes that had seemed to come alive when he saw Aurora the other day. He must've relished in the thought of being able to take another close family member away from me.

Walking down each row of wolves, he whispered something to them. Even with my amplified wolf hearing, I couldn't understand what he had said because it sounded like a dead, ancient language but not quite Latin. Instead, the words came almost divine. *Almost.*

After he strolled back and forth down all the rows, he stood in front of the fallen, lifted his hands to the ceiling, and waited. The white orbs sank into the bodies of the dead wolves and disappeared inside of them.

Toward the right, one dead man's toes twitched.

And then, suddenly, at least half of the wolves started moving.

4

Aurora tensed beside me and grasped my hand.

The wolves stood to their full height, their fatal wounds still carved out of their bodies. Some wolves were mere bones held together by the thinnest shred of tendons and ligaments. Yet … these weren't normal wolves anymore. A murky haze lay in their eyes, the same kind that *all hounds* had.

I stared at them in complete shock, my heart pounding inside my chest. *How has he …*

"More," Mom's rapist shouted. "Make me more!"

"Aurora," I said through the mind link, pulling her closer. *"We have to go now. We can't stay."*

Hounds, rogues, demons, or whatever abominations they were, there were too many of them for us to stand around here, just waiting to be caught. We couldn't fucking defeat them all by ourselves. We needed backup—warriors, packs, a damn army—to defeat the undead hounds.

The group of basically soulless hounds marched through the cavern and disappeared down one of the desolate pathways. While most of the wolves had come back to life, some didn't. Scattered around the cave, bones lay in piles with the white orbs pulsing above them still.

Mom's rapist walked to one, absorbed the orb through his fingertips, and brushed his callous fingers against the decaying and dry bone. And that was when I smelled it.

Mom.

I didn't have to see her to know that those were her bones lying in that cave or that he had removed her skeleton from her grave or that the hound who had destroyed her was trying to bring her back to life.

A growl ripped its way from my throat at the mere scent. The hound lifted his nose, stared right up at me through the small hole in the ceiling, and roared back in return. If he wanted to disturb Mom's peace as she ran with the wolves in the clouds with the Moon Goddess, then he'd have to fight me for it.

Aurora grabbed my hand, yanked me toward the exit of the cave, and sprinted toward home. "We're going to die," she said, running into the sudden fog. It had been sunny mere moments ago. "You said it yourself, Ares; there are too many of them to fight. Calm down."

Though I wanted to stay and kill that man, I hurried after Aurora. I needed to protect her, especially because she couldn't protect herself. It would take her at least five minutes to shift if we had to fight, and there were hundreds of undead hounds down in that cave.

I scooped up Ruffles in my arms. "Faster, Aurora."

Weaving in and out around trees, hopping over roots, ducking under branches, Aurora ran faster than I had ever seen her run as she easily retraced the steps back to her mother's pack house, which was closer than ours.

Birds flapped their wings, hurrying to get out of our way, and disappeared higher up into the trees. Paws hit the ground hard behind us, becoming louder by the second. We were screwed, fucking screwed.

"Aurora," I said through the mind link, *"can you shift?"*

I was itching to shift, seconds away from turning around and killing this hound once and for all. Thick, unruly rage pumped through my veins as the urge only intensified in me.

"No, I can't shift that quickly. They'd catch up to us."

Ruffles climbed up my chest and peered over my shoulder, hissing in my ear. I plucked her off of me and tossed her into Aurora's arms. She clawed her way up Aurora's chest, wrapped her arms around her shoulders, and bared her teeth at the woods behind us.

"Then, you have to run," I said. *"No matter what you hear, don't stop until you reach our pack. If I'm not back in ten minutes after you arrive, prepare our warriors for battle. We are not going to die this way."*

Losing all control, I shifted into my monstrous brown wolf.

After digging my heels into the dirt and sliding against sharp rocks and branches, I turned around to glare into the dense white fog that sat heavily in the forest, almost making it impossible to see.

Defying everything I'd commanded her to do, Aurora grasped Ruffles and stopped beside me. I growled at her, warning her to leave. Instead of listening, she drew her silver dagger from her back pocket and crouched in a fighting stance, holding it in front of her. Ruffles jumped down between her legs, head low and ass wiggling, as if she was getting ready to attack.

"We do this together," Aurora said.

I growled again in both wicked rage and immense pride. Our mate was a warrior, our luna was a protector, and if we somehow survived today, our pack would be stronger than every other pack in Sanguine Wilds.

Five hounds barreled through the forest with their paths headed straight for Aurora because she was the one with the stone in her back. They were attracted to that thing for some ungodly reason—a reason we needed to figure out as soon as fucking possible.

Taking the brunt of their attacks, I killed one hound at a time.

They should've been weak and recovering from the hound attack last week, yet their strength today far exceeded their strength a few days ago. It didn't make sense, but it didn't matter right now. All that mattered was protecting my mate and Ruffles.

With the dirt in my claws, I cut through each one and trusted that Aurora and Ruffles could kill off any ones that slipped past me. As I grabbed another one in my bloodied paw, I scanned the woods for others. There were at least a hundred hiding within the trees. Where were they now?

Yet while I couldn't hear anyone, I could feel the gaze of their leader on me.

He watched me from somewhere deep in the woods, making my fucking blood boil. The ache to slaughter him grew more intense with every moment that went by. I let out a low, threatening growl through the fog.

"Keep one of them alive," Aurora said, standing over two dead hounds. "We can use him."

I sank my teeth into the third hound's arm, broke his bones, and ripped his limb right from his body. Howling in pain, the hound fell to the ground. After I was positive that nobody else was going to attack, I shifted into my human form and snatched him by the neck.

Infused with whatever kind of dark magic this was, the hounds were becoming stronger and more violent. We needed to mobilize our pack and other packs quickly if we wanted to survive because it was clear that the hounds had already begun raising an army ...

An army of the dead.

The eerie feeling of Mom's rapist scrutinizing us disappeared. Aurora snatched Ruffles in her arms and patted down her puffed-up fur, whispering to her that we were safe for now. And while we might be, one thing was certain.

I'd be back to slaughter that man even if it was with the last breath I took.

CHAPTER 2

AURORA

*L*ong after we'd killed those hounds, I clutched the silver dagger to my chest and walked onto our property with Ares. The fog had almost instantly cleared, but still, my mind was clouded with so many questions. Were hounds really created from the flesh and blood of innocent wolves? Was that what Jeremy had wanted me to find out? He had said that the hounds were out for some kind of divine revenge, but ... this was more than I'd expected.

And what about Mom? Mere days ago, I'd laid her to rest behind her old pack house while hundreds of her pack wolves looked on. The hounds had cold heartedly dug her up from the ground, brought her down into that cavern, and made her a monster. What would I tell my old packmates?

The hounds were raising an army of undead wolves for a battle, which seemed to be against us for some reason.

Ruffles rubbed her face against my neck, her soft fur only slightly calming me. Townsmen and women whispered to each other as we walked with the hound almost lifelessly dragging behind us. Warriors scrambled to prepare a prison cell.

We needed to understand what this was all about before that army could attack us again because an attack by a pack of hounds that large would undoubtedly destroy this entire pack. Ares might be the god of war who thirsted for the blood of his enemies, but our pack wasn't zombie-hounds strong. Not yet at least.

When we walked by the training field, Marcel made announcements to the warriors, waved everyone off for the morning, and jogged over to us. Charolette sat on a small hill with her arms crossed over her chest and a scowl on her face as she glared at Marcel. Although I didn't know what they were fighting about *this time*, it was probably—definitely—about the Malavite Stone.

With his foot, Ares kicked the prison door open before the guards could get it for us. The hound smacked against each wooden step that Ares descended and howled in pain through his snout.

Marcel followed us down the stairs. "What's with the one arm? You do that to him, Roar?"

Ares growled at Marcel for nicknaming me and pivoted on his heel to posture over his strongest warrior. Since we'd left the cave earlier, Ares had been on edge and ready to slaughter anyone who stepped on his bad side. The smallest remark would set that man off.

Swinging open a cell door, Ares hurled the hound into the chamber next to Dad. Dad decided not to acknowledge my existence as he scraped his nails against the hard stone floor, sending a shiver down my back.

I tried to ignore him. Ruffles brushed her fur against my calf and waved her gray tail back and forth, watching with magically wide eyes as Ares snapped the cage's lock. Purring as if she thought it was the sexiest thing in the world, Ruffles rubbed against his ankle.

Ares relaxed just a bit. "We have a problem."

Marcel leaned back against the stone wall and crossed his big arms over each other, his greasy silver hair falling into his face. "We have a lot of problems," he grunted and nodded toward the cage Liam sat in. "Like, when you finally let me kill him, who will become the next beta? How will you convince Charolette to use the fucking stone? How are we going to find Charolette's father?"

Ares growled, "That hound did nothing to father her."

Ruffles meowed at me to pick her up. When I grabbed her, she did her infamous *look someone up and down and then look away* gaze, giving Marcel a sassy attitude, like she did with almost everyone who wasn't Ares.

"The hounds are raising their army, one dead wolf at a time," I said with a breath.

Marcel furrowed his brows, creasing his forehead. "What the hell are you talking about?"

"The hounds—"

"What is your damn problem, Marcel?" Charolette shrieked, storming down the creaky wooden stairs. Gaze fixed on Marcel and thin arms crossed over her chest, she turned her body toward Ares. "You want to know what he said to me during practice? He said—"

Ares growled to silence her, the sound echoing through the small red-lit dungeon. "The only thing I want to know is when you're having your surgery," he said to her.

Everyone in the room fell into a deafening silence; even the mice that Ruffles liked chasing around at night didn't squeak.

Fuming with anger, Charolette balled her hands into fists and stormed back up the stairs. Liam glanced at her departing figure through the cell bars. When she slammed the door, unused cuffs and torture equipment attached to the ceiling by silver chains clattered against the side stone wall.

Though I wanted to ask her why she didn't want the surgery done, I couldn't get myself to follow her.

I'd asked her about twenty times to have the surgery to insert the stone in her spine, and I was tired of hearing the words, "No, I don't want it."

Strongly against using any sort of divine rock in her back, she either had already accepted her death or just really wanted to piss off her brother. It was important for her to live, but it was even more important to protect this whole pack from an unavoidable war that could kill us all.

Ares stepped toward the exit and sighed. "Can you talk to her?" he asked me.

Ruffles meowed in response for me, hopped out of my hold, and walked up the stairs. I rolled my eyes at her *more dramatic than usual* ass and followed her toward the heavy stone door.

"You should call a meeting with the other alphas in the region. We need more than our pack for this war," I shouted before I left the prison.

After shoving the door open, Ruffles and I hurried after Charolette. "Wait up!"

"Please don't try to convince me, Aurora. I've made up my mind. I just need someone to support my decision," she said, refusing to turn around.

Once I caught up to her, Ruffles looked at her and meowed.

"Stop it, Ruffles," I said down to her. I grabbed Charolette's hand. "Why are you against it? I talked to Elijah and his doctor. They're willing to do it to help you get better."

Charolette stared at me with a blank face. "Why don't you use the stone to shift more easily? I don't need it. It won't even help me," she said as if she already knew the outcome. "Ares looked for that thing for years when I told him not to. I don't want it."

"It might help you," I said, desperate for her to consider using the stone. If Ares lost his sister after losing his mother, he might just break. And I honestly wanted Charolette to be able to live a worry-free life. "You might be able to grow older with Marcel and have pups and—"

She gagged and scrunched her nose. "Marcel? Are you serious? I would never date him. He's a man-whore; he fucks anything with a freaking pulse." She looked at her socks, stained with dirt from practice, and clenched her jaw. "It's not like he wants me anyway."

"Oh, come on. I know you two are mates."

A breeze blew slightly, making the first withering leaves of autumn break off the trees and fall to the ground. Ruffles ran ahead to swat at the brown leaves with her paw and then jumped on them, listening to the crunch.

Charolette snapped her head toward me. "Did he tell you that? He's such a—"

"No," I assured. "He didn't tell me anything. I can just tell."

Suddenly, she fell quiet and looked down at her feet, shoulders slumping forward. "We're never going to be together, so it doesn't even matter." She waved it off as if it were nothing, even though I could feel the desperation in every one of her words.

She wanted there to be more, and I knew there could be if she took the stone.

After another moment of silence, she grabbed my hand and intertwined our fingers. "Soooo, the Luna Ceremony is soon!" she said, changing the subject and squealing. "Are you excited to officially become our luna? I cannot wait for it! We have to go dress shopping! I've had this day planned for Ares's mate since I was seven."

The Luna Ceremony—the night I would officially be announced and recognized as Luna of the Ironmane Pack to others in Sanguine Wilds—was in less than two weeks. And neither Ares nor I had time to even prepare for a party, especially not amidst a war with divine intervention.

"I don't think you should get too excited," I said, tucking some hair behind my ear. "We might not be able to have it. We spotted hounds today—too many hounds to take much of a break."

Charolette grasped my hands and held them to her chest. "We'll have it, no matter what. Don't you worry. Ares is going to want to properly introduce you as his luna. Mom always dreamed of it. He won't let her dream die with her."

After Charolette had easily weaseled her way out of using the stone, I bought some chips from Mad Moon Grocery for Ruffles. She had been eating more than usual lately, and I thought she had even hooked Ares on them.

I readjusted her blue hat and swung the pink plastic bag by my side as we walked back toward the pack house. Preoccupied with thoughts about how we could defeat a growing number of hounds, I almost missed when Ruffles came to a sudden stop at the head of an alleyway.

A Siamese cat popped his head out of an empty Pringles can and glanced over at Ruffles. They looked at each other for a few moments, until he finally walked over and sniffed her butt. Ruffles glanced back at him. After allowing it for mere moments, she batted him across the face with her paw and then walked away, swaying her ass from side to side, like she did with Ares.

The Siamese cat meowed at her. She looked back at him, gave him her signature *don't fuck with me* stare, and continued walking back home. I smiled at the cat, watching him return to the Pringles bottle before I continued the walk home with Ruffles.

"So, Ruffles," I said, shutting the pack house doors behind us. "Did you finally find your own man?"

Instead of answering me like she normally did, she sprinted up the stairs to her bedroom, like a teenager would after being confronted about dating someone for the first time. I smirked at the empty wooden stairs and crossed my arms over my chest, smelling Ares's sweet aroma drifting through the house.

Ares wrapped his arms around me from behind and stuck his nose into my hair. "Are you jealous of our cat?" he asked, his voice all rough and edgy. It made me warm in all those sinful places.

"No."

Maybe.

Wrapping his hand around the front of my neck, he pushed me against the wall. "I'm all yours, Kitten." Ares sucked on my mark between his lips and drew his tongue over the small scars from his canines, making me shiver in delight. "Especially after this morning."

"After this morning?" I asked, digging my claws into the wall until the white paint chipped.

"You don't know how turned on I was when you took out this little dagger of yours"—he pulled my silver knife from my back pocket and tossed it onto the side table—"and killed those hounds with me." He pressed his hardness into my backside, slipped his hand into my pants, and gently teased my clit. "It made me want to take you right then and there."

Heat gathered in my core. I pushed him away and walked backward up the stairs. "What happened to you, *Alpha*? The Ares I met at the lake would've taken me right then and there. He wouldn't have waited."

Ares growled lowly and stalked up the stairs toward me with darkening brown eyes. "*Kitten*, don't taunt me."

Wanting to tease him just a bit today, I shrugged my shoulders and tried to suppress a giggle. "I guess that man is gone," I said, and immediately sprinted up the rest of the stairs, knowing that Ares would catch me and make me his.

Before I could make it into the hallway, Ares caught my wrist, twirled me around, wrapped his hand around my throat, and pushed me down the hallway. I stumbled backward and stared up into his glowing golden eyes as his hand tightened around my throat.

He let out a guttural growl from deep within him and roughly brushed his thumb over my jaw. "Keep talking, and you'll end up on your knees."

I'd take kneeling in front of Ares as punishment any day.

I seized his wrist, my cheeks flushing, and said, "So ... *weak*."

After shoving me onto my knees in the middle of our hallway, Ares clutched my chin and forced me to look up at him. He stepped closer to me, so his bulge in his gray sweatpants was inches from my mouth. "I don't have to tell you what to do, do I?"

Deciding to play with him, I *innocently* stared up at my alpha through my lashes, my core clenching in anticipation. All I wanted was for him to take me savagely, like he had the morning he marked me in the prison.

After a few moments of my defiance, Ares grabbed me by the throat again, pulled out his hard cock, and rubbed it against my lips, coating them in his pre-cum. "Open your mouth and suck it," he demanded. And when I didn't, he slapped his dick against my swollen lips. "*Open.*"

Needing it now, I parted my lips and stuck out my tongue. He slapped his cock against it over and over as the heat built in my core.

He grasped my jaw to hold my mouth open, pushed his head into me, and then pulled it out. "You're going to have to beg for it now."

"Please."

He gifted me with another inch and pulled himself out again. "Beg."

"Please, Ares."

Another inch. "Louder."

"Goddess, Ares, please give it to—"

He shoved his cock all the way down my throat until his balls pressed against my lips. And even then, he forced more of himself into me until they were in my mouth. I stared up at him through big, teary eyes, gagging and slobbering on his cock, just like how he wanted me to.

Ares lightly smacked the back of my head with his hand, ramming his cock even further down my throat. After pushing deeper into me, he wrapped his hand around the front of my neck and jerked himself off inside of it.

I placed my hands on his thighs to push him away, but he held me tighter against him.

"Let me see your pretty eyes, Kitten," he purred.

I glanced up at him through my lashes, my cheeks flushing.

"You look so damn sexy with my cock down your throat."

Goddess, I love this so fucking much.

"Tell me you love it, Aurora."

When I parted my lips to get out those words, I could only manage a few throaty gargles as Ares decided to start pounding into my throat. He wrapped his hands in my hair, pulling me toward him with every thrust.

"What was that, Kitten?" he asked, taunting me like I had done with him.

I closed my eyes, trying to form coherent words this time.

He pulled himself all the way out of my throat and slapped his cock against my lips. "Eyes on me."

I collapsed onto my hands and looked up at him through glossy eyes. He bent down, roughly snaked his hand around my throat, and pulled me to my feet. After pinning me to the wall, he rubbed my spit and drool off my chin and then stuck his fingers into my mouth.

"Touch yourself," he ordered, "While I watch."

Not having to be told twice, I slipped my hand into my underwear and rubbed my fingers against my clit. My legs trembled slightly, and I curled my toes, the pressure rising in my core. He stared down at me with those hungry golden eyes and held himself back.

"Faster, Aurora."

My fingers moved faster and harder against my clit. The pure intensity of an orgasm was about to rip its way through me. I closed my eyes but reopened them when he tightened his grip on my neck.

"Please," I whispered, my cheeks flushing.

"Harder."

All I needed was him inside of me. Thrusting into me. Taking me. Making me his. I imagined his cock sliding into my pussy until all of him disappeared, his cum leaking out and running down my thighs.

Just as I was about to tip over the edge, Ares growled, "Stop."

I furrowed my brows. "Stop?" I asked in a breathy whisper.

"Touch your pussy but don't come, or there will be fucking consequences for you this time."

I rubbed my clit again, almost immediately returning to the brink of an orgasm. Ares brushed his fingers against my breast and trailed it over my nipple through my shirt, teasing me. A wave of pleasure rolled through me, yet I held myself back from unraveling. When he pinched my nipple, I moaned out loud and clenched hard.

"You're not coming, are you?"

"No, Alpha."

He growled under his breath. "Good. Now, stop."

After forcing myself to pull my hand away so I didn't come without his permission, I took a shaky breath. I stood there, shifting from foot to foot, trying hard to ease the ache between my legs. "Ares, please, give it to me."

I begged for him. Straight-up begged.

He stepped away and smirked at me. "Is my little Kitten begging for me now?"

"Ares ..." I whimpered.

"I'm not fucking you again until the Luna Ceremony."

My eyes widened. "The Luna Ceremony? That's almost two weeks away."

He slapped my ass and winked. "Better control yourself, Kitten."

But he was the one who would have to control himself because I couldn't wait two weeks for him to fuck me again. I would get under his skin, break his will, make him desperate to fuck my pussy again.

I stood on my tiptoes and placed a hot, lingering kiss on his mouth. "Better control yourself, *Alpha*."

CHAPTER 3

MARS

*L*ying in bed beside Aurora, I smiled at her sleeping figure. She shifted in my arms and curled into my chest, resting her head in the crook of my shoulder and mumbling something about Ruffles in her sleep.

I rubbed circles with my thumb across her bare forearm and inhaled deeply. Mixed with the scent of salt from pretzels we'd had earlier, she smelled like lemons on Sunday mornings when Mom used to bring Charolette and me to Buckleberry Farm to pick fruit.

After sinking into the sheets, I turned onto my side and laid one arm around her waist to pull her closer to me before I slept. The Luna Ceremony was over a week away, and this woman made me want her more and more every single damn moment.

I didn't think I'd be able to resist her. I'd barely gotten through tonight.

Either way, she'd be ours, and she would forever be ours. In just over a week, we'd announce her to Sanguine Wilds as the new Luna to the Ironmane Pack. And she'd finally get the respect that she deserved.

My only wish was that Mom could be here to meet her. I wanted to make her proud.

CHAPTER 4

AURORA

*O*range sunlight glared through our bedroom window, bouncing off the mirror on the other side of the room, and reflecting right into my eyes. After stretching out in our bed, fit for gods and goddesses, and mumbling that it was too early, I rolled over to wrap my arms around Ares but instead got a face full of pillow.

I curled into the pillow anyway because I loved how Ares's scent seemed to linger on everything he touched. The unmarked side of my neck burned slightly, forcing me to groan. Goddess, this Luna Ceremony couldn't come sooner. I had been craving Mars's bite, his mark, his claim on me for so long now. But my Mars had way more self-control and restraint than the rash god of war Ares.

Mars would *try* to hold out until the Luna Ceremony. *Try.*

"Kitten," Ares said from the doorway, white V-neck thrown over his shoulder, body covered in a layer of thick sweat, pronounced veins in his arms teasing all the dirty parts of me.

Pushing myself to a seated position, I gazed down my mate's body and clenched my jaw, so I wouldn't jump him. By the looks of it, he was *trying* to get me riled up for him. And he was too damn good at it.

It drove me insane.

"Looking for me?" he asked with playful gold eyes.

After I hopped out of bed and stripped my shirt, I walked to the closet to scavenge for one of his oversize shirts. "As if ..." I tugged on one that read *The Flaming Chariot* across the chest and ended just below my ass. Then, I tossed him my shorts *and* my panties, and walked to the kitchen.

I wanted payback for last night.

Drenched in a layer of maple syrup, two heaping stacks of pancakes waited for me on the granite kitchen tabletop. I pulled one plate closer to me and stuck my fork into one pancake, bit down, and closed my eyes in bliss.

Ares followed me in, stuffing my lacy panties into his jean pocket, and hopped onto the counter. He opened the chocolate-colored cabinet and pulled something out, lips set into a small smirk. "I bought you something while I was out."

"You did?"

He tossed me a white plastic bag. I placed my fork down, hesitantly peered inside, and fished out the item.

"Are you serious?" I asked, a giggle escaping my throat as I stared at the human-sized blue cap that matched Ruffles's hat to a T.

"Put it on."

"Ares! No!"

After snatching the blue hat, he slapped it on my head and flicked the bill with his index finger. "Thought I'd get you one," he started, and for a moment, he sounded like Mars. He gazed at me with the brightest eyes, and my heart felt warm. "You know, since you've been jealous of Ruffles."

My lips curled into a smile I couldn't stop. Though Ares was violent, arrogant, and so rude sometimes, he always tried to make me smile. He was mine, and along with Mars, he made me feel things I'd never before thought I'd experience.

"Hey, Ruffles!" Ares grabbed his plate of pancakes and dunked a piece into the pool of syrup. He leaned against the counter and gave me a lopsided smile as he looked between the door and my hat. "Get your ass in here and bring your hat!"

Usually, Ruffles came sprinting down the hallway faster than a damn wolf when Ares called her, but she didn't.

After waiting another moment, I furrowed my brows, leaned back in my chair until the front legs hovered off the ground, and peered into the hallway. "Ruffles?"

No response.

"Ruffles!" Ares shouted in his alpha tone.

Still nothing.

With the hounds fresh on my mind, I leaped up and sucked in a gasp of air. Then, I shook my head, knowing that Ruffles wouldn't get herself into any *real* trouble without warning me first. Every time she used to take off in the woods when we lived with Mom, she would always meow at me while staring at the woods, as if to say, *I'm leaving.*

Either she was taking a really good catnap or she had eaten one too many chips this morning and was nursing the best hangover of her entire life.

Nonetheless, I hurried down the hall to her open bedroom door and peered inside, just to make sure. But Ruffles wasn't lying on the bed, hiding in the closet, or lounging under the bed frame. She was nowhere to be found.

What if Ruffles had gotten out, hadn't warned me, and was now battling a hound deep in the forest? Though she had always been careful, Ares had brought out her wild side. Ever since we'd met him, she'd been acting more adventurous.

"You open the window for her?" Ares, who stood behind me with his plate and a huge doofus-like smile, said.

Last night, I'd cracked the glass open just a few inches because she kept meowing at me, but now, it was at least open six inches, and the screen was pushed out just enough for Ruffles to squeeze her fluffy gray body through.

I muttered under my breath and hurried to the window, gazing down at the two-story jump that Ruffles could have definitely made. After sighing under my breath, I threw a hand over my face. "She's been getting wild ever since she met you."

Ares scarfed down another bite of the pancake. "Are you saying I'm—"

"Don't even start." I paced in front of him, thinking that the hounds would have killed her by now. Even with her wild self, she never left without warning me. Not once. I rubbed my sweaty palms together. "Do you think she got far? Will she be back? She doesn't just leave without telling me."

Placing his plate on the mattress—*on the damn mattress, where it could tip over and spill easily*—Ares looked under the bed, where she usually kept her blue hat. "Looks like she was off on a mission. Put her hat on by herself and left."

Though my lips curled into a half-smile, I shoved his shoulder. "This is not the time for your jokes. That's Mars's job. You should be angry that she left and help me go find her."

Ares arched a thick brown brow. "I can be lighthearted. I have to be the big, bad alpha for you all the fuckin' time?" The words came out harsh, but then he smirked at me and shrugged his shoulders. "Remember how you want me to act, Kitten. I'll do nothing less."

I rolled my eyes and took a deep breath, calming slightly. At least, Ruffles had had a plan when she left. She wouldn't go anywhere that she hadn't been before or anywhere that she considered dangerous. Hell, she'd warned us away from the cave.

Ares rested his chin on my shoulder and clutched me tightly, claws digging into my flesh. "If she's not back by tonight, we can go look for her. But … everyone in our pack already knows who she is. They'll return her if they think she's lost."

"Everyone already knows who Ruffles is ... but not me?" I asked, crossing my arms and tapping my foot.

Ares and Ruffles went out so much together that it was, as if *Ruffles* was his damn mate sometimes.

"Of course they know who you are. The Luna Ceremony is to introduce you officially." He roughly grasped my jaw in his hand and pulled me closer to him. "There are far too many warriors in this pack who'd die to take you away from me. When they see my mark on your neck during the Luna Ceremony, they'll know not to even think about touching what's mine. And if they do, my teeth will be in *their* fucking necks as I rip out their throats."

Pressing my thighs together, I sucked in a deep breath and tried to calm my wolf.

Exhibit A as to why Ares was the biggest tease.

After a few moments, he shrugged. "Ruffles, on the other hand, can be a ho."

I nearly snorted and handed him back his pancakes, so they wouldn't tip over on the bed if he decided to push me onto it and break his promise of waiting until the Luna Ceremony to fuck me again. "If she's not back by five, then we're going to go look for her. But now"—I placed my hands on his sweaty chest and pushed him out of the room—"we have an alpha meeting to attend."

Unable to defeat thousands upon thousands of hounds ourselves, Ares had called a meeting with fourteen of the strongest packs in the region. It had definitely been short notice, but this issue was bigger than us. We needed other warriors and packs on our side for this problem. Hell, we probably needed a god or two on our side to conquer those soulless monstrosities.

After we dressed, I walked downstairs to the meeting room and hopped into one of the oh-so-comfy black office chairs, spinning from side to side.

"You're wearing my shirt in the meeting?" Ares asked me, eyeing The Flaming Chariot shirt.

"Would you rather I take it off and be naked?" I asked, knowing that it would get on his nerves. For good measure, I added, "In front of all the other alphas?"

A guttural growl rumbled from his throat. He clenched his jaw, eyes intensifying into golden suns. The aggressive and quick-tempered Ares was back—my favorite parts of him. They might not be the most attractive features to the average person, but they made Ares himself.

"Don't push me, Aurora," he said through elongated canines.

I sauntered around the empty meeting room, drawing my finger down the brown table and then across Ares's shoulders. "And if I do?" I asked, trailing my fingers down the center of his chest, down his abdomen, down the front of his pants before grabbing his cock inside his jeans. "What's the big, bad alpha going to do to me?"

From the meeting room, I listened to the rustling down the hall. Knowing that I only had a couple moments before the other alphas came into the room, I stroked his hardening cock and smirked against his neck. *Ares* definitely wouldn't be able to last until the Luna Ceremony.

He loved savage, rough fucking.

Wrapping a large, callous hand around my throat, he pulled me closer until our lips nearly touched. "You don't want to know how I'd wreck your little pussy, Kitten." He growled again, this time lower, "I'll leave you a sopping mess under the table if you try anything during this meeting."

Just before the other alphas came into the room, Ares pushed me away and smoothed out his jeans, which had the biggest damn imprint of his cock. I swallowed hard, sat, and pressed my thighs together, hoping to hide my arousal from the other men and women as they piled into the room.

Alpha Vulcan and Alpha Minerva from nearby packs walked

into the room, followed by their betas and strongest warriors. Skilled in the craft of weapon creation, Vulcan stood stoically, nearly six feet tall with dark red hair and bronze skin. By his side, Minerva—one of the few female alphas in Sanguine Wilds—pursed her lips and softened her brown eyes at me.

They smiled at me—the lovely mate of the most ruthless man in all of Sanguine Wilds—which earned them a growl from Ares. I smiled back *just to be nice*, and Ares cut his eyes to me, large canines dripping with saliva emerging from under his lips.

"I decided to go braless today," I teased through the mind link and winked at him. I hopped up from my seat, let Ares watch my nipples harden against my shirt, and squeezed his shoulder. "I'm going to go see where Elijah is."

After walking into the hallway, I passed three more alphas and hurried to the front door to scan the woods for Elijah. I expected more alphas to come but didn't see any in the woods. Not even five minutes after the meeting began. It looked like five alphas were the only ones to respond—or the only ones to take this threat seriously.

Ten minutes later, with disheveled hair and tired eyes, Elijah ran to me from deep in the woods. He shifted from a dark brown, almost-black wolf into his human. "Sorry I'm late. I was up all night." He ran a hand across his face and stepped in through the back door. "I haven't been able to sleep."

I handed him clothes and glanced out the door. "Did you see anyone else on your way here?"

"No. Why?"

"Not even half the alphas we'd invited showed up."

Elijah pressed his lips together. "That's what happens when you tear up the entire world to find the stone. Nobody trusts Ares not to hurt them. Maybe at one point, they would've shown up to show their support. Not now."

I groaned internally at Ares's past. I had a mess to clean up, and I needed to restore peace quickly because these hounds weren't a joke. A war was approaching faster than I'd originally thought it would.

Before Elijah could walk toward the meeting room, I caught his slender wrist. "Before we go in"—I gnawed on the inside of my cheek and teetered from foot to foot—"I want to talk about the stone. You'll still put it in Charolette, right?"

He stuffed his hands into his pockets. "I heard that she didn't want it."

"She doesn't, yet." I had tried all week to get her to agree to the surgery. Even after everything that Ares had done to find the stone for her, she didn't want it. I swallowed hard, knowing that the worst was coming for her. "I'll convince her. I just want to be sure that you can."

"You know …" He lowered his voice, the hallway light glimmering off his sweaty, dark skin. "You know that *you* can always use the stone. Nobody will judge you for wanting to use the stone that kept your brother alive, so you can shift easily. If you do, you'll always have a part of him with you."

The thought had crossed my mind more than once this past week. A piece of Jeremy … it *was* the only thing I had left of him. But I couldn't accept it. I wanted it more than anything, but I had survived as a cripple for over a decade; I could survive longer. But without the stone, Charolette wouldn't survive the next few years, never mind the rest of her life.

"No. I can't do that to Ares. He hurts too much already."

"Look, all I'm saying is that if you use that stone, you'll be stronger than Ares. This war with the hounds means life or death for so many of us, and you might be the only one who can stop it. Jeremy said they're after you for *divine revenge*. You shouldn't go into battle without being as strong as you can be, especially if they want to kill you. With the stone, you'd be smarter *and* stronger—a deadly combination."

At the thought, I sucked in a breath. *Me? Stopping a war this huge? No way. I just couldn't.*

"Just think about it," he said. Then, he walked down the hallway toward the meeting room, leaving me with one notion that even I had considered before ...

If I used the stone on myself, I wouldn't just be stronger. I would be alpha-strong, maybe even as strong as a divine.

"Elijah!" I called before he could disappear into the meeting room. I hurried down the hallway and frowned up at the dark circles under his dull eyes. It broke my heart. "I'm sorry that I didn't ask you before, but ... are you okay?"

Jeremy's death had broken him the first time, but experiencing it for a second time must've been hell. Seeing his fated mate alive after over a decade of believing he had left this world for good, and then, in the same moment, watching him die again ... that pain had to be so much worse than how I'd felt about killing my brother. That pain scarred for decades, centuries maybe.

Elijah pressed his lips together in a weak attempt to stay strong, and then his chin quivered. "I'm fine."

"No, you're not."

"It's just hard sometimes, Roar. Really hard." He sighed, shoulders slumping forward. "Every time I close my eyes, I see his face. I see every moment we spent together, every time he smiled at me. I think about what our lives could've been like if ... if he hadn't died. I wanted to spend every waking moment with him. But that's just a distant dream now."

"If you ever need to talk to someone, we can always get smoothies at Pink Moon Tavern, share stories of Jeremy, celebrate his life." My lips curved down further, and I inhaled deeply. "Don't be a stranger, Elijah. You know, Jeremy would have appreciated if we celebrated his life rather than grieved over his death."

After a moment of silence, he nodded. "I would like that. Every Sunday, like we used to."

Suddenly, the door opened. Ares glared down at us with his jaw tight and his golden eyes fixed on my proximity to Elijah. I ushered Elijah into the room and followed after him, plopping down in the seat across from Ares.

For someone who didn't want to fuck me, he sure had been tense lately.

"Anyone else?" Ares asked through the mind link.

"No," I said, the word so utterly heartbreaking as I thought it.

I completely understood the reason the other alphas didn't attend, but this problem was so much bigger than Ares. Yet if I were an alpha and Ares had invited me over to chat about hounds, I would have declined too. Ares had the worst reputation around Sanguine Wilds. The news and gossip made him out to be a monster.

Sinking in my seat, I listened to the terrible thoughts racing through Ares's mind. Some were from Ares himself, thinking about how stupid those alphas were for not showing up, but others were from Mars, scolding Ares for losing control on every pack they had fought.

But as if it didn't affect him, Ares went on with the meeting. He had a bad habit of holding things inside of him until he broke into a thousand tiny silver pieces. I feared that one day, he'd lose his battle to the haunting thoughts and do something unspeakable.

"What about the stone?" Alpha Vulcan asked.

It seemed that the alphas were more interested in the stone than with the hounds.

Elijah and I tensed. While Ares wouldn't allow anything to happen to me, telling other people that we had the stone was beyond dangerous. Who knew if they would sell us out to the hounds or attempt to steal the stone from me or Charolette?

"You've found it, I suppose," Vulcan continued, strumming his claws on the wooden table. "If you hadn't, you would still be out there, trying to rip each pack piece to piece." He stared pointedly at Ares. "So, where is it?"

The words didn't faze Ares, and this was the first time I'd

really seen him doing alpha business. Not tearing apart packs. Not being the violent man everyone thought he was. A calmer, more collected, still *don't give a single fuck* Ares.

"Yes, we have it," Ares said. And then he carried on as if he hadn't noticed the entire room tense when he admitted to hoarding the divine-like sphere somewhere. "We have bigger problems than the stone. We have undead hounds who are—"

"How do we know you have the stone?" Alpha Minerva asked, drawing her fingertip against her golden ring shaped like an owl. "And how do we know that we can trust you? How are we supposed to trust a man who can't control his temper in war?"

Ares slammed his palms down on the table and growled, "We are not talking about me."

From the frustration radiating off of him, I could tell that he was about to break, about to show them that they *should* be afraid of him and that they shouldn't trust him so blindly. And I didn't blame him for becoming irritated either. We had an enormous problem on our hands that nobody seemed to be taking seriously.

I stood up from my seat and grazed my fingers across his shoulder. It was dangerous to say and dangerous to do, but if I wanted everyone to trust what Ares said, I had to tell them everything. We had a forest, a pack, and a species to protect from this divine war.

"I have the stone," I admitted.

Everyone quieted down. The alphas' eyes glazed over to chat to their betas through their own personal mind links. Elijah's eyes widened, and he shook his head, telling me to be quiet. But I couldn't.

This needed to be done to save the entire fucking world from these monsters.

"I have the stone, and I have patience," I said, trying hard to get everyone to trust me.

If they couldn't trust the rageful Ares, maybe they could trust his nearly crippled mate.

"I will not let Ares blindly destroy anymore. I am only interested in annihilating the hounds. Now, if you don't like that, you can leave and have your entire pack slaughtered by hounds like mine was, or you can stay and we'll talk about what we're going to do to defeat them."

After shifting my gaze to each alpha and beta in the room, I waited for them to react. And when they nodded their heads, I sat back down to give my full attention to my mate. That misunderstood man deserved it.

"You said that they are raising wolves from the dead?" Alpha Vulcan said, disrupting the silence. When Ares nodded, Vulcan scratched his claw so hard against the wooden table that the paint came up. "There is a necromancer that I'm aware of about five hundred miles south, whose family specializes in raising people from the dead."

Eyes widening slightly, I glanced at Ares. I hadn't even thought necromancy was real, but I couldn't unsee what I had seen in that cave. It was more than real. If we found a necromancer who could help us understand how it was done or how to reverse it, we could be one step closer to stopping the hounds from destroying the world.

"Get me more information," Ares said to Vulcan. Then, he looked at Elijah. "We also held off on killing a hound this morning. He's locked in our prison. Take it back to your pack and study it."

Elijah perked up, his eyes actually glowing for the first time since he had seen Jeremy alive. Excited, he quickly nodded in acceptance. Though he was an alpha, he and his pack specialized in the sciences, and he was the biggest dork for anything medical-related. He'd been obsessed—*hard-core obsessed*—over the stone and begged the doctor to let him into the room during my first surgery.

As the alphas fell back into a discussion about how we'd tackle the hounds, one thing was clear to me. We might've made some progress today, but it wasn't enough. We needed to work faster before the undead beasts started to wreak havoc across the lands.

I feared that once they did … nobody would be able to stop them.

CHAPTER 5

AURORA

"*R*uffles!" I shouted when I got home. I hurried to her yellow-accented bedroom with the cracked window, empty bed, and her blue hat missing. She hadn't made it home yet, which made me even more nervous.

With autumn sweeping across Sanguine Wilds, the sky became darker earlier in the day. I didn't want Ruffles to get lost somewhere in the woods, not knowing how to get home. She'd be an easy prey for a hungry hound.

After grabbing a light-purple jacket, I rushed down the stairs and mind linked Ares—who was still meeting with the other alphas—that I wasn't waiting any longer. I needed to make sure Ruffles was safe. If I lost her, *I* would lose it. She had been with me since Jeremy died the first time.

Stomach in tight knots, I rushed down the asphalt streets toward town. Ruffles never stayed out this late. If she left, it was only for an hour or so ... not for the entire day. Some wolves ran past me, bowing their heads toward me in respect. Feeling weird about asking about my cat, I politely nodded back and continued to peer into the alleyways.

Ruffles was too prim and proper to hang out in back alleys, but she'd stopped in one yesterday after our walk. Maybe she had come back for some ungodly reason. Maybe.

Wind whipped through the town, blowing my hair in all directions and making me feel like the mythical woman Medusa, who had restless snakes for hair. I pulled my hood up to shield my face from the blistering breeze.

Couples walked past me on the sidewalks toward The Flaming Chariot. High schoolers gathered outside of Mad Moon Grocery. I weaved between herds of people to try to find my damn cat. She must've really wanted to give me a heart attack or something.

Hurrying past an alleyway, I stopped dead in my tracks. I stepped back and peered around the corner of a building, staring wide-eyed at Marcel, who had Charolette pressed against a wall, his nose buried deep in her hair, one hand posted on the brick wall, the other brushing against her hip.

When he touched her, I shivered and nearly squealed in excitement. I felt like a total creep, peeping on them, but ... it was *finally* happening! I had waited for so freaking long for this damn moment that it felt like Ares was touching *me* for the first time.

Marcel inhaled deeply and pressed her harder against the wall, growling into her ear.

My heart pounded against my chest. I waited in anticipation for one moment, then another, then another for them to just kiss already. Since Liam was out of the picture, Marcel could finally step in and tell her that he liked her. After. So. Freaking. Long.

Marcel's white hair hid their faces, so I couldn't see much, but he leaned down and—

"It's not luna-like to spy," someone said into my ear.

I jumped back, my heart racing from being caught, and turned on my heel, expecting to see Ares.

36

Instead, I came eye-to-eye with a young man with devilishly sharp cheekbones and dark brown glasses, who couldn't be any older than me. Dark brown locks blowing against his forehead, he rocked back on his heels, stuffed his hands into his jean pockets, and gave me a sheepish smile.

"Sorry. I didn't mean to scare you."

I parted my lips, and then pressed them back together. Though I was certain I hadn't met him before, he looked so familiar. My cheeks flushed, and I stepped behind the building, so Marcel and Charolette wouldn't see me gawking at them. "It's okay."

"I'm Adrian," he said, sticking out his hand. "Thought I'd properly introduce myself."

After giving him a once-over and concluding he wasn't a threat, I placed my hand in his larger one. It felt even more callous and rougher than Ares's.

"Aurora," I said. I furrowed my brows at him, knowing that I had to have seen him somewhere. He looked way too familiar. "Have we met before?"

"You've probably met my twin sister, Ariana. She works at the pharmacy with Alpha Barrett." An awkward moment of silence fell upon us, and then he nodded to the alleyway. "So ... you're stalking your mate's sister?"

I took a few steps down the sidewalk, away from the alley. "No. Are you stalking her?"

He chuckled and followed me. "No, I'm trying to find my cat."

My eyes widened, and I clenched my jaw. Oh, Ruffles, the ho, had probably gone to meet that cat we had seen last night. That was why she had been out all day, trying to strut her stuff for Mr. Siamese Beauty.

"Is your cat a Siamese that frequents alleyways?"

Adrian nodded his head, and I arched my brow. First, that damn ho had been all over my man, and now, she was out on a hunt for another. Couldn't even keep her men straight anymore. She needed some cat therapy or something.

"Lead me to his favorite alley," I said, glancing around the town. I couldn't remember where we had seen him last night.

We walked down the sidewalk against the searing wind, looped around the pharmacy, and snuck around some buildings to peer into a surprisingly clean alley made of bricks. Sure enough, Ruffles sat right on a green dumpster with her blue hat on, her little ass right up in the air, back arched—*stretching*. Adrian's cat sat near the closest building with intent wide eyes, as if he were watching a stripper.

Oh Moon Goddess. Who taught this damn cat to be such a slut?

I stifled a laugh and watched Ruffles parade around with that blue hat. She loved it so much that she wanted to show it off to other cats too. My mind wandered to Ares for a moment, heart clenching. Goddess, I couldn't wait to tell him this. He'd be so proud.

"Pringle," Adrian called behind me.

The Siamese cat glanced over as Ruffles continued to prance around on top of the dumpster. He stood on all fours, the silver bell on his neck jingling in the breeze.

"Pringle? That's your cat's name?"

"His nickname." Adrian rubbed the back of his neck. "Used to get his head stuck in Pringles tubes when he was younger."

My lips curled into a smile, and a giggle escaped my lips. Of course, Ruffles would go for someone named Pringle. Out of all the cats in the entire world, she would find someone who loved chips almost as much as she did.

After stifling another laugh, I cleared my throat. "Ruffles, what are you doing?"

She snapped her head in my direction, eyes wide in fear. She hopped off the dumpster, gray fur blowing in the wind, and rubbed herself against my shin, her tail sticking right up in the air. She stood between my legs and stared at Pringle.

Adrian nodded to Pringle. "Come on. Let's walk your new girl home."

Pringle took charge and walked ahead of us toward the pack house, as if he knew exactly where he was going. Ruffles let him walk in front of her, prancing by my side and glaring at Pringle like she hadn't just been trying to seduce him a couple minutes ago.

"So," I said, smiling at beams of moon through the trees. While hundreds of hounds were being raised from the dead, tonight was oddly quiet—too quiet. It frightened me. "What do you do?"

"I'm an engineer," Adrian said. "Been working on this pack for a few years now."

"You're an engineer?" I asked, raising my brows. Though Ares commanded a huge and thriving pack, he had been focused on building an army, not so much on any other disciplines. "I haven't met any here yet."

Adrian nodded. "I'm probably one of the only ones you'll find here."

When we reached the pack house, I noticed our bedroom light on. The alpha meeting must've been over by now. Ruffles ran to the door, scratching at it for Ares to let her into the house, and I turned toward Adrian. "Can you build underground bunker-like tunnels?"

"I can design something like that, yes."

"Good…"

This would be the perfect chance to get the same underground tunnels like the ones back home done here *with* improvements. Pack members would have a safe place to hide their pups when we were attacked by the hounds. And this time, I would make sure that all the pups would be saved. There would be entrances at all corners of this pack, so we wouldn't lose anyone else.

"I have something that I want to discuss with you. Are you free tomorrow night?" I asked.

He scrolled through his phone calendar. "Yeah, anytime after four. Here." He handed me his phone. "Put your number in. We can meet at Pink Moon Tavern at seven."

After typing in my number and handing him his phone back, I clapped my hands together, my stomach fluttering from excitement. "Perfect!"

Ares let out a guttural growl behind us and snatched the back of Adrian's neck, lifting him. My eyes widened as Adrian dangled in the air.

Ares bared his canines. "Making plans without me, *Kitten?*"

"We were just …" Adrian grasped Ares's hand as it tightened around his neck, his cheeks flushing a deep red.

Ares had Adrian a foot off the ground, his bicep flexing so hard to hold him in place that I thought the muscle would burst out of his T-shirt. He stood so stoic and strong with that infamous look of golden fury on his face, so godlike and divine under the moonlight.

"Ares, let go." I tugged on his arm to pull him away or at least to loosen his grip on Adrian's neck because a god could snap a mortal's fragile neck so easily. "We weren't doing anything."

Ares yanked Adrian closer. "Planning a date with *my* mate and *your* luna?"

"We were … talking … about …" Adrian's wolf tried to force him to shift to break out of the death hold, but Ares held him tighter and refused to let him move.

"About fucking what?" Ares said through his canines.

"Ares, stop," I said through clenched teeth, pulling his arm harder.

After snarling one last time, he thrust Adrian against the nearest tree. "Listen to me." He pinned Adrian and tightened his grip around his neck. "Aurora is mine. All mine. Nobody takes her away from me. And if you try it again, you'll be sorry you did. Do I make myself clear?"

Adrian nodded furiously. When Ares let him go, Adrian fell onto his hands and knees, gasping for air. I hurried to make sure Adrian was okay, but Ares snatched my wrist before I could touch him and lifted me into the air.

"No."

One single word.

One word that held so much power.

Ares dragged me to the front doors. I stared back at Adrian, who stumbled to his feet and leaned against the tree. He offered me a weak wave, as if to say that he was okay, and Pringle jumped onto his shoulder. Before I could tell him good night, Ares shoved me into the pack house and slammed the doors behind us.

He shoved me to the wall by my throat. "I told you not to fucking push it, Aurora," he growled into my ear, canines grazing against the mark on my neck.

My entire body shivered at the memory of Ares marking me in that spine-chillingly cold prison a couple weeks ago.

"We didn't do anything," I said.

Jaw twitching, he glared at me with golden eyes and balled his free hand into a tight fist. I gathered all the damn sanity I had left and thought about swaying this in *my* favor. If Ares was mad ... maybe I could get him angry enough to fuck me because I couldn't wait any longer. I had been needy all damn night.

"Maybe if you weren't such an overly possessive asshole, you'd be able to see this situation for what it was—nothing."

He chuckled so menacingly that I clenched, and he brushed his fingers against my cheek. The touch was soft and inviting and such a facade because a moment later, he snatched my chin hard in his hand and stared down at me with dark, devilish eyes.

"Such an overly possessive asshole? If I were an asshole, I'd have you on your knees in front of Adrian as he watched me fuck this pretty mouth of yours." He roughly pushed his thumb into my mouth. "But I spared you that embarrassment."

"Embarrassment?" I asked, brow arched hard.

He pushed his throbbing cock against my stomach. "You're my luna and an alpha. I don't want just anyone seeing how easily you submit to me … but it seems like you need a reminder," he said into my ear, fingers brushing against my breast through my shirt. "Get on your knees."

Moon Goddess, I needed it so fucking bad, and he knew it. He fucking knew it.

"Knees," he said between clenched teeth.

"What makes you think I'd submit to you so easi—"

Before I could finish my sentence, he shoved me to my knees, pulled his hard cock out of his sweatpants, and rammed it into my mouth. My breath caught in the back of my throat as he slammed himself into me. I dug my fingers into his thighs, my eyes watering as he snatched my chin and the top of my head and pulled me toward him, making me take every inch of his cock down my throat.

"All of it, Kitten. I know you can do it."

Furrowing my brows, I pushed more of him down my throat until my lips met at the base. Not because I was submitting to him, but because I wanted him to break and finally give me what I wanted. Sucking him off until he was desperate enough to ram his cock into my pussy was my only plan.

"Fuck," he grunted and pushed his hips closer to my lips, tracing the outline of his cock in my neck with his index finger. Then, he slowly started to jerk himself off inside my throat, his hand moving up and down the column of my neck.

After grabbing my hand, he placed it on my throat and made me rub him off too. I clenched and tightened my hand around myself, a wave of heat warming my core.

"Do you like my cock inside of you, Kitten?"

I moaned on him, pleasure rushing through me. This was

pure agony, pure fucking agony. My pussy pulsed, aching to be filled by my mate. But I had to hold out, just for a little longer. I had to get him just a bit angrier.

"*No,*" I said through the mind link. "*I don't.*"

We both knew that I fucking loved it, but that still didn't stop Ares from losing total control to his wolf. Furious, he thrust quickly and harshly into me, holding nothing back. Spit and slobber ran down my chin as I choked on his big cock.

"Well, I fucking love when your tiny little throat talks to me, Aurora."

"*Harder.*" I stared right up at him through teary eyes, letting him destroy my face, and pushed a hand between my legs to ease the ache. All I could think about was making him angrier and angrier, making him lose it. "*It doesn't seem like you love it to me.*"

Ares continued, his hand traveling down my neck to squeeze his cock in my throat. "*Don't* fucking touch yourself," he demanded.

But I didn't listen. I was too damn close to coming—something I needed more than ever tonight. I wasn't going to give up now. Pressure was building up in my core, and my mouth was stuffed full. I felt so fucking good.

When I didn't move, he pulled himself out of me, jerked me to my feet, and pinned my wrists to the wall. "I said to stop." His voice was low and taut and full of fury. "Only I get to touch this pussy tonight."

"Well, Alpha," I said between raspy breaths, "let's get one thing straight. Just because I get on my knees for you doesn't mean I submit easily. All you're doing is giving me what *I* want—for you to break, bend me over the bed, and fuck me senseless."

After growling again, he stepped closer to me and trapped me with his hips. "You don't think I have you tied around my finger, *Kitten?*" His cock throbbed against my stomach. "I can smell your wet cunt. I know just how much you want me to thrust my cock into your tight pussy."

I sucked in a deep breath and tried hard not to let him mess with my head.

Control the damn situation, Aurora. You're his luna. You make the deci—

"You *will* submit to me willingly tonight," he said without leaving room for argument. He picked me up off the ground and walked with me to our bedroom. "I don't care how long it takes. You're mine." He tossed me onto the bed and *let* me scurry to the headboard to catch my breath.

Trying to ignore the throbbing between my legs, I stared down the bed at that godly man with hungry eyes, sharp canines, and claws that could tear me to pieces. He crawled up the bed toward me, pulled off my pants, and forcefully spread my legs. Resting his forearms on the sides of my hips, he pressed his mouth against my clit and lapped at my pussy with his tongue.

"Don't come unless I tell you to," he ordered, his slight stubble tickling my inner thighs as his tongue moved in tortuous circles around my clit, driving me higher and higher. When he pushed a finger into me and curled it in a come-hither motion, I grasped the bedsheets in my fists and bit my lip to hold back my moans.

I was so close, so damn close. All he had to do was—

His fingers hit my G-spot, and my whole body stiffened.

Just as I was about to come, he pulled away from me and slapped my pussy hard. "I said not to come."

"I wasn't going to," I lied right through my damn teeth as I teetered right on the edge of a body-trembling orgasm.

"Yes, you were." He slowly rubbed his fingers against my clit, not fast enough to tip me over, but enough to make me clench. After a few moments, when the pressure subsided, he dipped his head and flicked my clit with his tongue. "Your whole body tenses right before you come, *Kitten*. I know your body."

He pushed a finger into me again, and my pussy wrapped around it almost instinctively. I moved my hips against his hand, so close to another orgasm, and tugged on my nipples through my shirt. A rush of heat hit my core, and I curled my toes in pleasure.

Ares slapped his palm against my clit again, and my body jerked into the air.

"What did I say?" he scolded.

I didn't even try to deny it this time. Instead, I stared down at him with my brows furrowed together, my legs spread wide, and my pussy pulsing as the cold air hit it. *Desperate* was the only word I could find to describe how I felt at that moment.

"Tell me what I want to hear, and I'll give it to you," he ordered.

I swallowed and shook my head, refusing to submit to him now. He was close to breaking. I could see it in his eyes. I just needed to hold out for a couple more moments.

After realizing that I wouldn't submit willingly, he sat up. "Turn around and get on your hands and knees, ass in the air."

While I wanted to refuse again, I couldn't stop myself from turning onto my hands and knees. He crawled behind me and dug his fingers into my hips. He wrapped one arm around my waist to rub my swollen, sensitive clit again, the smallest sensation making me jump.

After pressing his hardness against my bare pussy, he grabbed a fistful of my hair and drew me closer to him. "Is this what you want?"

My lips curled into a smirk. "Yes, Alpha."

He rubbed the head of his cock against my wet pussy and groaned into my ear. I listened to the sloppy, wet sounds my pussy made for him and waited for him to plunge himself inside of me. But instead, he pushed another finger in. I pressed my lips together, trying to suppress a moan as he moved it around inside of me.

Cock continuing to rub against my entrance, he made my wolf insane. I ached for one damn release—one, that was all. I didn't care what it was from anymore. I just needed him to push me over the edge and send me into divine serenity.

"Doesn't my mate want to make me his? Doesn't he want to make me submit?"

With his free hand, he dug his claws right into my shirt and ripped it right down the middle. My breasts bounced out, and I clenched hard. *Oh Moon Goddess.* He groped my breast in one of his large, callous hands and then tugged my nipple between his fingers, making me cry out in pleasure.

After shoving another finger inside of me, he continued to thrust them in and out, moving them in a rhythmic fashion while pulling on my nipple with his other hand. I clenched around his fingers, the pressure growing in my core. My whole body tensed, and I lingered on the edge, but he growled lowly in my ear, fingers stilling.

I tried so desperately to move my hips, but he held me in place and refused to let me come. This was sinister.

When the pressure in my core subsided, he curled his two fingers and hit my G-spot. Over. And over. And over. And over. Until my legs were shaking. Until I collapsed on the bed, unable to hold myself up. Until I squeezed my eyes shut, knowing that this would be the orgasm I would come to, no matter what.

He grabbed a fistful of my hair, forced me back onto my hands, pulled his fingers out of me, and stuffed them into his mouth, sucking off the juices. "Kitten, your pussy tastes so good." He hovered his fingers closer to my core again. "Do you want a taste?"

"The only way I'm tasting myself"—I pressed my lips together and wiggled my hips, feeling his cock press against my entrance, and his fingers slipped inside of me—"is if it's off your dick."

Pounding his fingers into me, tugging on my nipples, pushing me so close to the edge again, he sucked on his mark. Heat pooled between my legs. When he pinched my nipples harder and harder and harder, and the pain became almost unbearable, I whimpered.

"You think you have a choice, Kitten?" He pulled his fingers out of me and shoved them into my mouth. He pulled them back out and rubbed his fingers against my lips, his dick pressing at my entrance. "Good girl ..."

I growled low. He rolled us over, so he was lying on his back, and I rested on him. With one hand, he groped my breast, and with the other, he rubbed his cock against my wet pussy.

"Who do you belong to?" he asked.

"Not you."

He slapped my clit hard, and a wave of pleasure rolled through me.

"Who do you belong to?"

I clenched my jaw, trying to displace the pain. "Not you."

He slapped my clit again, and I squirmed in his embrace. I gazed at him, watching him stare at me with those golden eyes and a smirk that told me I was *his*—whether or not I admitted to it.

All I wanted was for him to thrust his cock into my pussy, to fill me up with his cum, to make me tremble and scream out his name. And by the light in his gaze and the tenseness in his jaw, I could tell that he was so close to letting me have it too.

Ares hated being defied. He'd want to prove me wrong.

"Why don't you make me yours? Thrust yourself inside of me and take it," I whispered, watching his eyes flash gold. I slid myself down, closer to his cock, and rubbed myself against him. "Make my pussy yours."

When he didn't move like I'd thought he would, I growled and started to buck my hips against his. Moon Goddess, why did he have to make this so difficult? Didn't he see I was so fucking—

"Oh, Kitten," Ares said into my ear. He stretched my legs further apart and stared at my reflection in the mirror. "Look at you ..."

I gazed at myself in the mirror, watching my pussy pulse as I desperately moved my hips. The head of his cock pressed against my aching entrance, teasing me and putting pressure in just the right place.

"Please, Ares."

Ares slapped his cock against my pussy, coating it in my juices. "I've never seen you so desperate for me," he said, golden eyes locked on mine.

Though he was controlling himself quite well, I could see the tenseness in his eyes. But … I didn't quite have the strength to fight back anymore.

"Give it to me," I said.

"Are you submitting to me, Aurora?"

I swallowed hard, feeling his head just about to slip into my pussy. "Yes, I'm submitting."

He pushed his cock harder against my entrance and rubbed my clit. "Good girl."

"Please, put it inside of me already."

"I told you that we're waiting."

My pussy clenched, and I tried so desperately to move around in his hold to slide his cock inside of me myself, but Ares just held my legs further apart, making me watch him.

"Jerk me off. Make me come all over your pussy, baby."

"Ares," I whimpered, the pressure in my core rising.

"Do it. I know seeing my cum spread all over your pussy lips will make you come."

I reached between my legs, took his cock in my hand, and stroked him almost as quickly as he rubbed my swollen clit until his cum sprayed across my sopping pink pussy.

"Alpha!" I whimpered, loving the way his cum looked on me. "Can I come?"

"Yes, Kitten. Come for me."

My legs trembled, and I stared at him in the mirror, wave after wave of pleasure pumping through me. He pushed the head of his cock right against my entrance, feeling it pulse on him, and grunted in my ear. More cum pumped out of him and into my hole.

"Push my cum inside of you," he said into my ear, watching it roll down my thighs. "Do it for me. I want to get you pregnant with my pups, Aurora. I want to see your belly swollen with my children."

And so, I took two of my fingers and pushed his cum inside of me because I was Ares's desperate mate, who wanted nothing more than any part of him to be inside of me.

CHAPTER 6

AURORA

"*H*ow was your night last night?" I asked Charolette the next afternoon at practice during our infamous five-mile run. I jogged alongside her through the woods, leaping over fallen branches and stepping on withering orange leaves in my human form.

I *definitely wasn't* prying about what had happened with Marcel. Pack lunas *never* wanted to get involved in pack drama. And not knowing about them *definitely wasn't* eating me up on the inside. Note the sarcasm.

A fog sat heavily in the woods just above the trees as other warriors sprinted through the narrow paths far in front of us. The chilling morning air vaguely reminded me of Hound Territory, making me uneasy. Or maybe I was uneasy because Ares *still* hadn't broken yet.

I'd be getting sweet revenge on him today though. He had it coming after last night.

Charolette shrugged her shoulders, breathing heavily out of her nose. "Good."

I slowed my pace to meet hers. "Do anything fun?"

"No, not really."

The last of the warriors disappeared through the woods, but Marcel hung back and glanced over his shoulder at us. I waved my hand to tell him to move along and to train the rest of the pack as we continued by ourselves. Charolette gazed at him, a small smile on her face, and then she looked down at her shoes and continued beside me.

When Marcel finally ran ahead, I grabbed Charolette's slender wrist and stopped her. Almost immediately, I dropped my hand because her bones felt so brittle and weak. I didn't want to accidentally break one. No matter how much Marcel denied that he liked her, I knew that if I accidentally broke Charolette's wrist, he'd try to beat my ass for it.

"Okay, spill. Tell me what's going on between you and Marcel." I crossed my arms, arched a brow, and smiled at her flushing cheeks. "And don't say nothing because I saw you and him together last night."

Her eyes widened. "You saw us together?"

"I was looking for Ruffles but found you two instead."

"At the coffee shop?"

"In the alleyway."

"Oh Goddess, no ..." She threw her hands over her face. "You didn't tell Ares, did you?"

My lips curled into a smile. "No."

She sighed, her shoulders falling forward. "Thank Goddess. Okay, I'll tell you about it, but you have to promise me that you won't tell anyone anything, especially Ares. He would have Marcel's ass if he saw him all over me. He knows how much of a player that man is."

After pinkie-promising her that I wouldn't say a word, I stared at her in excitement. I'd been dying to know exactly what was going on because this tension was driving *me* insane. I could only imagine how she felt about it all. "So?"

Glancing through the trees at the pack gathering in the field, Charolette smiled softly. "Marcel and I are ..." she started, getting sidetracked when Marcel pulled his shirt over his head, his thick muscles glistening with sweat. When she looked back at me, her entire peppy demeanor changed into one of sadness. "We're mates."

Something about the way she'd said it made it seem so sad.

Mates weren't supposed to be sad or sorrowful. Mates made life better in every way possible.

I frowned as she jogged a bit ahead of me, keeping her eyes trained on the ground.

I caught up to her and nudged my shoulder against hers, hoping to lighten the mood. "Is that a bad thing?"

"No ... I just ..." She held back her tears. "I want to be with him. It's just difficult because of my cancer. I want him to be happy. I know that if he's with me, he won't be. He'll have to take care of me and ..." She tugged on the edges of her fake hair. "And there are so many other pretty girls out there he could be with ..."

I stopped in my tracks and snatched her wrist. "Stop it, Charolette. You're beautiful."

"I have a wig, Aurora," she whispered, huge eyes trembling with tears. "I ... I don't feel pretty. I haven't felt pretty in years. Why would he want to be with someone like me? I only come with problems."

Lips quivering, I pulled her into a hug, so she wouldn't see how much it hurt *me* when she said it. I knew what it was like to think that you weren't good enough for someone. Thoughts like that had eaten me up for years.

"Having cancer or a wig doesn't define who you are. Marcel will love you for it either way," I said, stroking her smooth blonde hair.

She sniffled into my shoulder and wrapped her arms around me, holding me tight. I rested my head against hers and glanced through the trees at Ares, who stood in the middle of the field, peering around the woods to find us.

When his eyes locked on mine, he furrowed his brows. *"Is she okay?"*

"She's fine," I said through the mind link.

Lie. She wasn't really fine and was hurting a lot. But this was girl talk.

After pulling away from her, I tilted my head toward the field. "We should get to practice."

She nodded and followed me through the woods to the field. I pushed some branches out of the way for her to walk through and stepped onto the grass, heading toward the other warriors.

"Why don't you use the stone?" I offered, desperate for her to take it. If she wanted to heal, *wanted to live*, she needed to take the stone. "It will heal you."

She pushed away tears and shook her head. "No."

I swallowed hard and clenched my jaw, so I wouldn't flip. Why was she so against using it? Why did she refuse over and over and over? After everything that she had been through, I'd think she'd want to use it to survive, especially if her cancer was getting worse, like Ares had said it was.

Charolette looped her arm around mine and strolled to Marcel. "Enough about me. Let's talk about the Luna Ceremony! I am so thrilled for it! It's almost in ten days!" She pushed some strands of blonde hair off her sweaty forehead. "I made an appointment at Lucy's Boutique for Tuesday morning at ten a.m., so we can get you the best dress ever!"

Though I wanted to spend more time convincing her, I nodded and smiled along, stomach filling with butterflies. Men, women, and children always raved about Luna Ceremonies, when I was growing up. Everyone loved attending and officially adding a new member to the pack. And in just over a week, I would officially be this pack's luna.

But ... I wanted to be more than just a luna.

Since Jeremy had died, I'd had my sights set on being alpha. Training relentlessly every day, I'd tried hard to be strong, to fight with such aggression, to one day be able to lead, but I had consistently let my pack down.

Elijah's words about me using the stone rang through my head. With the other half of the Malavite Stone, I could be everything that I hoped to be *and more*. I'd be more than a luna, and I'd have more than just the title of *alpha*. I could be an actual one—dominant, possessive over what was mine, and ready to kill whoever threatened my pack.

If Charolette wouldn't accept the stone, then maybe I'd have to use it.

My gaze shifted to Ares, who was fighting some vigorous wolves in our pack. We could be the most powerful couple around Sanguine Wilds. And we might, just might, be able to get rid of the hounds without everyone becoming the undead.

"Aren't you excited?" Charolette said to me, drawing me out of my thoughts.

I forced a smile on my face. While I wanted to be thrilled for the ceremony, other things like the hounds, chatting with Adrian about underground tunnels, and trying to control Ares's short temper as he tried so desperately to keep his hands off me, plagued my mind.

That last bit wasn't much of a problem. It just got him closer and closer to breaking. And to be honest, something about it was damn sexy. His possessiveness, the way he'd dominated me, how he had shown me that I was his last night, I couldn't get enough of it.

Tan skin glistening under the rays of light breaking through the fog, Ares glanced at me from across the field with darkening eyes. *"I can smell you, Kitten,"* he said through the mind link. He slammed a wolf onto his back and stood above him, veins in his arms prominent, as if he was *trying* to keep himself preoccupied.

I took a deep breath to calm myself down, but it wasn't working. I couldn't last another ten days without him. We hadn't been without sex for that long since we'd been together. Ten whole days was too damn long.

He growled low. *"Control yourself before I lose it."*

I smiled, ready for round two when we got home. *"No."*

"Kit—"

"About time," Marcel said, crossing his arms over his chest when Charolette pulled me toward him.

I threw Ares a cheeky smile and looked back at Charolette and Marcel.

Marcel gave Charolette an expression filled with the utmost guilt, and then turned stoic. "What took you so long?"

Charolette cut her eyes at him. "If you couldn't tell, we're both broken. You don't need to go so hard on us. We're doing the best we can." She stormed past him, smacking her shoulder right into Marcel's arm in a weak attempt to push him, and grabbed her water bottle from the grass.

Marcel raised his brows, his silver hair blowing in the breeze. "I do need to go hard on you because I know you won't try if I let you train by yourself," he said, lip curled in an ugly snarl. "You won't do anything if I don't hound you about it."

Charolette tossed her bottle down and started toward the corner of the large field, by a group of tall pine trees and fog. Nobody ever practiced that far away from the center, as it wasn't needed. The field was nearly two hundred yards long.

"Come on, Aurora. Let's go train."

Marcel caught her wrist. "No, you don't, Princess. You're training with me today."

I suggestively raised my brows at her and winked.

She rolled her eyes at him and crossed her arms over her chest. "Well, who will Aurora fight then? I *have* to be her partner or else she won't be able to train at all, and how could you let our soon-to-be luna not train? Do you—"

"Damn, you ask too many questions." Marcel turned to the pack, puckered his lips, and whistled.

Almost immediately, wolves stopped and glanced over. Ares emerged from the pack, thick strands of brown hair plastered to his forehead.

Marcel nodded to me. "Ares, you're with your mate."

Marcel wanted me to fight Ares?

It had been a while since I'd fought an alpha, and I had never once really fought my mate. But maybe it was time to test out my true strength instead of being pitied by wolves who knew I couldn't shift.

Marcel squeezed my shoulder and leaned in close, strands of his hair falling into his scarred face. "His weaknesses are left-ankle picks, his right calf, and getting sucker-punched right in the rib cage. Stay on him and don't let up. Make him tired." Then, he stepped away from me and smirked at Ares. "Let's see who the real alpha of this pack is."

Dressed in nothing but a pair of gray shorts, Ares sauntered over to me and eyed me like he did his prey. I had seen those hungry, vicious eyes too many times in the bedroom to know *that* was what I was to him at this moment—a piece of meat he'd try to chew up and spit out to prove his superiority.

I sucked in a deep breath—remembering every moment, every sensation, every touch from last night—and crouched in a wrestling stance, ready for him to destroy me—I mean, ready to kick his ass ... because that was exactly what I was going to do. I wasn't going to let myself get distracted by that chiseled abdomen or those golden eyes that had taken in every part of my body last night.

When Ares lowered into his stance, I analyzed his body positioning. Because he was at least twice my size, he'd toss me around so easily if I let him. But I needed to fight to get stronger, so we could have a possibility at defeating these hounds. He wouldn't have a chance of throwing me around.

Ares came at me quickly, shooting in for a takedown and snatching the backs of my knees. I sprawled back, driving my hips toward the ground, and hooked my arms under his shoulders to get a grip on him. After gaining leverage, I pushed him back and reevaluated my plan.

He stayed back for one fucking moment before coming at me again, this time faster. He hit me so damn hard that he knocked me down onto the ground, his hand cradling the back of my head before it could bounce off the earth.

I growled under my breath and squirmed out of his death grip to get to my feet, keeping a low stance. That wouldn't happen again. I wouldn't allow it to happen. I had to be prepared for anything.

So, while he circled me, I kept my distance and watched the way he moved. I kept up with him, sprawling and dodging his takedowns, pushing him harder than he'd expected me to. And when I finally saw the opening, I grabbed his right wrist, yanked him down, and snatched the back of his left ankle, executing the perfect ankle pick on him.

With all his muscle mass, he hit the ground hard with an *oof*. I landed on top of him, immediately turning him onto his back to nail his shoulders to the ground. But before I could secure a position, he threw me off him, pulled me onto my back, and pinned my shoulders to the dirt.

After inhaling his scent, I vowed that I wouldn't let myself lose this fight.

I'd lost last night. I wouldn't be able to stand that arrogant face of his when we got home tonight.

So, I back-bridged out of his grasp and turned onto my stomach. From behind me, he hooked his legs around my thighs, spread my legs so I couldn't hold a strong base, and tried hard to break me back down.

It was *that* position that lost him the match because his cock was pressed against my ass. Instead of actually fighting—because, let's face it, I was still way too horny to think straight—I ground my hips back against his. When I felt him harden against his shorts, I elbowed him hard in the ribs and turned us over, so I was on top.

Straddling his waist, I swung my leg around his right calf and squeezed hard, putting his right ankle into a tight lockdown with my legs. Almost immediately, he tapped out, a low, guttural growl exiting his throat.

"Fuck, Aurora. Let go."

"What's wrong?" I asked when I let go and he *still* looked like he was in pain.

He shook his head, and then showed me the large canine scar across his right calf. "It's from a battle I was in years ago with a hound," he said, rubbing it gently. It looked like the muscle had been chewed off and grown back.

"I should call you Achilles."

He growled under his breath and grabbed my hand to pull himself to his feet. "If you start calling me that, *Kitten* is going right out the window." He walked over to the sidelines with me and tugged on his shirt. Despite practice still running, he checked his phone. "Six p.m. Don't we have a date at Pink Moon Tavern to attend?"

"We?" I asked, wiping the sweat off my body with a towel. I glanced over at Marcel and Charolette bickering back and forth about something. "I don't remember you asking to go with me to meet with Adrian." I arched a brow and rolled my deodorant stick under my arms. "But you can come, as long as you apologize to Adrian for what you did last night."

"What did I do?" Ares asked, so seriously dumbfounded that I almost believed him. *Almost.* "Finger-fucked my woman so many times that she had to beg me to stop? Made sure she knew she was mine? Protected her from some asshole who could take her away from me?"

I rolled my eyes and waved good-bye to Marcel and Charolette. "Guess you don't want to go. You can always stay here and babysit Ruffles, so she doesn't go out ho-ing anymore. Will that do it for you?"

"Fine. I'll apologize but not because I'm sorry about it." He grabbed my hand and led me down to the prison, taking a detour before we ran to the tavern. "Only because you want me to."

Dusty and filled with cobwebs, the prison reeked of feces and days-old wheat. Dad sat in his open cell in the same bloodied clothes and barely looked at me. I stared at him for a few moments and frowned. I didn't know what to say to him anymore. I hadn't found the words, nor had the confidence to ask him to live in this pack with Ares and me. He didn't have anywhere else to go, so I thought it was kind of a given, but everything felt weird with him now.

"How's Liam doing?" Ares asked a guard.

Sleeping on the hard cement with chains binding each of his extremities, Liam lay on the ground two cells down from Dad. He was another problem that we needed to sort out as soon as possible. Ares needed a beta to take Liam's place. Marcel would fit perfectly, but he was already in charge of training the pack.

"Doesn't eat his food or talk to anyone here," the guard said, shrugging. "Sits in that corner and sleeps all day or just mutters to himself about how stupid he was for blindly trusting a rogue."

"And the rogue?" I asked, brows furrowed.

After glancing briefly down the hall in the opposite direction, he directed his attention to me. "She's ... self-harming. We've tried to stop it by using metals other than silver, but she continues to find a way."

Ares tensed and glanced down the hall toward her cell. This was a sensitive topic for him. He had done the same to himself

Goddess knew how many times. I didn't want him to even *think* about it.

So, I ushered him up the stairs, but before I followed him, I stopped in front of the guard. "Keep me updated on the rogue and give her a mental evaluation. She has a son. I don't want her trying to give herself fatal wounds."

After he nodded, I followed Ares up the stairs and out into the dark wilderness. I grabbed Ares's hand and let him guide me to the borders, trying to get his mind off the rogue and on something less ... sensitive.

"So, when are we having the pups over for your group therapy session?"

"Tuesday night." Ares intertwined his fingers with mine. "You're going to be there, right?"

"I wouldn't miss it," I said.

He paused, looked over at me, and smiled—a bit of Mars peeking through his solid, rocky exterior. "I wanted to talk to you about the Luna Ceremony. I heard you speaking to Charolette about it during practice and wanted to ask if you would wear my mother's—"

Before Ares could finish, the mind link started buzzing with wolves. *"The hounds are here."*

CHAPTER 7

AURORA

*O*ne quiet and almost-meek hound stood fifty feet away from our pack borders, staring at our prepared guards with dull, dead eyes. I furrowed my brows as Ares and I advanced from the east with caution. So far, the forest near the property line looked empty and clear of any other hounds.

Why was this one alone? And what was he doing here?

This could be a setup.

"Don't attack," I ordered through the mind link.

It was too weird to not only see one hound without his pack, but to also have that same hound not be aggressive toward other wolves. Hounds were undead beasts who attacked anything and everything they could find. To my knowledge, nobody knew the reason for their aggression. But maybe, just maybe, Jeremy had been onto something with all that *divine revenge* talk.

When we approached the guards, Ares growled and bared his teeth at the hound. The hound fixed his gaze on me and walked forward—slowly, steadily, and calculatingly. Though he looked harmless, something about him told me to be careful. This wasn't a typical hound who would've tried to kill me already. And he certainly wasn't a Jeremy-like hound.

Wolves whispered behind me, arguing about how to capture him without anyone dying.

"Stay back. This is a setup. It has to be."

Just as the words left my mind, the hound bolted toward me, slashing his claws through the air with a whoosh, growling deep into the night, and baring his blunt, blood-and-saliva-glazed teeth at me.

Ares shifted into his wolf midair, latched his canines into the wolf's neck, and jerked him side to side like a dog would a rag doll. The hound slammed against the forest floor over and over, the intensity making the tree branches above us shake. I stepped forward toward my warring mate, grasped the hound's neck, and snapped it myself with my bare hands.

Adrenaline pumped through every bloody vessel of my body. I backed up and glared around the forest with the hound's foul scent smeared all over my hands. I waited for more hounds to attack because they rarely fought alone. There had to be more.

And that was when my gaze landed on two piercing gold eyes deep in the woods.

The man who had raised wolves from the dead stood hundreds of yards away from us, staring at me. My heart raced, and I swallowed hard, unable to pull my gaze away. He was watching *me* fight, not Ares. It was extremely unsettling.

Without losing sight of him, I growled low. *"The hound who raped your mother is here,"* I said to Ares through the mind link, not knowing how else to refer to him. I didn't know his name, and I didn't think that Ares did either. *"North. Hidden behind that big pine tree."*

Muscles swollen, mouth bloodied, eyes dark under the night sky, Ares growled and looked north. As soon as he made eye contact, the hound sprinted away through the woods.

Ares went to follow, but I grabbed his hind leg and yanked him back. "Don't attack. He might be up to something that we don't know about."

Ares ripped his leg away from me and took off through the dark and foggy woods. Though I knew he was tired of the hound taunting him, something else was up with that man. I couldn't let Ares thrust himself into war and get killed.

I sprinted after Ares, jumped forward, and snatched his back leg again, landing flat on my stomach. For a moment, Ares dragged me through the woods and against the fallen leaves and twigs. Ares stumbled a bit, his claws digging into the dirt, and stopped.

"*Let go of me, Aurora.*" Ares seethed through the mind link. "*I'm going to kill that fucker. I'm done with his games.*"

Instead of letting go, I wrapped both my hands around his hind leg and pulled him back with all my strength. "You're not going," I said through clenched teeth. I crawled to my knees and pinned him to the ground. "Shift now."

Canines dripping with saliva, Ares shifted under me and wiggled out of my hold. "What was that? I could've killed him. This would be over with by now. We could've stopped a war before it started."

Crossing my arms, I refused to let him talk down to me. "He would've killed you. You don't know how many hounds he has in that forest, waiting to attack." I stepped closer to him and stared up into those wolfish golden eyes. "And I'm not about to let you get killed."

It would destroy me to lose my mate. I had already lost so many family and pack members. But Ares ... he didn't just have a special place in my heart. He owned my heart. Losing him would be like losing a piece of myself.

"We need to amp up our security, so this doesn't happen again." I placed my hands flat on his chest and curled my fingers into the bare muscle. "Please, calm down and think things through before you react. We have a pack to protect."

Vein pulsing wildly in his neck, he looked as if he wanted to rip that man piece by piece. And one day, I'd turn Ares loose, so he could do just that. That man deserved more than just death. But Ares couldn't do anything now. I wouldn't let him put himself in senseless danger.

"Fuck!" Ares hurled his fist into a tree next to us. It snapped and fell, the impact shaking the trees surrounding it.

Everyone stayed quiet, and Ares turned back to me, his eyes golden with a red tint to them. I sucked in a breath.

Though stories plagued Sanguine Wilds of Ares being a god, of his eyes blazing red when fury controlled his body, I had never seen it. After meeting him, I never thought the rumors were true. But maybe, just maybe, I was seeing things.

Most gods, besides our Moon Goddess, were myths created by wolves before us.

Ares wasn't immortal. He suffered wounds, had scars, lived life like everyday could be his last. But those eyes ... they were more vicious and terrifying than any hound I had met, and I loved them more than I thought I should. Something about them seemed so familiar, yet ... I couldn't place it. I didn't know where I had seen them before because it definitely wasn't in this lifetime. I'd remember it if it was.

Storming to a house at the border, where we kept spare clothes, Ares grumbled to himself and tugged on some pants. He snatched up my hand and led us in the opposite direction, toward Pink Moon Tavern. "I'm meeting with Alpha Vulcan about the necromancer in the south. He'd better have fucking information about this shit because I don't want to fucking wait."

"Hopefully." I picked up my pace, trying to keep up with his long strides.

"We are going to my father's for dinner," Ares said to me. "I need to figure out why they're targeting the lunas of this pack.

They targeted my mother, and now, they want my mate. And I will never let them have you."

I swallowed hard, believing that there was more than just that. The hounds were planning something; we just had to figure out what that something was. It wasn't like hounds to ever have a plan. They were ruthless. They were volatile. They were like Ares —personified into demonic hell-dogs. They didn't think before they acted …

But the hound who rose the dead seemed to have a plan. He'd waited and watched as I killed one of his minions. He was calculating, researching, trying to understand … me.

CHAPTER 8

AURORA

*W*olves from different packs gathered inside of Pink Moon Tavern, hooting and howling with each other. Ares led me into the neon-pink-accented building and around the groups of people until we saw Adrian. Typing on his phone and sipping on a chocolate milkshake, he sat alone in a teal booth.

Dark purple claw marks from last night decorated his throat.

When he glanced up, he dropped his phone and held his hands into the air. "I promise I wasn't going to try anything with Aurora. She just asked me to meet her here for—"

"You don't have to explain yourself, Adrian," I reassured, pushing Ares into the other side of the booth and sliding in next to him. I narrowed my eyes at my mate. "Ares has something to say to you. Don't you, Ares?"

Pressing his lips together, Ares flared his nostrils and refused to speak. I elbowed him hard in the ribs, remembering that

Marcel had said it was his weak spot. He winced and cleared his throat.

"I ... apologize for how I acted last night," he said through clenched canines. When Adrian's eyes widened in surprise, Ares added, "But I don't regret it because you shouldn't be ogling your luna."

I glared at Ares's profile. "What he means is that he let himself lose control and that it will *not* happen again." Or else he would not get any of this pussy, even after the Luna Ceremony. "Isn't that right, Ares?"

After Ares grumbled, he sat back in the booth and crossed his arms over his chest, making them look so damn thick that I had to tear my gaze away before my wolf urged me to rip his clothes off right here and now.

A light inside a charred mason jar swung above the booth as some rowdy kids behind us knocked into theirs. I steadied the light and sipped the water that Adrian had gotten for me.

"So, I wanted to talk to you about underground tunnels. There is a war coming that we can't stop, and I want our pups to be safe."

"Your pups?" Adrian asked with wide eyes. "You're having pups?"

My eyes widened, cheeks flushing. "No, not me."

"Not yet," Ares added.

"Not ever, if you don't want to fuck me," I reminded him through the mind link.

I blew an annoyed breath out of my nose and pulled up the blueprints for my old pack's underground tunnels on my phone. "I mean, the pack pups." I handed him the phone. "This was my old pack's blueprints for the tunnels. We had a central shelter under the pack house and some various tunnels leading from different areas of the pack. Since this pack is much bigger, we need to make improvements."

Adrian studied the blueprints for a couple moments, and then nodded. "Who mapped this out? It's very detailed and a smart idea for protection."

Unable to hold back my grin, I beamed in my seat. "I did."

"Damn, I'm impressed." He sipped on his milkshake and handed me back the phone. "Send me these, and I'll see what I can do under the landscape we have already. What kind of improvements do you want to make?"

"More hidden entry points, so hounds can't find them. Also, I need you to evaluate the landscape to make sure there are no tunnels already underground. When we went to the cave, we saw hounds in an underground lair. If there are already tunnels within fifty feet of our property—whether or not they belong to the hounds—I want the walls to be made of cement, not dirt, so the hounds can't claw their way into it."

Ares placed his hand on my thigh, golden eyes glimmering under the dull light. His rageful red-tinted eyes from earlier had disappeared and were replaced with softer, prideful ones. "You've really thought this out."

"Of course I have."

I'd had so much time at my old pack to think about improvements. To be honest, that was all Mom *let* me do. I thought that *she* thought of it as busywork to keep me out of her hair. But I believed that having a hidden escape was essential, and it'd proven to be.

I wished Mom had made the improvements before the hounds attacked our pack, so we could've saved more than a handful of pups. But things would be different this time around. I was now a pack's luna. I vowed to protect them as much as I could even if that meant with my life.

"This project needs to be done as soon as possible. How long will it take you?"

"If I stop all production we have elsewhere"—Adrian paused to think—"and there aren't tunnels underground already, I would say it'd take six months because we're on a huge plot of land." He furrowed his brows and leaned back. "But I think—and I'm not positive—that there used to be a bunker underground after the fallout of 1754, during the War of the Lycans. If there still are some tunnels, it should take significantly less time. Say ... two months, max."

I glanced over at Ares. "Are there tunnels already under your property?"

"I believe that there is a bunker under the pack house, not sure if there are tunnels."

"Start work on this immediately. Drop all your other projects. We need this done as soon as possible. We don't have time to waste. If there are already underground tunnels or even just bunkers, expand on them. We need a safe space within the next few weeks. We can broaden the tunnels sections later, if we have time."

Behind us, the Pink Moon Tavern door opened, its bell jingling. Adrian glanced up, his pupils suddenly dilating. He sat up in the booth, pushed his shoulders back, and inhaled deeply, canines emerging from under his lips—not in a vicious way, but a hungry one.

I glanced over my shoulder at Elijah, who stopped in the middle of the packed diner and stared at Adrian with lustful eyes under his thick-lensed glasses. Pink neon lights glimmering against his dark skin, Elijah pushed his shoulders back and recomposed himself.

"Second-chance mates?" I asked through the mind link to Ares.

Ares eyed them, leaned back in his seat, and relaxed for the first time tonight. *"Goddess, I hope so. Get two guys off your tits. I don't have to go after them."*

I narrowed my eyes at him and slapped him on the chest. *"Stop it."*

He gave me a big lopsided smile and pulled me into his hard chest. *"You know how crazy I am about you, Kitten."*

"More like psychotic."

Elijah stuffed his hands into his pockets and sat in the booth, right beside Adrian. Adrian fumbled to scoot over and give the alpha some room. My lips curled into an even wider smile as I watched them. Goddess, if they weren't second-chance mates, I would shed a damn tear. They looked so cute together already.

"Didn't expect to see you two here," Elijah said, wiping his palms on his black jeans. He glanced over at Adrian and offered him the same smile he used to give my brother. "I'm Alpha Elijah."

Adrian swallowed hard, cheeks turning the lightest shade of pink. "Adrian."

Unable to hold back my excitement, I smacked Ares on the thigh and grinned. Goddess, I loved love and fated mates, destinies that were bound to collide. My stomach fluttered with butterflies. Ares side-eyed me and rested his hand on my thigh, squeezing lightly.

After a few moments of staring at each other, Elijah tore his gaze away and gave me that *don't even think about it* look. I had nagged him for years to find another man or woman who could make him happy. Maybe he'd finally found him.

"So," Elijah started, "we're preparing to dissect the hound tomorrow."

"Already?" I asked. "Aren't you going to run tests on him?"

"We ran some tests on him today. Everything came back normal, but there was something off about his blood. I haven't been informed on what exactly it was, and my doctor hasn't figured out much either. As soon as we do, I'll let you know."

I paused for a moment. "Have you ... done any research on Jeremy?"

He tensed and looked at his hands. "I want him to rest in peace, Aurora. He deserves it."

"You know he'd have wanted you to study him," I said.

It was wrong to want to study my brother, but I needed to figure out how they'd brought him back to life. When the hounds had attacked, he had been ripped piece by piece. Even with necromancy, it would be a struggle to raise him from the dead. Sure, the stone might've played a part, but something else must've helped him too—the same things that'd helped all those other undead hounds.

"Let me study this hound first. I'll see what information I get. If my doctor and researchers can't find anything, I will consider it. But I'm not making any promises. He went through so much. I want him to run in peace with the wolves above."

I nodded. If worse came to worst, we would need to use Jeremy to understand the hounds and give us some insight into this divine revenge because nobody understood it, especially me. But by the way that hound had watched me so intently earlier, I had a bad feeling this retribution had to do with me.

CHAPTER 9

ARES

*T*hank the fucking Goddess that Elijah and Adrian seemed to be mates because I'd loathed seeing Adrian with Aurora last night. I'd wanted to kill the bastard for even walking her home, never mind inviting her out tonight.

"Elijah"—I cleared my throat—"I need to speak with you."

Elijah paused and glanced from Aurora to me, breathing hitched. The last time I'd *talked* with him alone, I'd beaten his ass for keeping the Malavite Stone a secret from me. Now, I needed to chat with him about something twice as important.

"Now."

Aurora looked at me oddly but scooted out of the booth. I walked to the other side of the Pink Moon Tavern, near a group of rowdy wolves drinking to the new moon, so Aurora wouldn't hear.

Elijah stopped a few feet away, pushing his hands into his jean pockets. "What do you want to talk about?"

"My sister doesn't want the stone. I've asked her a hundred

times over. I've had everyone ask her …" I started, my chest tightening. I'd searched long and far for that stone, so I could heal Charolette, and she refused to take it. "And if she doesn't want it, I can't force her."

Elijah raised a dark brow. "You could force her. You're Ares."

"I'm not the man people think I am."

So many rumors ran rampant around Sanguine Wilds about me, ones that had terrified my own mate at one point. And because of me and the way I acted sometimes, we were in a dire situation with little to no help from other alphas.

"So?" Elijah asked. "What do you want from me?"

"If she doesn't accept the stone by the Luna Ceremony, I want you to place it in Aurora."

Elijah crossed his arms and chuckled. "You want *me* to put the stone, which you tore every pack to the ground to get for your sister, inside your mate now?"

Growling, I lengthened my nails into claws and dug them into my palms to keep my anger caged. "Listen to me. I know that you and she have talked about it already. I know that you want to give it to her too. Aurora is … getting stronger every day with proper training. With the other half of the stone, she will be stronger and faster than me. She'd be unstoppable, and that's exactly what we need with these hounds showing up all the time."

Since she'd left her old pack, she had improved every day with Marcel training her. I found it astonishing that her mother never trained her as hard, especially because she was to be the next alpha. For years, her parents had thought of her as weak, as a burden, not able to be a true alpha because she couldn't shift.

They were wrong. I had known it from the beginning.

"I can do that," he said, leaning toward the window. The pink neon lights from the *Open* sign glimmered against his dark skin. "I told Aurora that I would rather put the stone into her than your sister. As long as she agrees to it, my doctor would be happy to do it."

"Ares!" Aurora called over the busy tavern. She stood up in the booth, waving me over and tapping her wrist, as if to hurry me up. "We have dinner with your father!"

After I thanked Elijah, we walked back over to the table.

Aurora pushed Elijah into the booth next to Adrian. "Well, we're off to Ares's father's house for dinner. *So sorry* that we can't stay longer. Hope you both have a good night." She winked at them, giggled, and pulled me out of the tavern.

When the door closed, she didn't head for the woods but peeked in through the tavern window and ogled at Adrian and Elijah. "Oh, they are definitely mates."

I grasped her arm and pulled her away, shaking my head but feeling warmth on the inside. "Kitten, you can't peep on people." I dragged her through the woods and watched her roll those big eyes of hers.

"I wasn't peeping. I was, uh, fixing up my best friend with a man."

"You're a matchmaker now?"

She hummed to herself, a huge smile on her face. "Mayyybe."

Chuckling to myself, I tightened my grasp on her hips and continued through the woods. No matter what she said about rumors and gossip, she loved it so much. Or maybe she just loved seeing people happy and in love because she hadn't gotten that affection, growing up.

When we reached Dad's house, he stood on the front porch, slapped me on the shoulder, and hugged Aurora. "How is my favorite couple doing?" he asked, ushering us into the house.

"Good, Mr. Barrett," Aurora said.

"Everything okay?" he asked me when Aurora disappeared into the dining room.

"No."

When Dad had been alpha, he hadn't had to deal with the hounds. After the War of the Lycans, they had disappeared for hundreds of years. Now, they were back and were building an army for what we thought was to destroy Sanguine Wilds.

Without saying more, I walked into the dining room and saw Charolette and *Marcel* sitting at the table, tensely chatting with each other. I eyed them suspiciously and glanced at Aurora to see her smiling widely again, and then at Marcel.

"What are you doing here?"

Aurora playfully shoved my shoulder and pulled me down next to her. "He's here to eat," she said. Then, she took my hand and trailed it all the way up her thigh to her pussy, knowing exactly how to distract me. *"Like you should be doing."*

My wolf howled inside of me, barking at me to shove Aurora into the back room and eat her wet little cunt until she couldn't stand. Even after I'd told her I wanted to wait until the Luna Ceremony so her first time as luna would be relatively special, she continued to push and push and push me about fucking her. She knew that I didn't have the patience or tolerance for her teasing. And her pussy smelled fucking amazing. I had imagined drawing my tongue up and down those folds so many times today.

Walking into the room with four boxes of pizza, Dad sat at the head of the table and across from us. Cheeks flushing, Aurora quickly pushed my hand away from her pussy, thinking that she was only going to give me a tease.

But I wanted more.

I always wanted more of her.

I slid my hand up her thigh, gently rubbed her pussy through her thin leggings, and drew my fingernails right down where her folds were. When she gushed through her panties and leggings, I slipped my fingers into her pants and nearly groaned at the way her juices coated her soft pussy lips.

"I heard the hounds attacked," Dad said, grabbing a piece of pizza from the box.

"One hound. Northern borders," I said.

Aurora stayed quiet next to me and pressed her lips into a tight line. I cupped her pussy in my palm and pushed my middle finger into her hole.

"Aurora killed him."

Dad turned to Aurora with wide eyes.

She dug her claws into my wrist—a weak attempt to make me stop—and nodded. "Yes, I-I did."

Wanting to ruin her in front of my family, I sank two more fingers into her pussy. *"What's wrong, Kitten?"* I asked through the mind link, rubbing my thumb over her swelling clit.

She squeezed her thighs together, but I forced her legs apart to give myself even more access.

"Spread your legs and keep them spread. Be a good pup for your alpha."

Aurora spread her legs for me without making it obvious to everyone else. As her pussy tightened around my fingers and her legs started to tremble, my cock twitched in my pants. I imagined slipping into her pussy right here and right now, taking her so ruthlessly. I'd had to stop myself so many fucking times lately. I had even jerked off and taken a cold shower this morning before she woke up.

I stared at the bare side of her neck, where Mars would mark her one day. I hoped it was fucking soon because part of me wanted to do it again and feel that rush of adrenaline pump through my veins. Though I respected Mars, I was a greedy bastard and still wanted to keep Aurora as mine.

Quickening my pace, I pumped my fingers in and out of her until she scooted to the edge of her seat and was trembling. *"Is my Kitten going to come for me at my father's dinner table?"*

"Ares ..."

"Alpha," I corrected.

She glanced over at me, cheeks flushing. She parted her lips to say something, but when I curled my fingers around her G-spot, she pressed them back together to hold back a moan and stared down at her lap.

"Ask me for permission to come," I said.

She shut her eyes tightly, her heart thumping so loud that I could hear it. My dick felt so fucking hard in my jeans, pressing against the restrictive material. I wanted Aurora to touch it, suck on it, slide onto it until my load pumped into her cunt.

"Please, Alpha, can I come?"

"Come for me."

Pussy pulsing on my fingers, she started to tremble. I decided to toy with her a bit and draw all the attention to us. She had teased me one too many times.

Still playing with my mate's pussy, I turned to Dad. "There is something I've been meaning to ask you."

Dad wiped his mouth with a paper napkin. "What is it?"

Aurora squeezed my wrist and growled through the mind link at me for drawing attention to her, but I loved seeing her embarrassed and panting for me. I continued to move my fingers in and out of her, letting her ride out her orgasm.

"When Aurora and I went to the cave, they were trying to revive Mom," I said, pulling my fingers out of her pussy and shamelessly sucking them into my mouth to calm myself. "Why do you think that hound wants Mom back?"

The thought of seeing Mom as nothing but bones had been haunting me for the past few days. All I wanted to do was go retrieve her bones, so she could rest in peace. But our pack wasn't prepared to face that kind of challenge. We needed more information on the hounds and to build a larger army. I hoped that the necromancer in the south could help us in some way.

"Son," Dad said, glancing nervously at Charolette. When he returned his gaze to me, I saw fear in his eyes. "There is something that I've never told you about your mother." He paused and sucked in a deep breath. "I loved your mother more than anything else in this entire world, but I was your mother's second-chance mate. And—"

Unable to hold my wolf back, I growled and ripped my claws into Dad's wooden dining room table. I had a bad fucking feeling about what he was about to say next, and I knew I wouldn't be able to handle the truth.

"Don't say it," I said through clenched teeth. I ripped a chunk of the table off and crumbled it into dust in my fist. "Don't fucking tell me that the bastard hound was her original mate. I'll fucking lose it."

Dad cleared his throat. "Fenris was your mother's first mate."

My body shook, trembled, twitched. I stared at the wall with fury pumping through my veins and terror running through my mind. I saw red. I saw blood. I saw betrayal. *This couldn't be fucking happening. It fucking couldn't.*

Charolette gasped. "Oh my Goddess ..."

Aurora placed her hand on my shoulder, rubbing gently. "Calm down."

"Why the fuck didn't you tell me about this sooner?" I seethed at him and postured over him, my own father. I couldn't believe he hadn't told me about that hound sooner. If I had known that they were second-chance mates before, I would've ... I would've ... I didn't know what the fuck I would've done.

"I only ever heard stories of Fenris," Dad said. "And I wanted you to see your mother and me differently. Second-chance mates or not, there was nothing but love between us. I wanted to show you strong love."

"You knew the whole time who the fuck he was?" I shouted. "You knew?! I've been trying to figure it out for fucking years. Why didn't you fucking tell me? Save me some time, so I could kill his fucking ass."

Charolette kicked her leg under the table and slammed it into my shin. I growled at her, baring my canines, and shook my head in disbelief. Yet she didn't back down and almost looked … offended about what I had said.

"Ares, please, relax," Aurora said. "You've been looking for this man for years. Knowing his name wouldn't have done you any good. He's a hound. They come and go as they please. Don't blame your father for this."

"And he's dangerous," Dad added, motioning for me to sit back down. "More dangerous than anything this pack is ready for. Not even you. You don't know what that man is capable of."

Filled with rage, I ripped the tablecloth from the table, the boxes flying off the table and pizza spilling everywhere. "Don't tell me what I'm ready for. I have an alpha mate. She has the stone. We will defeat them whether or not it kills me. And if it does, then she's strong enough to lead our pack to victory."

Aurora widened her eyes and sucked in a breath. "Ares," she whispered softly, tugging on my hand. "Please, listen to what your father is saying. I can't lose you. I won't let you fight blindly anymore."

"I'll kill the fucking bastard with my own two hands," I said.

Charolette growled loudly, eyes glowing a fiery gold and fingers trembling in anger. "Stop it, Ares. Just drop it," she said, voice sharp.

"If it wasn't for him raping our mother, she'd still be alive."

"He's my father!"

I balled my hands into fists and glared at my sister. Charolette pushed her chair out, the legs screeching against the hardwood, and ran down the hall and up the stairs. Marcel watched her disappear and clenched his jaw, staring back and forth between me and the staircase.

Aurora stood up and walked to the hallway. "I'm going to see if she's okay."

CHAPTER 10

AURORA

"Charolette," I called, walking down the wide hall and gazing at family pictures in wooden-carved frames.

After knocking on her door, I stared in awe at a picture of Mars with his mom, his arms wrapped around her thigh and him grinning from ear to ear, his front two teeth gone but his canines poking out through his gums. My lips curled into a frown as I listened to Ares scream at his father downstairs about keeping this secret from him for years.

While part of me wished Mars could be that happy again, I had little control over that man, and I didn't blame him for blowing up at his father. I had always been fond of Mr. Barrett, but knowing that his son would become the alpha … he had to have expected Ares would find out sooner or later.

I knocked twice and placed my ear against the door. "Charolette, can I come in?"

Letting out an exasperated sigh, she opened the door. Almost instantly, she enveloped me into a huge hug, rested her head on my shoulder, and tugged me into the room. "I miss her. I miss my mom." Tears streamed down her cheeks, staining my clothes but I didn't care. "I hate when they talk about her because it makes me so sad."

Not knowing what to do, I wrapped my arms around her and gently stroked her hair. I wasn't going to tell her that it was okay because what had happened to her was devastating and losing a loved one was hard. Goddess, I didn't know how many times I'd cried over Jeremy.

"I-I—" She hiccuped and slumped her shoulders even more, as if she were sinking in on herself. "If I wasn't born, Mom would still be alive. She-she-she wouldn't have taken her life. I am a constant reminder of—"

"Stop it," I demanded in my alpha tone. I pulled away, grabbed her chin, and forced her to look up at me. My heart pounded against my rib cage, hurting so bad that my friend thought this way. "Don't you dare finish that sentence."

She covered her face with her small hands. "B-but it's true."

"No. It's not true. Don't blame yourself for how your mother felt or what she did. You didn't cause her to do that." I shook my head and took her face in my hands. "It wasn't your fault, and it will never be your fault, so don't think like that."

After she pulled herself away from me, she grabbed an orange pillow shaped like the moon, held it to her chest, and curled into a ball on the bed, staring off into space. "Ares and my dad—*my adopted dad*—would be so happy if she were still here."

Sitting on the edge of her bed, I gently rubbed her arm. "They're happy that you're here. They love you so much. Ares has gone to hell and back to find you the stone, so you could survive. Don't think for a minute that they'd be better off without you."

Charolette opened her mouth, and then snapped it closed. I frowned and glanced down at her cream star-covered blankets, wondering what life would've been like if their mother hadn't committed suicide. Would Mars just be Mars? Would Ares have emerged? Would I have even met him yet?

As a silence fell upon us, I heard growling downstairs from Ares.

Charolette pulled the blanket over her head and sniffled. "Do you think my dad thinks about me?"

"Your father always thinks about you. He does so much for you."

"No, I mean, my real father, Fenris."

I parted my lips and pressed them back together, completely taken aback. While I didn't want to talk about Fenris because of how shitty of a person he was, I couldn't deny the fact that Fenris was her biological father. She had been the product of rape and abandonment from him, yet she still wanted to know more about the hound leader.

"Do you think that he'll raise my mother from the dead? I heard that he has her bones and was trying to bring her back."

My whole body tensed. "Where did you hear that?"

"Marcel."

Marcel. I would have to beat some sense into that boy later. I didn't want him telling anyone about this. If the average wolf found out the true nature of the hounds, everything would end in chaos.

Charolette curled up next to me and stared up at me with bright eyes, like I had all her answers—how I imagined many people would look up to me once Ares and Mars officially announced me as their luna. "Do you think he thinks about her still? Loves her?"

"I don't know, Charolette."

Because, well, I didn't. When we had seen him trying to bring back those bodies, he'd looked so determined to bring Charolette's mother back. And I wasn't sure if it was to hurt Ares or for his own selfish reasons. Whatever it was for, I couldn't get hers hopes up. We had to kill Fenris to end this; he had taken so much from us.

CHAPTER 11

ARES

*A*s soon as Charolette and Aurora disappeared upstairs, Dad cleared his throat. "There's something else too." He paused for a moment until he heard Charolette shut her door. "I didn't tell you when you became alpha because I thought that it'd ended with your mother."

Knowing that there was more bullshit that I needed to listen to, I sat in the chair. "What?"

Dad peeled a piece of fallen pizza from his lap and wiped a napkin over the sauce. "During the War of the Lycans, hundreds and hundreds of years ago, a divinity prophesied the future of our pack."

I growled under my breath and clenched my hands into fists on the table. Marcel looked at me, and then back at my dad, tensing. Dad raised his brow at me and gave me that stern look he had used when he wanted Mars to calm down when he was younger. But I didn't know how to calm down without Aurora.

"What's the curse?" I asked him outright, voice teetering.

Dad never beat around the bush. He said what he needed to say, like true alphas did.

"The prophecy was that a luna from this pack would be taken by the leader of the hounds."

"What do you mean, she'd be fucking taken?"

"Some people believe she would be taken as a mate. Others think that version of the prophecy has been bastardized and that the true prophecy means that the luna would become leader of the hounds."

"No," I growled, unable to displace all my rage. "She will not."

"What's the entire prophecy?" Marcel asked with the same bewildered expression.

Dad threw a dirty napkin into the center of the messy table. "The prophecy is that we'd lose our luna to the hound leader and that being with the hounds would kill her, but when she dies, this war with the hounds would end for good." He gulped and stared emptily at the table. "I thought this woman who'd end the hounds for good was your mother, but they're back."

I shook in rage. Nobody would take Aurora from me. Not physically. Not sexually. Not emotionally. Aurora was mine and only mine. Nobody would lay a hand on her body. She wouldn't leave. Mars and I wouldn't let her.

Marcel cleared his throat and stared down at the table. "It's just a prophecy," he said, trying to play it off lightly. But it didn't feel like just a prophecy. It felt fucking real. "We can stop it from happening. You can always stop prophecies from happening. It is the first thing that we learned in warrior training."

"The divinity who spoke the prophecy provided a way to end it, but you're not going to like it." He blew out a deep breath. "If Aurora is the one the hounds will take, you can find that man's weakness and kill him with it or offer an alpha in place of Aurora." He paused. "Because Aurora is an alpha, you can replace her life with someone else's to protect her. I believe you must speak with someone in the underworld named Hella, though I'm sure if an alpha is actually willing to sacrifice himself while fighting Fenris, it could work and stop him, especially because he takes direct part in the prophecy."

"I'll do it."

It wasn't even a question. I would do anything for that woman. She was my entire world.

Dad's eyes hardened. "I'd prefer the first option."

"Me too, but if sacrificing myself is what it takes to keep Aurora safe, then I will." I thought about all the nights I had spent with Aurora, all the early mornings, watching her shift in her sleep, the way she smiled up at me when I whispered her name. I wouldn't ever let her die.

Marcel cleared his throat. "Let's focus on finding his weakness."

"My mother was his weakness, but she's gone." I glanced over at Dad. "If you thought this prophecy was about Mom, if you knew that they'd try to take her away from us, why didn't you surrender yourself for her?"

Dad glanced down at the table in guilt. I wanted to hate him for not doing it himself, but I wouldn't be half the man I was today if he hadn't grown up to teach me the way to lead. No matter how hard he was on me, he always made me stronger.

"I had to choose between my children and this entire pack, and your mother." Tears welled up in his eyes. "If I had known for sure that your mother would be able to raise you and wouldn't end up taking her life in the end, I would've. But your mother was unstable after he raped her. I didn't want you and Charolette to grow up without parents." He wiped a tear off his cheek. "I should've done things differently, but I have to live with my decision for the rest of my life."

Letting it all sink in, I paced the room and ran a hand through my hair.

"What do you plan to do with the other half of the stone? Charolette isn't going to take it. She hasn't budged once, and I don't think she will." Dad glanced over at Marcel, who clenched his jaw, as if he was genuinely angry at Charolette's decision. It wasn't an expression I saw often from him. He and Charolette fought all the damn time.

"You think Fenris wants Aurora for the stone, don't you?" I asked, worry plaguing me.

After a curt nod, he said, "Yes, but I think giving her the other half of it would do her more good than harm. I was watching her fight you in practice earlier. She's extremely talented and already so strong. With the other half of the stone, she'd be able to do more than just shift easily."

"I think the same," Marcel said. "Charolette really doesn't fucking want it."

"Maybe with the stone, you will be able to defeat the hounds without her being taken," Dad said. "I don't know though. There wasn't any mention of the stone in the prophecy. I'm not even sure that they knew about it at the time. It could be another loophole. Just be careful. There has only been one person to ever wield the entire stone in their body. She—"

Upstairs, the door opened. Aurora's and Charolette's scents drifted down the stairs.

I furrowed my brows at him, waiting for him to continue. "What?"

"I'll tell you later. I just wanted you to know that I couldn't protect your mother, but you must protect Aurora at all costs, especially because she has the stone. But most importantly, because if she has the other half of the stone, she will be the strongest werewolf to ever grace these lands."

CHAPTER 12

AURORA

On our short walk home, Ares clutched my hand tightly and repeatedly scanned the forest, as if he was on guard for someone or something to attack. Moonlight flooded the cracked street pavement while tiny lightning bugs floated by, dodging falling leaves.

"You know I love you, right?" Ares asked suddenly. "That I'd do anything for you?"

I stopped, chest tightening, and stared up into his golden eyes. Ares didn't get affected by many things very easily. The conversation with his father must've been worse than I'd thought.

I grasped his hand to let him know that I did. "I'd do anything for you too. I love you and Mars."

Though a strained expression flashed on his face, he forced a half-smile. "I can't wait to make you our luna, but you must do a few things before. I can't lose you." He ushered me closer to the pack house, glancing around the forest again. "I can't fucking lose you, Aurora."

Ruffles sat in the window, swaying her tail and watching us— or maybe she was staring at Pringle, who sat in front of some hedges and chased his tail. Ares grimaced at him and opened the front doors.

"What's going on, Ares? What'd your father say?"

After pushing me inside, he shut and locked the doors behind us. "That you should have the stone," he said, the look on his face telling me that he wanted to say so much more. But instead, he cupped my face and drew his thumb across my cheek. "And I agree."

"You agree?" I asked in disbelief, laying my hand over his. "I thought you wanted me to give the stone to your sister? I *want* to give the stone to your sister."

I couldn't bear to see her die. I had already lost my brother twice. I couldn't lose Charolette too. Within the past few weeks, we had grown so much closer to each other.

"You need the stone, Kitten." He rested his forehead against mine. "It will help you shift and make you stronger than anyone in this pack, including me."

When he blew an angry breath from his nose, I knew that there was more. He wasn't telling me everything.

"What is it? Why the sudden change?"

"The hounds," he said quietly, eyes glazing over for a moment as he mind linked with pack warriors, telling them to increase border security and guards around the pack house. When he turned back to me, he grabbed my hand and walked me up the stairs. "They're going to try to take you away from me. Fenris, my mother's *mate*"—the word came out of his mouth with so much distaste, as if he didn't think the hound deserved such a title—"he plans to make you his."

While I had the urge to laugh because I would never in a million years leave with that hound—I'd kill him before he touched me—I instead pressed my lips together because I had only seen Ares this terrified once: after the hound attack at Mom's pack.

"I have lost everything. My mom. Maybe Charolette. I can't let them have you. You're my life, Mars's life, too."

Butterflies swarmed inside my stomach, all those feelings I'd had on the night we met making me smile. Every single day, Ares surprised me with another side of himself, and my love for him grew stronger.

Though I didn't want to take the stone from Charolette, she didn't want it. The reason she'd refused broke my heart, but she seemed way too adamant to change her mind. I had tried desperately. Mars and Ares had tried desperately. Hell, Marcel had even tried desperately. Yet she still refused it.

And I couldn't let a power like that go to waste.

A war was barreling toward us at lightning speed, and using it might be the only way to stop it.

Or at least, it'd give Ares and Mars peace of mind.

"Okay," I whispered. "I'll do it. I need to ask Eli—"

"I already talked to him at the tavern."

My eyes widened. "You're serious about this."

"Dead fucking serious, Kitten," he said, eyes flickering a hundred shades of gold. He took my hand and led me to our bedroom. "Come. You're going to wear something of my mother's for the Luna Ceremony. I want to show it to you."

Unlike Mars, he wasn't going to ask me to wear it. Ares demanded.

After rummaging through his dresser, he pulled out a black box with a sparkling emerald-green gemstone on a necklace encrusted with silver. Although hesitant at first, I didn't think the silver would be in direct contact with any of my skin.

"It's beautiful," I whispered.

"My family has passed this down for centuries," he said, handing me the necklace.

Under the moonlight, the emerald flickered. I brushed my thumb across the gem and smiled.

He swept his fingers against the chain. "Let me help you try it—"

Suddenly, he paused, gold eyes glazing over as he talked through the mind link. A moment later, someone knocked on our front doors. He pushed the necklace into my hand and wrapped my fingers around it.

"Go take care of whoever is at the door. And when you come back, I'll have it on," I said.

When he slipped out of the room, I walked into our bathroom and shut the door behind me. I clasped the necklace around my neck and slipped out of my clothes, lips curling into a smirk, standing completely naked on the marble floor.

Payback's a bitch, Ares.

Ares wiggled the bathroom doorknob a few moments later. "Everything is taken care of. Come out. I've been waiting to see this on you for so damn long."

My lips curled into a smile. "Sit and be patient, Ares. You're going to love it on me."

"Kitten, you know I don't have patience."

"Well, if you want to see it on me, you'll sit, Alpha," I said, hand wrapped around the knob. "Be a good boy for once."

Hearing the bed dip, I peeked my head out and smiled at Ares as he lounged against the mattress, his shirt in the hamper and his taut abdomen braced hard.

"Are you ready to see your luna?" I asked.

"Don't make me wait."

Heat gathered in my core, and I pushed the door open and sauntered over to him, loving the way he tensed suddenly at my nakedness. I spun slowly for him and brushed my fingers over the necklace.

"Do I look like a luna?" I asked, my wolf purring loudly so her alpha could hear it.

"Kitten ..." he said through clenched teeth, as if he was trying desperately to control his beast.

"Still a kitten to you?" I crawled onto the bed, laid back against the headboard, and spread my bare legs for him. Then, I slipped my fingers between my legs and teased my clit. "How about now, Alpha? Am I good enough to be your luna? Hmm?"

The most ferocious, menacing growl rumbled from his throat, his canines extending under his lips and eyes glowing gold. "You don't know who you're teasing."

Rubbing my clit in sweet, torturous circles, I moaned softly and stared at him, taunting him to come take me. I had been begging for him to thrust himself inside of me for days now. I didn't care how ruthlessly he took me.

"I know exactly who I'm teasing," I said. "The big, bad wolf."

Ares let out another monstrous snarl, tilting his head down and staring at me through hooded eyes. On edge and impatient, he had been wrapped around my finger since I stepped out of the bathroom.

So, I pushed him even more.

I spit on my fingers and rubbed my pink clit, making it glisten. "I know you want it."

His sharp canines lengthened even more under his lips, and I wondered what it would feel like if Mars marked me tonight. How much closer would I feel to him? How much pleasure would pump through my body as he pounded into me from behind? Would he be ruthless with me like Ares had been, or would he take it slow?

"Kitten," Ares said, standing at the end of the bed with his hands on the mattress and his shoulders flexed. "You know I can't control myself around you."

"What? My hungry alpha can't control himself around me?" I trailed my toes down his abdomen to the front of his pants and then against his hardness.

He snatched my ankle and yanked me to the edge of the bed, spreading my legs and staring down at my pussy.

Oh, Ares is going to break for me.

He drew his fingers down my inner thighs so softly, making me shiver. I purred and arched my back, waiting for him to touch me. He inhaled deeply and placed his lips on my knee, brushing them down my thigh and right to my pussy.

And just as he was about to lay his hot mouth on my wetness, I set my foot on his chest and pushed him away. "The only way you're getting my pussy tonight is if you finally give me what I want. No eating. No touching. No tasting unless you give it to me."

"Aurora," he growled low, warning me not to test him.

But I wanted to test him all day because I could handle everything he gave me. He just wouldn't be able to handle himself—before becoming a wreck in his pants.

I stared up at him and pushed a finger into my wet pussy, moaning softly. "All you have to do is shove your big cock into me ..." I drove in another finger and clenched. "Thrust me hard against the headboard." I thrust my free hand into his hair and forced him to watch my fingers as I pleasured myself. "Pump all your cum into me until I'm full with *your pups*."

When all he could do was tense, I smirked and pulled my fingers out of my pussy, shoving them into his mouth. "Here's a taste."

After I pulled out my fingers, I pressed my legs together and rolled away from him and off the bed. "But if you don't want it, I can go play with myself in the other room, let you listen to my moans all night long, let you stroke your cock to me, wondering how good you'd feel in—"

Before I could continue, he seized my hips, tossed me onto the bed so I landed on my stomach, and climbed on top of me from behind. A rush of heat warmed my core. Alpha Ares was exactly how I wanted him—on the verge of losing complete control.

He thrust my legs apart and ground his hard cock against me from through his pants. "Is this what you want, Kitten?" he asked into my ear, grabbing my hand and forcing me to grope him.

My pussy clenched, and I nodded my head. "Don't you want to please your luna?"

After swiftly pushing down his pants, he rested the head of his cock against my entrance and pressed me hard against the mattress, leaning over me and curling a hand around the front of my neck, his lips by my ear. "You want me to lose all fucking control? Is that what you fucking want?"

Instead of giving me time to answer, he shoved himself into me until his hips met mine. I clenched around him and whimpered, my pussy full with his huge, veiny cock.

He growled into my ear, "Fucking answer me."

"Yes," I breathed out. "I want to see you lose control."

He slowly pulled himself out, and then pushed himself back into me in one long stroke. After curling his hand around my thigh, he rolled us over, so my back rested against his chest. He held my legs open wide and slammed himself deep inside of me, my pussy clenching.

"Harder, please," I moaned out, pleasure pumping through me.

When he brushed his callous fingers against my swollen clit, I moaned. Wave after wave of pleasure pumped out of me, yet he continued to tease my clit, holding my legs far apart and peering over my shoulder to watch my pussy quiver.

"Mine," he said into my ear.

"Yes," I breathed. "Yours."

He picked up his pace, thrusting faster inside of me, and snaked a hand around my throat. "You've been waiting for this, haven't you?"

He slapped my clit, and I released on him again and nodded my head.

"Yes," I cried out. "Yes, I love it. Fuck me harder. I want to feel your cum. All of it."

He groaned against me and pounded harder inside of me. He growled into my ear and sucked harshly on the bare side of my neck, right where Mars would put his mark soon. "I promised Mars that I wouldn't mark you, that I'd leave this side of your neck bare."

I leaned my neck away, his canines pricking my skin. He let out a guttural growl.

"I won't sink my canines into it and claim it as my own"— Ares strummed his fingers against his mark on my neck—"like I did here." He sucked harsher on the skin, definitely leaving love marks. "But tomorrow, Mars will see that every part of you belongs to me; even his mark will lay atop the skin that I had in my mouth, skin that you want me to mark." He lifted his nose and parted his lips right by my ear, stilling inside of me. "Fuck, Kitten."

Shifting his hips so he pushed more of himself up into me, he rolled us onto our sides.

"You can take it out," I said, wiggling in his hold. "You came, didn't you?"

He wrapped his arm around me, cupping my pussy in his large hand. "This is my pussy, Kitten. You told me if I fucked you, I could do what I wanted with it," he said, smirking against my neck. "So, I'm going to keep it inside of you, making sure all my cum stays inside of your tight cunt for as long as I want."

My entire body tingled, and I clenched on him again, trying to stop my racing thoughts. I rested my head on the pillow and closed my eyes, breath hitched, wolf pleased, and thoroughly fucked.

He was right. He could do whatever he wanted with me tonight, and I'd let him.

CHAPTER 13

MARS

*W*ith my white Flaming Chariot T-shirt hanging off her body in shreds, Aurora struggled to squirm away from the hound bastard at the foot of the bed. He snatched her ankle and yanked her to the edge of the mattress, forcing himself between her legs and fondling her in places only I should touch.

"Stop!" she screamed, tears streaming down her face. Blood dripped down her throat from the large claw marks in her neck and pooled by her collarbone, her skin paling. "Please, stop! Don't touch me!"

I roared at Mom's rapist and tried so hard to move, but I felt glued to the spot near the door. With heavy legs and a racing heart, I clutched my chest. Aurora ... he couldn't take Aurora from me.

She screamed and kicked him, punched as hard as she could. But she wasn't strong enough to push him off of her. He grabbed her tighter, claws digging into her skin and ripping the rest of her clothes off to leave her bare to him.

Half of the Malavite Stone glowed brightly on our nightstand, and I cursed myself for not giving it to her sooner or forcing her to take it. We had thought Fenris was after the stone, but he had been after her the whole time. He wanted to do to her what he had done to Mom as I watched helplessly from the door.

Fenris flipped her over so she sat on all fours facing me, pushed himself between her legs, and shoved three sharp claws into her. She shrieked and grasped the sheets as droplets of blood spilled down her thighs.

"Please," she pleaded, hiccuping, "please, stop ..."

After thrusting his fingers into her harder, he pulled out and gripped her left shoulder in one hand and dug his claws into the back of her neck with the other, right above the Malavite Stone that helped Aurora live a decent life. She froze—almost instinctively—as if she couldn't move, as if she was immobilized from the action.

My heart pounded in my chest, and I growled at her to move, to struggle, to do something to get away from him. I didn't care if he ripped the stone out of her. I didn't care if she couldn't walk anymore. I didn't care if she was paralyzed for the rest of her life. I could make that better for her as best as I could.

But I couldn't take away the pain I'd see on her face every day if he raped her, the shame, the guilt that she shouldn't ever have to feel. He couldn't destroy someone else that I loved just for the hell of it.

"Come here, Kitten," I begged, my lips trembling. I tried to move but couldn't. "Please, Kitten."

She stared at me, her entire body frozen, except her eyes, which looked so helpless and so glossy.

"Don't stop struggling."

For a second time, I found myself unable to help the one person I cared about the most. I was weak. Totally and utterly weak. This couldn't be happening. This couldn't be happening. I needed to protect my mate. It was what I had been made to do. If I couldn't do that ... I didn't deserve to fucking walk this earth anymore.

As she knelt, incapacitated and defenselessly with a look of sorrow on her face and trembling lips, he rubbed the head of his dick against her entrance and thrust himself into her. A tear slid down her cheek, yet she still couldn't move her limbs.

"I-I'm so-so-sorry," she managed.

"Stay strong, Kitten ..." I pushed myself to move. I had to move. I had to help her. "Stay strong for me. Please." My feet felt like stone, heavy and anchored. "Don't let him win. Don't let him take you too. You're so much stronger than you think."

Aurora's body jerked back and forth as he raped her. Blood flowed down her thighs and down her back and around her ribcage from his grasp on the Malavite Stone. More tears streamed down her face, staining our bedsheets.

Fear ran through every one of my veins, as I could do nothing but watch. I saw Mom in her eyes, the look of shame she had worn on her face every day, her dead body lying in the bed with a good-bye letter to her children and her mate.

"No," I whispered, crouching down in the corner and wrapping my arms around myself. "No, Goddess, no."

Fenris used Aurora to thrust deeper into her, his claws sinking further into her flesh. The life faded from Aurora's eyes, all that liveliness and hope and happiness completely gone. Just gone. Just like Mom.

After grunting, he pulled out of her and made me watch his cum mix with blood dripping out of her pussy. With his hand lodged in her back, he tossed her around like she was a rag doll.

"Mine," he said to me, kissing her on the neck but staring at me. "She's mine. Not even an alpha like you can stop me from taking her. With or without Ares, you're weak, Mars. I'm coming for her."

Then, he tore the stone out of her spine and snapped her neck, letting her lifeless body smack against the bedpost with a thump and onto the ground. Blood leaked from her throat, creating a sanguine puddle underneath her.

Fenris disappeared into thin air, and I finally found the strength to move my legs. I doubled over Aurora's dead body and clutched her to my chest.

"No!" I pressed my hands against the back of her head and her neck *to stop the blood, but it kept pouring out of her. "No," I said softer this time, body trembling back and forth. "Please, Aurora, don't leave me. You're the only thing I care about, my only reason for living anymore."*

"Mars," she said softly. But her eyes weren't open, and her heart wasn't beating.

"Someone, help me," I screamed. But I was all alone. "He killed her. He killed my mate."

"Mars," she said again.

I squeezed my eyes shut. How was I hearing her? How was I—

Aurora wrapped her arms around me from behind and cradled my head. "Mars, stop. It's just a bad dream," Aurora said into my ear, pulling the hair off my sweaty forehead. She rocked us back and forth in our bed. "I'm here."

Blinking my eyes open, I looked at the foot of the bed.

No body. No blood. No dead Aurora.

Realizing that I'd had the worst nightmare of my life, I squeezed her hand tightly, as if she would disappear if I didn't. Her heart beat evenly against my back, her sweet scent drifting into my nostrils. She continued to rock us until I could finally breathe again.

"I'm here," she whispered, kissing my neck. "I'll always be here for you."

I turned in her hold, cupped her jaw, and stroked my thumb against her cheek. "I'm sorry," I said, so desperate to hear her forgiveness. It had just been a dream, but it'd felt too real, too damn real.

"There's nothing to apologize for." She stood, pulled me to my feet, and walked us to the bathroom. "A warm bath always calms you down. We can talk about your dream, if you want." She turned on the water and stopped it when the tub filled halfway. "Come on."

Seconds away from a panic attack, I stood by the bathroom

door with trembling fingers and a racing heart. I swallowed hard, stared between her and the bath, and pressed my lips together. I wanted to protect her from the truth—that Fenris was coming for her—but I needed to tell her everything.

I wasn't strong enough to face this alone. Neither was Ares.

Aurora walked toward me in her Flaming Chariot nightshirt and grasped the waistband of my shorts to pull them down. She crouched down to the floor and grabbed for my sock. "Let me take these off you," she said, stripping them off when I lifted my foot. After she removed both socks, she grasped my shaky hand and led me to the bath. "Get in."

"You first."

She glanced at me for a few moments and then stripped off her shirt and sat in the bath, scooching forward so I could sit behind her. For the briefest moment, I imagined her sitting in a tub of her blood similar to the pool of blood where she'd lain life-lessly inside my dream. I closed my eyes, shook my head, and sat behind her in the sudsy water.

Wrapping one arm around her waist, I took the soapy loofah from her and drew it across every inch of her bare chest. She leaned back, rested her head on my collarbone, and stared up at me, the ends of her brown hair wetting in the water.

After a moment, she frowned. "Do you want to talk about it?"

Trailing the loofah across her neck, I imagined scrubbing the blood off it and reminded myself it had been a nightmare and nothing more. It wasn't real life, but it could be. It damn well could be one of these days.

Releasing the loofah from my grasp, I let it float in the tub and gently caressed Aurora's skin. This woman was my mate. She was the only thing that mattered to me. I couldn't let her continue to walk about the pack and through the forest without thinking about her safety.

She needed the stone. She'd be strong with the stone.

"Fenris is coming for you, Aurora," I whispered.

A lump formed in my throat. The monsters that my therapist, Denise, had called anxiety and panic slithered up my spine like unwanted serpents. They weren't so much monsters to me than they were part of my damn soul. I couldn't remember a day in my life I had gone without them. It was almost as if they had been ingrained in me since the beginning of time, even before this lifetime.

She turned in the water and straddled my waist, tucking some hair behind my ear. "What do you mean?"

"My father told me at dinner. Our pack is cursed. Fenris is coming to take you away from me, and I can't protect you." I licked my dry lips and looked between us, ashamed that I couldn't save her in my dream. "Just like I couldn't save my mother from his wrath."

"He wants the stone," she said. "He doesn't want me."

I pressed my lips together, so they wouldn't tremble. I couldn't stand losing this woman. She was everything to me. She gave me so much strength to get through the days. If I lost her, I'd fail at being a mate, a wolf, and an alpha.

Somehow, someway, I felt like I'd had these thoughts before. Something inside of me knew and understood how much heartbreak the loss of Aurora would bring us, like we had lost her before in a past life.

"He wants you, Aurora," I whispered, holding her tightly. "We have to be careful. Please, be careful for me whenever you're out. And ... I need you to think about using the other half of the stone for your own safety. Charolette won't take it, so you have to."

"But, Mars ..."

"Just think about it, please."

She nodded in agreement. "Okay."

"You know that I would do anything for you, right?" I asked, placing my lips against her knuckles and offering her my best smile. "Anything I have to do to protect you, even sacrifice my—"

"No." She shook her head. "Don't even finish that sentence."

"I'm speaking the truth," I said, wanting her to be ready for when the time came. I'd fight like hell before I let anyone kill me, but I'd fight even harder to make sure what had happened in my nightmare would never happen in real life.

Aurora was a queen, a damn goddess.

I glanced down to the unmarked side of her neck and let my canines lengthen under my lips. Ares had claimed her so viciously and violently, but now, it was my turn. I didn't know when I'd have another chance like this. Forever wasn't promised.

I'd thought I'd have eternity with Mom, but she was gone in the blink of an eye.

"Let me mark you," I said quietly, pushing some hair behind her shoulder.

"You want to mark me?" She stared up at me with wide eyes. "I thought you wanted to wait until the Luna Ceremony."

I inched closer to her and pushed more hair behind her shoulder, giving me a clear view of her beautiful, bare neck. Ares had kissed her there so many times last night, had left a red hickey right where we wanted to mark her.

"I don't want to wait anymore."

She brushed her fingers against my forearm and moved closer to me, the water sloshing over the edge of the tub. Orange sunlight flooded in through the window, and I inhaled her sweet scent, positioning my teeth at the base of her neck.

"I love you," I murmured against her, and then I sank my canines into my mate.

CHAPTER 14

AURORA

"Goddess, Mars …" I whispered, tilting my head to the side and allowing him better access to pierce me with his immense, razor-sharp canines.

Ecstasy crashed through me, hitting me almost as brutally as Ares had jerked that hound around the other night. I curled my fingers into his chest and moaned as droplets of blood rolled down my bare chest and permeated through the bath water.

Forget the sex, the lust, the need for this man. I had ached for Mars to claim me since Ares had that night in the prison. Unlike Ares's, there was no hastiness, no recklessness, and certainly no jealousy behind the bite. Mars's mark was made with care, caution, and most of all, love.

Mars inhaled deeply and grunted against me, all his thoughts, doubts, and insecurities suffusing my mind. And while Mars almost had more memories than Ares, a distant vision of me being bent over our bed and screaming for something to stop was the only thing I could seem to focus on.

Maybe this was his nightmare last night, one of me being ... raped.

I sucked in a breath as the vision became clearer. Mars stood in the corner, unable to move and desperately calling my name, while I lay on the bed, paralyzed with Fenris taking me forcefully from behind.

After a few moments, he tensed and pulled his teeth out. "Sorry you had to see that."

Shoulders slumping forward, he licked my wound and covered the gash with a thick layer of saliva. Almost immediately, my skin sealed the lesion shut and healed the wound. Yet I still felt the swell of his mark, the epicenter of his love, the part of him rushing through me.

I ached when Mars pulled himself away but relished in the pain.

Wrapping my arms around his shoulders, I moved closer to him and kissed him. "Take me out for breakfast. Let me show everyone your mark. I want them to know that I'm totally and completely yours."

Mars tucked some hair behind my ear, drawing his fingers across my cheekbone. "You've always been mine, Kitten, since the moment I met you at the lake and you let me love you." He sucked my bottom lip between his teeth and tugged gently. "You own my soul, Aurora, every damn part of me, of *us*. Ares and I would do anything for you."

After pulling his lips into one more kiss, my heart fluttering at the thought of spending my life with Mars, I stood up and handed him a towel. I swiped my hand across the steamy bathroom mirror, wiped the beads of water off my chest, and smiled at the reflection of my swollen love bite. Surrounded by an onslaught of purple bruises, four large canine marks decorated my neck on each side.

With a towel wrapped around his waist, Mars stood behind me and admired his mark, drawing a finger down the side of my throat and stopping right before he touched the scars. Though I could still faintly see those nasty thoughts of Fenris inside his mind, he actually smiled and pulled me into a hug.

"You're mine," he murmured into my ear, staring at my reflection in the mirror.

"*Meow.*" Ruffles appeared at the door, looking directly at Mars and swatting her tail.

Mars cracked a smile and strummed his fingers against my stomach. "You're mine too, Ruffles."

Ruffles purred, her tail slowing to a sway. She disappeared, and then a moment later, she reappeared with her blue hat between her teeth. She dropped it in front of our feet and stared up at Mars. "*Meow.*"

"Sorry, Ruffles, you're not invited to our date."

Licking the chip dust off her whiskers, Ruffles ignored me and mewed at Mars again.

"You're always welcome to come with us, Ruffles. Don't listen to Aurora. She's just *jealous.*" He leaned down, fastened the hat on her head, and sneezed, scaring Ruffles in the process.

I tugged him into our bedroom and tossed him some clothes. "We should get you more allergy medication when we're out. We're running low." I pulled on some shorts and a sweatshirt, knowing that though fall had just started, the strong breeze and fog would block any warmth from the sun.

Ruffles padded to the front doors, her booty swaying back and forth. Something told me that she didn't want to come with us to go out on our date. She was on the prowl for her new man, Pringle.

Mars wrapped his arm around my waist and held me against him as we walked out the front doors and down the driveway, heading straight for town. I wanted to say that he held me close because of his mark, but I knew deep down that it soothed him and Ares to know I was close to him in case a hound attacked.

As we ambled downtown, I brushed my fingers against my

newest mark, savoring the feeling of it. Don't get me wrong; I loved Ares's mark, but Mars needed the extra love, more than Ares ever did. Being the shield and the spear, Ares knew Mars needed that protection too.

When we rounded the corner into town, Pringle walked right past us with a gray mouse in his mouth. He saw Ruffles and immediately changed his direction, stopping in front of her and placing the mouse at her feet, as if he were making a sacrifice to a goddess. After giving me a sassy smirk, Ruffles sniffed it and glanced toward the alley behind Moon's Cafe.

Looked like Ruffles was going to have her first official date.

"Don't get any diseases," I shouted, crossing my arms over my chest.

Mars leaned over my shoulder. "And she's not talking about eating the mouse."

I playfully pushed his chest and told Ruffles not to go far. She had our scent all over her tiny cat body. If Fenris found her out in the wild, there was no telling what he'd do to her to get at me. Mars had said Fenris wanted me and my stone, and I wouldn't let Fenris win this little game he wanted to play.

Ruffles nudged Pringle, and Pringle picked up the mouse, following her into the back alleyway behind Moon's. After ensuring that Ruffles wouldn't leave the alley, I walked toward the café with Mars in tow.

Beautiful white-painted silhouettes of the Moon Goddess decorated Moon's black walls. Star- and moon-shaped lights dangled from the high ceiling. Mars grabbed my hand and found a seat at one of the white couches and wooden tables that lined the outskirts of the small room. To the average human, this was just another café, but to wolves, this was a café dedicated to our goddess, the woman who had breathed life into us and chosen our fated mates.

"The pups are coming over tomorrow night," Mars said,

trailing his nose up the side of my neck near his mark as we waited for our Chai moon tea.

I shivered at his touch and eyed the torch-like candle flickering in the center of the table. "Are you going to show me how well you act around them?"

He wrapped his arms around my waist, sprawling one hand over my stomach. "Of course I am, Kitten." He curled his fingers into my flesh. "I want your belly swollen with my pups soon. I want little Auroras running around our pack house."

"Being tormented by a little Ares?"

"No, we're having girls, and they're going to be the strongest female alphas the world has ever seen." He chuckled into my ear and placed his lips on his mark. "Besides their mother, of course."

Talking about having children with my mate made my stomach tighten. While I wanted pups, now wasn't the right time, especially with everything going on in this uncertain world. But I also knew that Ares *and* Mars felt differently about it all. They both wanted to give me pups.

Mars leaned in closer. "So you'll have a piece of me when I'm gone," he whispered in my ear.

Tensing, I pulled away and suddenly felt defeated. I didn't want Mars to think that way because we were going to survive these attacks and this war. Maybe Mars was letting his nightmare frighten him too much, or maybe his father had said something to him last night about Fenris because it wasn't like him to … to act so conquered by fear.

"Don't be sad, Kitten," he whispered, taking my hands. "I didn't mean to make you sad."

I nodded and wiped away some tears. "I know."

Unable to take my eyes off him, I frowned at his goddamn perfect face. He had always been more than I'd ever asked for, and I wanted to be with him forever. He wasn't going to sacrifice himself for me. I wouldn't let him. I'd use the other half of the damn stone on him if I had to.

CHAPTER 15

AURORA

"*T*omorrow, I will talk to Elijah about the stone," I said after breakfast.

"About putting it inside of you," Mars clarified.

"Maybe ..."

Did I want to use it? Maybe. Would I rather have Charolette use it? Definitely.

Charolette didn't want it though. She didn't want to be a burden on anyone, thought she didn't deserve this life, and she believed her mom had committed suicide because of her. Just like Ares and Mars, Charolette had grown up living in a harsh reality. She deserved the stone more than I did, but nobody could force her to take it.

"Soon," Mars suddenly demanded. A darkness flashed through his eyes, and he thrust his shoulders back and ripped open the pack house's front doors and stormed in. Ares was back in control, about to tear me to shreds for not agreeing. "You'll get it done soon because I'm not letting Fenris fucking touch you."

I blew a breath through my nose and gently placed my fingers on his abdomen. "Soon," I reiterated, hoping it'd calm him down enough for him to think straight.

Alpha Vulcan was here to talk with Ares about his information on the necromancer.

Marcel walked out from Ares's office, arms crossed over his chest and white hair in his face. "About damn time you showed up. Vulcan has been waiting for fifteen minutes." He glanced down at my neck and smirked. "Like the new scar, *Princess*."

My ruthless god of war growled low and stormed past Marcel and into his office. I patted Marcel on the chest, thanking him, and followed Ares into the grand room.

With one ankle kicked up on his knee, gelled dark red hair, and sleeves rolled up his forearms, Alpha Vulcan sat in one of the plush red velvet chairs. "Two marks?" Vulcan asked, eyeing my neck.

With his lips parted slightly, I saw his canines in his mouth and noticed how much smaller they were compared to Ares's.

Ares had the largest teeth I had ever seen on a wolf—good for ripping an enemy to shreds and warning other suitors away from his mate. For another wolf to *try* to claim me, those teeth promised them death.

"Don't you think two marks is a bit much?" Vulcan asked.

To Vulcan, two marks from Ares probably looked greedy because not many people knew about his second personality that seemed to shine around me. It was the best-kept secret and one that I wished more people knew about. Ares and Mars weren't bad guys, like the world thought Ares to be.

"No, they're not too much," Ares said, keeping his gaze surprisingly steady on me.

He was controlling himself—at least, *trying* to control himself. But these marks were driving him crazy. I could see it in his eyes. Something had changed him last night. Maybe it was the talk with his dad or the nightmare or having Mars mark me, but he couldn't seem to keep his eyes off me.

After swiping his tongue across his saliva-covered canines, Ares growled under his breath and sat, turning his attention to Vulcan. "What'd you find out about the necromancer?"

Vulcan rubbed his forehead with his thumb and pointer finger, and sighed through his mouth. "She's from the Gargan family, the only magic family who survived the War of the Lycans."

My eyes widened slightly.

Fought between werewolves and hounds, the War of the Lycans was far more deadly and savage than anyone alive could ever even imagine. Some records stated that gods and goddesses had taken a role in the war and that it was divine by nature. But not many people believed that or even *cared*, as our Moon Goddess hadn't taken any part in it.

My history teacher had described the war in three words: magic, ruin, and slaughter. It'd proven to be more fatal and dangerous than a nuclear war or the end of the world. Yet nobody knew how it'd ended or how it had begun.

Some speculated the end had resulted from an entire pack mysteriously turning to stone. Rumor had it that each and every warrior in that pack had been preserved by the gods, each in their fighting stance—some lying on the ground, others about to be attacked by the unseen beasts.

Nobody knew how or why or if someone had just sculpted replicas of their bodies for their pack to mourn. Some packs believed the former, others the latter. Dad, whose ancestors had won arduous battles against the hounds, had always told me that those people had been real and turned to stone. But packs like Vulcan's didn't believe that. Hell, it was hard for me to believe it too.

Maybe I could ask Dad about it later. It'd be a chance to visit him to patch our relationship up or to just tell him to leave if he didn't want to stay here anymore.

"She lives in the south, near Syncome Mountains," Vulcan continued.

"Near Syncome Mountains?" I asked. "That place is a breeding ground for hounds. They kill anything that lives on the land—the rodents, the birds, the trees. It's the underworld on earth. How does she live there?"

Vulcan grimaced and shrugged. "Not sure. That's all the information I could get."

After pondering for a few moments, I nodded in response. It didn't matter. I had to be okay with running into hounds. I had to protect my mate, my pack, and myself. If we didn't end this now, the hounds would eventually come to us.

"We have to go," I said.

We needed to squeeze as much information out of this necromancer as we could before things around here became worse. My stomach tightened at the thought of being on the brink of another war that could last lifetimes. It might not be as bad as the War of the Lycans, but it could be damn close to it.

I glanced at Ares and frowned. I didn't want our pup or others' pups to grow up in war. I wanted them to prosper, to be free of fear, to live their lives to the fullest because being a werewolf in Sanguine Wilds was the best feeling in the world.

"Will you come with us?" I asked Vulcan.

Ares seethed through the mind link. "No. He's not coming."

I narrowed my eyes at him. "We need packs to trust us. We need to make friends, Ares, not more enemies. Maybe if he comes with us—and you don't kill him—it'll show all the other packs that we can be trusted."

Ares let out a boisterous growl but didn't push it. If another great war was coming, we needed to be prepared and to join forces with other packs who had different strengths, like medicine and science.

"We're not going until you have that stone in your back," Ares said out loud. He didn't hide the fact that he wanted to put the stone inside of me. He wanted Vulcan to know, even gazed over at Vulcan to challenge him about using it.

Vulcan shrugged. "As long as she doesn't become *you*, I don't have a problem with her using the stone. All I care about is that it doesn't end up in a hound's hands. They would have unimaginable power." He paused. "If Aurora does use it, you have to be prepared not only to kill for her to protect it, but also to kill her for it."

My heart tightened. Vulcan hadn't said the words lightly because they needed to be said harshly. He needed to get the point across that the hounds could never have the stone, just as Jeremy had warned me. Ares needed to be prepared to kill me. Not only kill for me, but *kill me*. To protect it.

And while I would beg him to kill me if it ever came to that, like it had with Jeremy, I knew that he would never lay a hand on me.

Ares slammed his fist down on the table and split it in two pieces, a loud crack echoing throughout the room. I pressed my lips together, knowing that he couldn't even begin to process the kind of responsibility he would have once the full and complete stone was inside of me.

He couldn't kill me now without the complete stone, and he wouldn't be able to kill me when I had both pieces.

To lighten the mood, Vulcan cleared his throat and winked at me. "If Ares isn't strong enough to do it, I will do it."

"Get out," Ares said through his teeth, glaring him down.

Vulcan raised his hands in defense. "Hey, all I'm—"

Ares stood over the broken desk with fiery and wrathful eyes. The god of war, vengeance, and wrath didn't mix well together, but damn, did it look good on Ares.

"I said get out—before *I kill you*," he roared again.

After piercing Ares with a pointed look, I stood and opened

the doors for Vulcan. "We'll be in touch with a final decision on when we're going. It will be soon, whether or not I have the complete stone inside of me. Get your warriors ready."

I shut the doors behind Vulcan and Marcel, and turned on my heel to meet Ares, who suddenly stood closer than I'd expected. "Don't get angry with him. He was pushing you. It's what all alphas do." *Apparently.*

"I'm not losing you again."

"Again?" I asked, brows furrowed together. *When has he lost me before?*

An unreadable expression crossed his face, and then he shook his head, as if what he'd thought didn't make sense. "It doesn't matter." Ares stepped closer to me, snaked a hand around my neck, and brushed his fingers against both of my marks. "You wear both of our marks now. You're ours to look at, ours to handle, ours to ogle whenever we want. Nobody else gets to do to you what we can. And nobody gets to decide your fate."

CHAPTER 16

AURORA

"You have one last chance, Charolette. Take the fucking stone," Marcel said to Charolette before practice later that day.

They stood off to the side, the striking fall wind whipping their long hair into their faces.

Charolette scowled at Marcel and bared her blunt canines. "I've already made up my mind. Stop trying to force me to do something that I don't want to do." She moved closer to him and poked a finger into his chest. "You're supposed to be my mate and support me."

Marcel crossed his arms. "I'm supposed to keep you alive."

Snapping my eyes from side to side, I continued to watch until Ares walked over to me with a sweat-soaked shirt. After our chat with Vulcan, he had taken a run to clear his mind. Though, by the looks of it, he just looked angrier.

"Why are they always fucking fighting?" he asked me.

Not wanting him to find out about Marcel and Charolette

being mates, I shrugged my shoulders and ushered him to the group of warriors stretching in the middle of the field. "Probably about Marcel being a dick or something. You know how he is …"

Ares stopped mid-field and looked me up and down. "You're not ready for practice."

I gnawed on the inside of my cheek and scrunched the dry grass between my toes. "I'm going to see my dad. I need to talk to him." I zipped my jacket up a bit further, the trees blowing another harsh wind in our direction. "When I'm finished, I'll be back to train. I promise."

"You better be," Ares said.

After kissing him good-bye and shoving on some sandals, I swallowed my pride, my hurt, my anger, and my fear, and walked to the prison. My stomach tightened to the point that I thought I'd puke. I didn't know what to say to Dad or how to get him to talk to me about the War of the Lycans. He barely wanted to talk to me about the damn weather now or how the food was here.

Approaching the two prison guards, I clasped my hands together. "How's my father?"

They looked at each other and then back at me.

"Angry. Won't eat. Same old, same old."

Annoyed that he still hadn't eaten, I opened the door and stepped inside the dungeon. The stairs creaked as I walked down them. Lights flickering from above illuminated the many cobwebs that decorated the ceiling. When I made it to the bottom, the door shut behind me with a thud.

Dad sat in the same cell with his back against the stone wall, a scowl on his face and tightly clenched fists. I stepped in front of the bars and eyed the unlocked cell, dumbfounded as to why he hadn't left yet. Nothing stopped him from escaping without telling me good-bye.

Not knowing how to start a conversation with him, I asked, "Why haven't you left yet?"

He didn't have to live here in misery if he didn't want to.

When he didn't answer me, I pushed more to try to get a rise out of him. I needed something from him. It had been forever since I'd heard his voice, the same voice that used to sing me to sleep every night when I was a baby.

"The Luna Ceremony is in a few days," I said, hoping to see any emotion cross his face.

I hoped for happiness, but there wasn't any. It hurt me beyond words because I wasn't his little girl anymore. I wasn't the person he had sung to or played with or even cared about. I was nothing to him, and my own father would never look at me the same way ever again.

"I would really like you to be there."

"No."

I glanced down at my feet as a lump formed in my throat. All I wanted was for him to be happy again. He didn't have to stay here. He could go back home, join another pack. Some alpha would definitely take him in because he had a vast knowledge of war from his family history. He could start a whole new life.

"I don't want to see you mated to that fiend. I don't want to see you at all."

My chest tightened. From the moment he'd let Mom trade me for their safety, he had made it clear that he didn't want me. Yet, stupid me, I kept coming back like a lost dog, hoping he'd change his mind, wishing he'd be the father he always had been to Jeremy, wanting things to switch back to my childhood for just one more moment.

Hell, if he smiled at me again, I'd savor the memory for my entire life.

But he wouldn't, and I needed to get that through my head. My father despised me.

Not wanting him to see how weak I was, I crossed my arms and turned my back to him. "I'm going to Syncome Mountains with Ares, Alpha Vulcan, and some other warriors in a few days.

More hounds have been attacking our pack. We need information about how to stop them."

"Syncome Mountains?" Dad asked, rustling with something behind me. I glanced back to see him shuffling to his feet but still keeping a distance from me. "Syncome Mountains are where you go to die."

Being the pissy daughter that he'd made me, I almost asked if he wanted to come. But I quickly scolded myself for thinking such thoughts. I was turning into more of a monster than I already had been, thinking things only Ares—the god of war —would.

"Thanks for having faith in us," I said harshly, eyeing the bloodstained cement floor. Tears threatened to well up in my eyes. I hated feeling like such a loser; I hated it so much. "Maybe going to Syncome Mountains would be best for us. I'd be out of your hair once and for all, like you've always wanted."

Dad growled and stepped toward me. "I'm telling you that because I don't want you to die, Aurora. Those lands are cursed. An entire pack turned into stone three days after they went there. You have to be careful."

I bit my tongue to hold back the pain of my own thoughts. Dad had said he didn't want me to die, but if I'd died all those years ago instead of Jeremy, if it were me who had gotten ripped to shreds, his life would've been so much better. He would have had a son who could follow in his footsteps to become the most powerful warrior wolf on the entire planet, a force to be reckoned with.

Instead, he got me—Aurora, a woman who could barely shift, mated to Ares, the most powerful alpha on the entire planet.

"Any tips on how to stay alive?" I asked dryly, turning toward the stairs.

Originally, I had come down here for closure. Yet somehow, he had only managed to make me feel worse. Family wasn't supposed to hate you and not care about you. They were supposed to support you, no matter what. I guessed I'd gotten the short end of the stick in that department.

"Any tips?" He laughed emptily. "Don't go."

Balling my hands into tight fists, I stormed to the steps. *Fuck this.* I shouldn't have ever even come down here. I just wanted to have family who still loved me, who supported me, but I didn't have shit. All I had was a moody father and a dead mother.

"Aurora, wait."

I stopped on the stairs, knuckles turning white around the dry wooden railing.

"My ancestors were the wolves turned into stone. Only my great-great-grandmother survived. She was just a child and was taken in by another pack. They had all gone out to Syncome Mountains to fight hounds and never come back. I don't …" He paused, voice softening. "I don't want that happening to you."

Lips parting, I wanted to turn around. I wanted to run into his arms for saying the bare minimum, for telling me that he didn't want me to die. But I didn't let my emotions control me. I stood my ground on those stairs and didn't look back.

"You're going to go whether or not I tell you to, but if you don't listen to me and you do go, make sure you never let your guard down. There are fucked-up things on those mountains that I don't even believe I saw for myself when I visited the outskirts years back."

"Like what?" I asked, staring at the cobblestone step.

"Dark magic. Hellish zombies. Only things witnessed in your worst nightmares."

I tilted my head to the side and glanced back to see an expression on Dad's face that told me he feared Syncome Mountains more than he ever feared Ares and his wrath.

He grasped the silver bars and swallowed hard, brows furrowed. "Once you go there, you'll wish you never had."

CHAPTER 17

MARS

*A*urora had left earlier this morning to talk to her father, and then shop for dresses with Charolette while *I* had the honor of preparing for the pups to come over tonight. Between Ares, my family, and my therapist, Denise, I had other people helping me with my life. It felt refreshing to be able to aid these pups in their recovery process now.

"Don't stress about it, Mars. I'm sure you already have everything set out," Denise said over the phone, her motherly voice reminding me of Mom.

It had been months since I'd last seen her; usually, when she checked up on me, Ares had control. And Ares hated her.

I sighed through the phone. "You know me too well."

She paused. "What's wrong? You sound off."

"I have a lot on my mind." I pulled the broom out of the closet to clean up some of Ruffles's balls of gray fur. She shed like crazy all over our carpets. "I want Charolette to have the stone, but

Aurora needs it to become stronger. I can't let her walk around, helpless."

"She's not helpless, Mars. She's capable."

"But she could be stronger, so much stronger. She could shift with ease and run through the forest, not be held back by her disability."

Ruffles jumped right back onto the carpet and rolled under the coffee table, shedding her fur everywhere again. I rolled my eyes and swatted at her butt to move her, but she just rubbed against my hand. Deciding that she'd do it again if I swept, I put it back into the closet and lay on the ground with her.

"I know how difficult it is to live with a disability," I said, staring up at the high ceiling. "If this stone could change her life, then I want her to have it."

My lips curled into a smile. Though Ares wanted her to have the Malavite Stone for safety reasons, I wanted her to have it because living with a disability was so damn hard sometimes. And I wanted to make my mate's life as comfortable as it could be.

CHAPTER 18

AURORA

"We're going dress shopping! I have been waiting for this day forever!" Charolette squealed, curling her arm around mine as we walked through town. Sun rays beamed down upon us, a nice break from the thick fog Sanguine Wilds had been experiencing. "I have always dreamed of being Ares's mate's best friend and helping her pick out her dress, and—oh, I didn't tell you, but I invited a few people along!"

It was Tuesday morning, ten a.m. sharp. While I wanted to be excited to pick out my dress, all I could think about was my conversation with Dad the other night and the terror in his eyes, warning me to stay away from Syncome Mountains.

She pulled me into Lucy's Boutique, the only dress shop in town. Elijah, Adrian, Ruffles, and Pringle sat on the royal-blue couch near the entrance, talking and *meowing* to each other. I smiled at them, knowing that Jeremy would've loved to be here.

I leaned closer to Charolette. "I'm surprised you didn't invite Marcel."

Charolette shoved my shoulder. "Do you think I spend every waking moment gushing over him? Because I don't." She glanced away, chewing on the inside of her lip, and pulled me toward our friends. "I don't even think about him."

"You don't think about him ever?"

"Nope."

"You're a liar. You're probably thinking about him now."

Though she tried, she couldn't hide her smile. Goddess, she was head over heels for Marcel, and it was the cutest fucking thing I'd had the chance to witness—aside from Ruffles and her man, Pringle. Now that Ruffles had her own boy to flirt with, we were back on good terms.

No more stealing my man.

"Definitely *not*," she said as we approached the guys.

"Aurora! Tunnels are underway," Adrian said, throwing one arm around my shoulders. "They started this morning. We're re-cementing the hideouts from the War of the Lycans. There are four located near the pack house, which we're working on first, and then a handful of others around the property lines. It should be done within a couple weeks."

"That's wonderful," I said honestly. It wasn't what I'd wanted to finish before a war, but it was something. Hopefully, the project—at least, cementing the hideouts—would be complete before we left for Syncome Mountains.

My gaze shifted to Elijah, who stood pretty damn close to Adrian, and I wiggled my brows. Dimples forming on his cheeks, Elijah looked at the ground and grinned. My heart warmed, and I vowed to bother Elijah about all the details later.

Dressed in a brown sweater dress and an orange blazer, Lucy, the store owner, walked out from a back room and grinned at us. "Luna!" she said, tucking some white-blonde hair behind her ear. "It's nice to finally meet you! I'm so excited you chose to shop for your Luna Ceremony gown here. I already have some gowns laid out for you to try on that I think would go wonderfully with your figure!"

Charolette pushed me toward her. "Make her even more beautiful. She deserves it."

Lucy took my hand and ushered me to the dressing room, presenting me with three silver-colored dresses—a silk column dress, a velvet mermaid dress, and a lace ballgown. And while butterflies fluttered in my stomach as I tried on all of them, none of them felt right.

After forcing Charolette to come into the fitting room with me and after trying on six more unsuccessful dresses, I grabbed a simple, strapless silver dress with lace near the edges from the hanger.

"When are you going to let Marcel finally bite you?" I asked Charolette, desperately trying to pull the dress over my hips.

I must've gained a few extra pounds from all the training that Ares made me do. I had to be putting muscle on in all the right places ... or maybe this weight was from all those late-night pretzel sessions with Mars.

"Marcel? Let him bite me?" she asked, fumbling with the zipper. "You mean, mark?"

I smirked into the mirror. "Or bite you in other places."

She wrinkled her nose, pulled the zipper up, and gave me a hard stare. "Gross." She glanced down at my dress to hide the sadness washing over her face. "I've told you before, and I'll tell you again, he's not my type."

"Is that what you really think?" I asked, turning around to face her. Strands of her blonde hair fell into her face, and I pushed them away. "Or do you think you're not his type because he has a new girl every week?"

Letting out an exasperated sigh, she shook her head. "We're totally different people. He's a warrior. I hate training. He's a player. I just want one guy who loves me. He deserves someone to be happy with forever. And I can't give him forever ... I don't even know if I could give him one more year," she whispered the last part.

My heart ached at her words. I grasped her face, forcing her to look at me through her teary eyes. And at that moment, I finally really understood what was holding her back and why she set herself on arguing with Marcel all the time instead of loving him.

"Stop it," I whispered, pushing fallen tears off her face with my thumbs. "You're good enough for him. It doesn't matter how long you have left. Make your life worth it. Do something crazy. Fall in love with Marcel and make this next year the best of your entire life."

More tears streamed down her face. "But ... I-I just ... I don't want him to hurt. I don't want him to care about me. I don't want to fall in love with him."

"Why not?" I asked.

"Because it'll make it harder for me to leave him. He makes me want to fight, want to get stronger. But I ... I miss my mom. I want to see her again. I don't want to be miserable forever. Nothing can heal my pain. Marcel can dull it, but it's always there, nipping at me, piece by piece until all I want to do is give in to it."

While I still pondered over Jeremy and his death, I had never once thought about life like Charolette did. I never thought about suicide or letting a disease take away my life, just to see him again. I didn't think I'd *ever* understand the pain and heartbreak both she and Ares went through every day.

I hugged her and assured her that she meant the world to her pack. Nothing could bring her mother back to life—except those damn hounds—but she cared about so many other people. What her mother had done wasn't her fault. And before I pulled away, I made sure she knew that Marcel would walk through hell for her. He had even seen her without her wig and not run away.

She rested her head on my shoulder and hiccuped. "Sometimes, I ... I think about what life would be like if my mom didn't kill herself. I wonder what a happy and whole family would be like with me, her, and ... and Fenris."

My eyes widened. "Fenris?" I asked, patting her back. "Why Fenris?"

"He's my dad, my real dad ..." She blew out a breath. "I wonder what he's like, if he knows who I am to him, and if he cares about me." She paused and looked up from my shoulder. "You're not saying anything. Do you think that's weird?"

Remembering the nightmare that Mars had had the other night, I swallowed hard. Why did Charolette want to know about the man who had raped her mother? If my mother had been raped by a hound, I'd have hated that man for my entire life, not wondered about him.

"Aurora?"

"Uh, no, I guess not."

What else could I have said to a broken woman who just wanted to live the rest of her life in peace? Should I have made her feel bad about it? Scolded her for even *thinking* that Fenris was a good guy?

Even after Dad had made it clear he didn't want me, I tried to find solace with him. If Charolette was just thinking about it, it couldn't hurt her, right?

I shook my head and pulled away, glancing back in the grand full-length mirror. I smoothed out my dress and frowned. "Why don't we go out for milkshakes at Pink Moon Tavern tomorrow night?"

"I'd like that."

What she didn't know about this milkshake date was that Marcel might *coincidentally* show up and it might *accidentally* become a double date. I was definitely *not* secretly planning every detail in my head at this very moment.

After grabbing my hand, she pulled me out of the room toward the guys and the cats. I stood on the stand and twirled around to see how terrible I looked in the mirror. Dressed in silver with white lace accents, I looked like a flop. The silver against my pale skin made me look even whiter somehow. Every dress I had tried on so far didn't complement me at all.

"Do you have any other colors? Maybe something pink, blue, something softer?"

"But the traditional luna dress is silver," Lucy said.

"I just ... don't think it's for me."

I wanted to make a statement with this dress. I wasn't just a luna. I was an alpha too.

Lucy smiled. "I finished stitching up a beautiful gown yesterday. Go get changed. I think it could be everything you are looking for."

She disappeared into one of the back rooms, and I waddled to the dressing room in this too-tight-to-walk dress.

A few moments later, Lucy handed me a blush-pink, baby-blue, and soft-yellow gown. Colorful wasn't normally my style, but something drew me to this dress, something I couldn't quite put my finger on. It reminded me of dawn mornings when Jeremy and I would go to the cave and watch the sunrise over the trees, the pinks and blues and tans mixing together in a breathtaking sight.

And yet, somehow, it reminded me of more than mornings with Jeremy. It reminded me of dawns with Ares that I was sure hadn't happened yet, in places far more tranquil than Sanguine Wilds. It was hope in a world of uncertainty.

As soon as I slipped the dress on, I grinned. It was exactly what I wanted and what I needed for my Luna Ceremony. This dress made me feel like a goddess, awakening the wolves every morning with soft pastels to start new days.

Elijah beamed when he saw me. "You look so damn beautiful, Aurora. Ares will love it."

Butterflies fluttered in my stomach. I brushed my fingers across the silk and grinned at my reflection in the mirror. I didn't care about my looks too often, but damn, did I look good in this dress.

It was me.

The alpha. The luna. The warrior. Me, Aurora.

After I settled on the dress and Lucy reserved it for the Luna Ceremony, I collapsed onto the couch next to Elijah. "When is the soonest you can put the stone in my back?" I asked when Adrian and Charolette started chatting.

Though I desperately wanted to give the Malavite Stone to Charolette, I didn't want to see Mars as defeated as he had been the morning after his nightmare. Screaming, trembling, crying in his sleep, Mars had broken me down to tears that night.

Elijah readjusted his glasses. "I think you should wait until after the Luna Ceremony. It's only a few days away, and you're going to need time to recover from surgery. We don't know how your body will respond to the other half of the stone, especially after it was inside someone else. You might react poorly to it. The Luna Ceremony is supposed to be a joyous event."

I stared at my feet and swallowed. The Luna Ceremony was a sacred tradition held under a full moon, where people not only celebrated a new luna, but could also fight to take the place of an alpha or luna position without consequences. I didn't think anyone would, but I couldn't ignore the whispering around town about how I could barely shift.

While the warriors didn't mind, that didn't mean everyone accepted a weakling as a leader. Ares's pack was filled with jealous women taken from wars and people who wanted to feel important. No shame to them at all, but nobody was going to mess with what was mine.

I'd fought damn hard to make it here.

"Let me think about it."

Ares wanted me to bind with the stone as soon as possible, but what if I was too weak to even defend myself from an attack?

Last time I'd had stone surgery, I could barely move for an entire week. I had been completely wiped out.

After a few moments of silence, Elijah grabbed my hand and led me to the opposite side of the room. "I wanted to talk to you about this sooner, but I didn't want to say anything in front of Adrian or Charolette." He paused and looked over his shoulder, as if to reassure himself that nobody was listening. "We ran tests on the hound's blood and found an unusual substance in it, like I'd mentioned before. We still haven't figured out exactly what it is, but my doctor looked back through some old files, and … and your blood matches theirs."

"What?" I asked, brow furrowed.

"Whatever kind of blood runs through those hounds' veins, it runs through yours too."

CHAPTER 19

AURORA

"What the hell did you just say?" I asked, having heard him clearly the first time. I just couldn't believe those words had actually come out of his mouth. I really couldn't believe it. "I have hound blood running through my veins?"

Elijah stuffed his hands into his jeans and nodded. "Yes."

"It's not possible."

I paced between him and the royal-blue couch in Lucy's Boutique and ran through everything Mom and Dad had told me about our family and about the hounds. None of this made sense. My blood was of Mom and Dad, two respected warrior wolves from the Sanguine Wilds, not of hounds.

"Luna, are you okay?" Lucy asked from her desk.

She, Charolette, and Adrian glanced over at us with worried expressions. And I didn't know how to even answer that question.

Was I okay? Who the hell knew what I was?

Instead of expressing my worry, I gave them my best smile. "Yes, of course. Thank you for all your help today. Adrian, please walk Charolette home. I need to speak with Elijah alone." I snatched Elijah's hand and pulled him toward the exit. "Oh, and, Charolette, don't forget our date tomorrow!"

After shoving the door open, I tugged Elijah out into town. "How do you know for sure?"

Elijah dropped my hand and nodded to a much quieter path leading to the pack house through the forest. Ruffles and Pringle hurried before us, chasing the leaves blowing in the wind and stomping on fallen branches.

"We only have theories about the hounds. We don't have vast knowledge about them ..."

"But?"

"But what makes hounds biologically different from rogues and wolves is their blood," he said. "At least, that's the only thing we've found so far. And that's only with alive hounds. Dead hounds have the same blood as werewolves."

I clenched and unclenched my hands. That didn't solve anything, but it wasn't Elijah's fault. He was just as clueless as I was about this entire thing. Still, this wasn't possible. We needed more information on the hounds to figure out why I had the same blood as them.

"You don't know any other reason?" I asked, desperate for answers. "Dr. Farral, the doctor who did my surgery, hasn't found anything else that could be the cause of my blood being different than normal werewolf blood?"

"The only other difference between you and regular were-wolves is the stone."

I swallowed hard. "You don't think the hounds have—"

"No," Elijah said. "There was no stone in the hound we studied."

A long time ago, Dr. Farral had told me that the stone changed my blood, but there had to be more to this explanation. My mind wandered to Fenris, the man who I thought was trying to take the Malavite Stone from me. While the stone was special, it might not be the reason Fenris was after me. Maybe he wanted me because I had the same blood as him; we were of the same kind.

Who knew? Sure as hell not me.

Though it didn't solve anything, that was better than knowing there was another stone out there that every hound had. If those beasts got their nasty paws on any sort of stone, they'd be unstoppable.

"We'll study it some more," Elijah said, stepping into my backyard. "We're working as hard as we can. I know the war is approaching faster than we'd like. I want to have some more information before that time." He glanced up at the kitchen window at Mars, who was furiously scrubbing a pan. "And let me know when you plan to have the stone surgery. I'll speak to Dr. Farral about it tonight."

After parting ways with Elijah, I blew out a deep breath and wondered how I'd tell Ares that I had hound blood. We had so much other shit to worry about, and this was just an added problem. What if I ended up becoming one, losing all sense of reason and murdering my mate in cold blood?

A few moments later, the backyard light turned on, and the door swung open. Ruffles ran to it, chased by Pringle, who had a brown leaf on his head. She turned around, swatted the leaf, and hit him in the face. Then, she walked right past Mars and into the house. Pringle followed after her.

I guessed Ruffles had a boy spending the night.

Dressed in a black T-shirt that hugged his biceps, Mars smiled at me with four pizza boxes in his hands and two bottles of soda stuffed between his bicep and chest. "Did you find a dress?"

"Yes," I said, grasping the sodas rom him and walking into the house to prepare for the pups to visit tonight.

Mars had been so anxious about this all day; he had texted me throughout the dress-picking session about not wanting to fuck this up.

"What's it look like?" he asked, setting the boxes down in the kitchen. "I want to see it."

"You can't see it until the Luna Ceremony," I said, wrapping my arms around his waist from behind and resting my cheek on his back. How was I going to tell him about the stone and then about my blood? I didn't want Ares to reemerge from his slumber and explode right before the pups came over tonight.

But I needed to tell him. The sooner, the better.

"Not even a peek?"

I forced out a laugh and shook my head. "No."

Mars turned around, brow raised, and grasped my chin, immediately sensing that something was eating me up on the inside. "What's wrong?" he asked, searching my face for any sort of response. "What happened?"

Fumbling with my fingers, I gulped. "I need to speak with you about something that I found out today ..." I stared up into his eyes, which turned more gold by the second, and grasped his hands tightly. "We're going out for milkshakes with Charolette tomorrow."

"And?"

"And Elijah said that the stone will make me weak if I put it inside of me before the Luna Ceremony," I admitted. While Mars didn't get angry that often, he furrowed his brows and scowled. But before he could say anything, I stopped him. "And he's right. Last time this happened, I could barely move for a week. I was so sore."

He tensed even harder. "You want to wait to put it inside of you? You'll be in danger."

"I've been in danger," I whispered, still not sure if waiting was the right choice.

But Ares and Mars both had been looking forward to this sacred ceremony for so long now. He'd even asked me if I could wear his mother's necklace because he knew it'd have made her happy. He wanted everything to be perfect. And if I couldn't attend the ceremony, there was no point of even hosting one.

"It's only a few days away."

He pulled away from me. "A few days is a long time."

"It'll take me even longer to recover." I grasped his hands to pull him back toward me. "I can fight the hounds now as I am. If I take the other half of the stone, I don't know how my body will react. We won't be able to go to the mountain and get information from the necromancer either."

"I'll go with Vulcan."

"You're not going alone," I said, voice strong, making sure he knew my word was final.

Ares went psycho when he was alone. He'd be a wreck, knowing that Fenris could attack our pack during his trip and that he wouldn't be able to protect me, especially after Mars's nightmare the other night.

"There's more. A bigger problem," I whispered, gliding my tongue across my lower lip. "Elijah found out that—"

"Elijah is just the damn bringer of bad news, isn't he?" Mars interrupted.

After shrugging in a weak attempt to convince myself that it wasn't *that* bad, I sighed. This was bad, damn bad. I didn't even know what this meant about our future, about possible pups, about if Mars would *want* to go through with the Luna Ceremony, knowing that I had hound blood.

"He ran some blood tests on the hound and found out that whatever is inside the hound's blood is also ..."

"Is also what?"

Staring down at our tiled floor, I shuffled from foot to foot. "In mine ..."

Silence. Frightening silence.

"You're a hound?" Mars asked, a tinge of annoyance in his voice.

I widened my eyes. "No! I just ... there's something in my blood that makes it similar to a hound's. Elijah's doctor doesn't know anything about it yet, but they're working on figuring it out and hope to have something soon."

Mars froze, realization darting across his face. "Dad was right," he whispered. "The curse ... you are who they're looking for. It wasn't Mom ..."

"The curse? What curse?"

Someone knocked on our doors, and Mars hurried over to it. "We'll talk about this later."

After he pulled the doors open, a woman with silver hair and flawless dark skin stepped into the house. "Goodness, it's freezing outside, and it's only the beginning of fall." She wrapped her arms around Mars. "How are you doing, Mars? I hope I'm not late. We haven't seen each other in a while. I usually get the plea-sure of speaking with Ares."

Mars beamed down at her, the tenseness from our conversa-tion still lingering in his smile. And for some reason, my heart clenched. Mars must've not come out as often as Ares did. But I guessed I was one of the lucky ones who had the delight of seeing Mars more than most people did.

She walked up the stairs and introduced herself to me as Dr. Denise Davis, but she told me to call her Denise. After offering her some coffee, I glanced out the window for the kids who'd be here for Mars's group therapy session. He walked over to me, shoulders tense and worry etched into his face.

"Why don't you relax, Mars?" I asked, grabbing his hand.

"How am I supposed to relax? My mate has hound blood and keeps getting attacked by hounds. We have about ten kids coming over, who witnessed the most horrific attacks in their lives. There is no relaxing, only stressing, Aurora."

I pulled him down into a kiss and brushed my fingers against his cheekbones. "Stop. We don't know about my blood yet. There is still so much to figure out. We're going to enjoy the night with the pups, and you're going to be great at it."

He grasped my hands and sighed. "What if I can't help them? What if they're already too screwed up, like I am, and become a monster like Ares?"

"You're not screwed up, and you're certainly not a monster," I said softly.

While I didn't know if he believed me or if he would ever believe me, I needed him to know that he wasn't a burden to me; he was not a monster, and he wasn't messed up. He was as the Moon Goddess had made him—a wondrous creation and my destiny.

After a couple moments, I wrapped my arms around his neck and tugged gently on the ends of his dark hair. "You're going to do great. Be who you are. If that's Ares or Mars, it doesn't matter. I'm sure the pups would love to meet both of you."

Denise glanced at us, lips set in a small smile and glasses low on her nose. Instead of asking me about my life like I'd thought she would, she looked back toward the front window and clapped her hands together. "They're here!"

As she hurried to the front doors, Mars froze.

I rubbed soothing little circles against Mars's back and ushered him to the doors. "Just breathe. These kids are like you. They need someone strong to help them get through this. And they look up to you. You're their alpha now," I said.

Mars relaxed slightly and nodded.

"And don't forget about those pups that you want to have." I stood on my tiptoes and kissed his cheek. "Show me how good you are with them."

At the mention of pups, Mars stood taller and with confidence, and walked to the doors to welcome all the pups into the pack house. About a fourth of his height, the pups waddled into the house one by one and gawked up at Mars like he was the most amazing godlike figure they had ever seen.

Oohing and aahing, all their little murmurs made me smile. I hadn't been around any pups for so long. Their innocence convinced me that I wanted pups as soon as we could. I'd love to have a couple little babies running around the house with Mars and Ares.

After grabbing plates of pizza, they sat on the floor in the living room and chatted with each other. I stayed back and let Mars take control. He needed this as much as they did, knowing that he was helping pups who were just like him.

Four hours later, Mars concluded the group therapy session and let the children run free in our living room. Leaning against our tan leather couch, Mars whispered something to the young pup in his lap, earning him a huge grin and a face full of hair from her when she nodded her head and her pigtails went flying.

My heart fluttered at the sight. One day, we'd have a pup like her as our own. She'd fall asleep on Mars's chest, her snores drifting through the pack house; she'd jump up onto his back, wrap her arms around his shoulders, and giggle into his ear. It was something I'd thought I wanted to wait for, but after seeing how natural he acted with the pups, I wanted it now.

Whoever had told me that Alpha Ares was a monster had obviously never seen this part of him.

"Mars adores you," Denise said as Mars grabbed the girl's hand and led her to the front doors, where her adopted mother, the owner of Moon's Café, waited to pick her up. She walked down the stairs, a jacket draped over her forearm. "I'm so grateful that he has you in his life."

"Leaving, Denise?" Mars asked.

She gently patted his shoulder. "I'll see you soon, hon."

When all the pups and Denise left, Mars shut the doors and turned to me, hands sliding around my hips. The pups' visit seemed to have helped him almost more than it did the pups because the pups didn't see him as Ares or as a monster; they saw him as a fearless leader and protector.

"So, how'd I do?"

"Goddess, Mars, that was amazing," I said, tugging on the ends of his hair and staring up at him in awe.

"Am I good enough to be the father of your pups?"

I playfully slapped his shoulder. "Stop it. You know you'd be great."

Unable to wait to take Mars to bed, I pulled him down the long hallways. When we passed Ruffles's yellow room, the door was closed, and she mewed. I decided *not* to interrupt Ruffles and Pringle because I had a sneaky suspicion that they were lying belly up on the bed with chip dust coating their whiskers.

After pushing him into our room, I pulled on his shirt. "Take off your clothes."

Ruffles bellowed in pain. I had heard the agonizing sound only once before—when I found her as a kitten in the bushes. She had been gnawed on by some kind of animal and nearly died. So, my first instinct was to check up on her, just in case.

"When I get back, you're going to fuck me," I called over my shoulder to Mars as I hurried to Ruffles's bedroom.

Another desperate yowl, and I pushed the door open. *Damn, this girl sounds like she is—*

"Ruffles!" I shouted, staring wide-eyed at her on her yellow bed.

Pringle stood behind Ruffles, doing the *nasty* with her, and Ruffles actually seemed as if she was enjoying it beyond belief despite her howls.

"Girl!"

Yet they didn't stop; they just kept going at it like wild animals.

"You'd better not ruin that bed," I said, scrunching up my nose and walking back to our bedroom.

I wasn't about to break that up and have two cats angry with me. At least this would keep Ruffles out of Mars's hair, so I could have him all to myself.

In nothing but a pair of gray sweatpants that clung to his hard-on, Mars leaned against our bed and crossed his muscular arms over his chest. Moonlight flooded in through the curtains, glistening off his sculpted abdomen. Something about him looked and seemed different tonight. I'd finally seen him as more than just an alpha tonight. He was a man, a damn good man, and would be a father to our pups one day. But most of all, he was mine.

"Ruffles?" he asked.

"She's fine," I whispered, trying to control my wolf who wanted to tear off his clothes and let him fill us with load after load of cum until I carried his pups in my belly. My cheeks flushed at the thought of Mars *and* Ares becoming even more possessive of me, knowing that his pups were growing inside of me.

"Mate," my wolf said through my mind. *"Mate now. Pups now."*

"Not—"

Before I could finish the thought, she took control of me and let out a possessive growl, staring our mate down like any she-wolf would in heat. Except we weren't in heat. We just craved him to be inside of us again. It had been way too long.

"Is my Kitten hungry?" Mars asked, his wolf recognizing mine. Brown eyes turning golden, he lay back on the bed with his legs hanging off the edge and one hand grasping his hard cock through his pants.

I clenched, heat gathering between my legs, and nodded at his throbbing cock. "Yes, Alpha."

"Eyes," he ordered, cocking a finger to his face. "Show them to me."

When I lifted my gaze to him and saw the wolfish fiend in his golden irises, my heart raced. Goddess, I wanted him to ruin every part of my body, to make me his, and to force me to surrender to the alpha inside him.

"Show me how hungry you are for this." He groped his cock through his pants, lifted it slightly, and let it smack against his hips with a thud. "Get on your knees."

I knelt, aching for his cock.

Mars smirked and stroked his bulge. "Crawl to me."

Crawling to him on all fours, I kept my eyes on his and watched his gaze slide from my face to my tits to my ass as it swayed. My juices coated my pussy lips, making me wet and ready and needy for him.

"Take off the shirt," he ordered when I knelt between his legs, "before I ruin that pretty face of yours."

After tugging off my shirt and bra, I let my tits bounce against his thighs. He moved closer to the edge of the bed, and I placed my hand over his to stroke him. Then, I placed my mouth on the head of his cock through his thin sweatpants and sucked.

Groaning, he shoved a hand into my hair and pulled me closer. I moved my mouth down his covered length, sucking. A wave of heat warmed my core, and my wolf purred for him.

When I pulled down his waistband, his veiny cock sprang out of his sweats and stuck into the air, curving down slightly. Grasping it at its base, I spit on the head, and then slowly sucked on him, bobbing my head up and down.

Unable to stop myself, I thrust my hand between my legs and rubbed my aching clit. He moved his hips, sending his dick deeper and deeper down my tight throat.

I stared up at him through teary eyes and gargled on him. "Ruin me, Mars. Make me beg for you to stop. Fuck my throat until it's sore. Be rough with me like Ares is."

Mars had always been gentle and passionate, but I wanted to see the wild and savage part of him. Over the past few weeks, I'd caught a few glimpses of it and been craving more. Nothing compared to a dominant alpha who knew when to lose control for his mate and claim her ruthlessly.

"Ruin you?" Mars growled and tossed me onto the bed, so my back was on the mattress and my head hung off the edge. He ripped off my pants and underwear with his claws, leaving me bare to him. With the torn clothing, he tied each wrist to the matching ankle, forcing my legs apart, and then he stood by my head and leaned over me, placing the head of his cock right against my lips and his hand between my legs to rub my pussy.

"Ruin me," I murmured.

Without another word, he shoved himself all the way down my throat and refused to move when I gagged on his cock. Instead, he fucked my face hard and fast, his fingers moving in torturous circles against my clit, sending waves of pleasure through my body.

Slobber dripped down my cheeks and nose. When he pulled himself out to let me breathe, he rubbed the head of his cock all over my swollen lips. A wave of pleasure rolled through me, and I dug my nails into the sheets.

"More," I said breathlessly, wiggling my hips to displace all the pressure building up in my core. "I need more. Face-fuck me, Mars. Give me everything you have. Make it hurt."

He rammed himself back inside of me, shoving all eight inches down my throat. Gargling, I opened my mouth wider to make room for as much of him as I could take. More spit slid down my face, making me a drooling hot mess for my mate.

Wrapping one hand around the front of my throat, he jerked himself off and face-fucked me even harder, using my throat as if he would use my pussy. He rubbed my clit in fast, tortuous circles, making me tighten.

"Is my Kitten hungry for my cum?" he asked, his balls resting against my nose.

Desperate to breathe, desperate to come, desperate for him to be inside me already, I sucked harder on him and nodded. Goddess, I needed it. Anywhere he wanted to give it to me, I would take it.

He jerked his cock off in my throat harder and tensed. "Do you want my load deep in this throat?"

My hips jerked into the air at the thought. I was so damn close to coming. He slapped my clit hard and pulled out of me. Spit and drool dribbled down my face, my nose, my brows, ruining me. He grabbed a pillow, tossed it onto the ground, and pulled me off the bed to sit me right on it.

"Use it. Grind your pussy against it. Pretend it's my cock." He grasped my chin and forced me to look up at him.

I ground my hips into the pillow, moving them back and forth quickly to feel any kind of friction that could tip me over the edge.

He trailed a finger down my bottom lip. "Open your mouth."

I took a deep breath, knowing that I wouldn't be able to last another few minutes before I came. My wolf ached for me to open my mouth, for me to obey our alpha, but I couldn't. I didn't want that. I wanted more. I wanted all his cum inside my pussy.

"Give me your pups," I pleaded breathlessly, knowing that he wouldn't be able to resist. My hips moved faster against the pillow, driving me higher. "Please, Mars, fill me with them. I-I-I can't take this any longer."

"Fuck, Aurora." He lifted me off the pussy-stained pillow, tossed me onto the bed like I weighed nothing, and pulled me toward the edge by the hips. He wasted no time, positioning himself at my entrance and shoving himself inside of me.

"Mars!" I screamed, immediately coming all over him.

Mars thrust into me only once more before he stilled and came deep in my pussy, refusing to pull out, even after he came.

He pumped into me a few more times, pushing his cum as deep and as close to my cervix as he could get it.

"Kitten, you're not leaving this bed until you're full with them," he growled into my ear, his cock softening inside of me, still refusing to pull out. He slipped a hand between us and rubbed my clit again. "I'm giving you all I have tonight. Everything, Kitten."

~

Outside, the soft colors of the dawn danced across the sky. I lay back in the bed, my swollen pink clit throbbing, like it had all night long.

I pushed Ares's hand away and whined. "Ares, please," I whispered. "It's too much. We've already fucked all night. We have to get some sleep."

After growling low, Ares kissed between my breasts and up my neck, stopping at his mark. He sucked on the skin, and I purred for him. Sure, it had been all night, but I was still wide awake, wanting and craving *him.*

At some point during our *ruin my pussy* fuck session, Ares had awoken and vowed to fuck me harder and longer than Mars had. Not that I minded. It was just that my pussy was aching to pause for a couple hours at least.

"You asked for the beast, Kitten," Ares murmured into my ear. "You fucking got him."

I gently wrapped my hands around his muscular shoulders and pulled him closer to me. Ares rested his forearms on the sides of my head, lightly brushing strands of hair off my face, and *smiled.* Ares—the big, bad alpha who had just railed me for the past five hours—smiled with such love and kindness and patience just for me.

"Get over here," he said, wrapping his arms around my waist, rolling onto his back, and pulling me onto his chest.

He trailed his nose up the side of mine and kissed me. I rested my head on his shoulders and listened to the ragged thump of his heartbeat.

After a few moments of silence, Ares cleared his throat. "We have to talk. If you're not going to put the stone in your back until after the ceremony, we need a beta now. I can't spread myself or Mars thin while trying to protect you. There are too many damn important and uncertain things we have to consider."

Drawing my fingers across the scars on his chest, I nodded in agreement. "Nobody knows this pack better than Marcel does. And though he's a dick sometimes, I think he could really step up and lead."

Out of all the wolves in this pack, I trusted Marcel the most. He had proven over and over again that he'd protect any person here with his life. He had protected me, stood up for me, taken charge when Ares was a mess. Hell, even when Liam had been beta, Marcel had seemed to be a better leader.

"If he becomes beta, he'll be with us all the time." Ares tugged on my hair to force me to look at him. "*With you.*"

"Don't worry about Marcel. He's seeing someone."

"Seeing someone, as in dating?" Ares chuckled. "Goddess, I feel sorry for the stupid girl who thinks he's dating material. He's always all over those damn women at The Flaming Chariot downtown."

I gnawed on the inside of my lip. Part of me wanted to tell Ares that Marcel was seeing his sister and that Marcel was more than just a man-whore. He sounded like one. He acted like one. But when he was with Charolette, he loved her more than anything.

Marcel was misunderstood, just like Ares was.

"Forget that," I said, playfully pushing him. "Marcel can and will lead."

"Why don't you be my beta?"

"Your beta, luna, and alpha?"

143

"A lot of titles for my Kitten," he whispered, gently biting into my shoulder.

As if he knew we were talking about him, Marcel voiced through the mind link. I thought it'd be a good-morning message or a gentle nudge to get to a last-minute early morning practice. But it wasn't. It was far from that.

"Ares, Aurora, get your asses to the prison. We have a problem. Liam has escaped."

CHAPTER 20

AURORA

"I'm going to kill that fucker when I find him," Ares said to me through clenched canines, glaring down at two murdered guards lying in a puddle of their blood in front of the prison.

Flies swarmed above them, nipping at the fatal gashes in their abdomens from what looked to be a wolf's claws—a wolf far larger than Liam.

But how the hell had Liam broken out through silver bars? Doing that without some kind of help was next to impossible. Silver was basically poison to wolves and burned our skin easily. And what about the guards in the forest? Someone would've caught the scent of Liam—their beta who had betrayed them— before he made it to the borders.

I leaned down to get a closer look at the claw marks and cringed. Their intestines had spilled out of their bellies and been ripped to pieces. Liam wasn't this violent either. He wasn't this ... this cruel to people.

After holding my breath, I walked into the prison alone and down the creaky steps. A musty stench filled the underground dungeon, similar to the way the cave had smelled when Ares and I witnessed the dead being raised from their eternal slumber. Burned into my memory, that scent haunted me every time I thought about the hounds being brought back to life, hundreds of them rising from the dead.

If Dad hadn't left yet, he had to have seen something, like someone coming into the room and helping sneak Liam out. Their cells were only a several feet away from each other, and while Dad might detest me, he was a warrior by heart. He wouldn't let someone who worked with the rogues and hounds escape so easily.

Like usual, Dad sat in the same spot with his eyes half-open and his head resting back against the concrete wall. He groaned slightly when I flickered the lights on, shielding his eyes from the blinding glare.

"What happened with Liam?" I asked.

He shrugged, yawned, and sat up taller. "I'm not sure."

"His cell is two down from yours. You must've been close to him," I said through clenched teeth.

It wasn't his fault that Liam had escaped, but he had to know something. He always talked about respect, about dignity and ethics that his decorated family of warriors had instilled in him, but I was beginning to think that was all a lie.

Or maybe he had forfeited the warrior side of him when he met Mom, Sanguine Wilds' first female alpha.

"How'd he get out? Did he say where he was going?"

"I don't know, Aurora. I was sleeping. It was dark. All I heard was growling. Thought it was Ares, beating his ass again for what he had done." Dad stood up and walked over to the silver bars, staring at me through them and not daring to open the gate. "I'm ready to leave."

My eyes widened, my chest tightening. "Ready to leave?"

Maybe it was bad timing. Maybe it made Dad look suspicious. Maybe I just didn't want to lose him. I had lost everyone in my family, and Dad saying he wanted to leave—even though I'd told him he could—broke my heart.

It was so sudden. Too sudden.

"Ares and I can set up housing for you. I know there are some empty cabins north of—"

"No, Aurora. I want to leave."

"Are you sure you don't want to stay?" I asked, heart clenching.

Goddess, I might hate him, and he might hate me, but that didn't mean he had to leave, right? We could provide everything that he could possibly need. Why would he leave me, his only daughter, the only family he had left?

"I'll leave tonight," he said.

"But where are you going to go?" I whispered, voice faltering.

This was what I had wanted—for him to be out of my hair and to stop talking to me about how shitty my mate was. But now that he wanted to leave, I didn't want him to go because once he was gone, I would have no family left.

All those memories of my childhood would vanish, the people who had made me who I was gone for good. Hell, even my pups wouldn't have anyone to call Grandma or Grandpa on my side of the family or to stare with wondrous eyes as my father told them old war stories.

"Anywhere but here," Dad said.

Before tears spilled down my cheeks, I turned away and curled my arms around myself. I should've felt relieved that he'd be gone, that I didn't need to tolerate his disrespect anymore, but … I felt like shit. Like I always did when I was with him.

"I hope you find whatever it is you're looking for," I whispered, walking to the stairs. After telling myself to fake it, to act like his departure didn't bother me, I thrust my shoulders back even though I wanted to ball up and cry into his arms, and said to him, "Love. Happiness. Family. Be happy. Stay safe. And maybe we'll meet in another life."

Gathering all the strength that I had left, I walked up the stairs as he called my name. I refused to turn around. I knew that if I turned around to face him, I'd break down in tears and be that weak alpha he always knew I was. I'd prove him right, which was probably what he wanted.

After piecing myself back together and pretending that whatever Dad had just said didn't affect me in the slightest, I walked back out into the sunlight and toward Marcel and Ares, who were talking tensely with some of the border guards.

"You didn't fucking see anyone on the property?" Ares roared. "Liam couldn't have just broken through silver bars strong enough to kill him. And he wouldn't have been able to kill two guards without anyone else noticing. Someone must've fucking helped him."

"They did." I swallowed the lump in my throat. "My father said he heard growling inside the prison last night. And when I walked down there, I smelled that musty stench from the cave." I paused and let reality set in. "Hounds ... the hounds were here."

The warriors broke out into a fit of gasps.

The hounds had been here last night. On our property. Without anyone noticing.

"Double security around the borders at night—at least until we find Liam. Don't brush the hounds off as easy targets to kill. The hounds might be wild and feral, but their leader isn't." I placed a hand on Ares's bicep and squeezed gently.

Ares cleared his throat, commanding attention. "Get three trackers to follow any musty or unusual scents. We're going to find Liam, and I'm going to kill him for fucking leaving and betraying us."

When all the warriors dispersed through the forest, I folded my arms. "We need to chat about this over lunch at Moon's and try to draw some conclusions about how the hounds made it onto our property and why they wanted Liam." I narrowed my eyes at Marcel. "You're coming."

Marcel raised his brow. "Are you asking me out on a date, Luna?"

I rolled my eyes and mind linked Charolette to meet at Moon's Café instead of Pink Moon. Pink Moon Tavern was too far away, and I wanted to stay as close as heavenly possible to our pack in case the hounds showed up again. We couldn't let anyone die.

~

"You think Liam is working with the hounds?" Marcel asked, sliding onto the white couch at Moon's. He sipped on a soda, scrunched his nose, and placed the can down on the table. "I don't think he has the balls for it."

Ares blew an annoyed breath out of his nose. "You think he wouldn't? He betrayed us once by sleeping with that rogue while he was dating Charolette." He shook his head and cursed to himself. "I should've seen this coming … I should've killed him when I had the fucking chance."

To my surprise, Marcel lifted one shoulder in an attempt to shrug. "He was your beta and best friend for years. I don't blame you for not killing him," he said with a tight voice. It almost sounded like he blamed himself for not ripping out Liam's throat.

I sat back in a chair and stared up at the twinkling star and moon lights hanging from the ceiling. If I were Marcel, I would've killed him as soon as I found out that Liam was sleeping with my mate. I didn't know what had held Marcel back from doing just that. His reputation perhaps?

"I don't like how there's a fuckin' hound on our property," Marcel said, staring out the window at the townspeople. He lifted his nose into the air and breathed in gently, as if he smelled something enticing. "How'd they even get onto the property without being detected?"

"I bet it was fucking Fenris," Ares said through clenched teeth, hands balling into fists. "He has more control than most hounds. He knows exactly what he's doing." Ares placed his hand on my knee and squeezed tightly, claws ripping through my jeans. "He wants to weaken us, and Liam knows all our secrets."

Trailing my fingers around the edges of the mason jar filled with my water, I laid my other hand on top of Ares's in hopes of calming him down. Fenris was the one who had taken my brother and raped Ares's mother, and now, he was sneaking onto our property.

He was getting more dangerous by the day.

Charolette walked into the café, hair in blonde curls on her shoulders. Marcel breathed in deeply again and instinctively sat up straight, his pupils dilating but his jaw tensing. She sauntered over to us, eyes narrowing at Marcel's back.

"Ares, I didn't know that you'd be here!" Charolette said after grabbing a bagel at the counter. She wrinkled her nose at Marcel, who glared at the window and acted as if he were ignoring her. Once she took a seat next to Marcel, so close that their forearms brushed against each other, she stabbed her bagel with a plastic knife. "I should've known you were up to something, Aurora," she murmured.

My lips curled into a smirk, and I mouthed the words, *You're welcome*, to her so that Ares wouldn't hear. While I knew today wouldn't turn out to be the double date I'd hoped for, I was still glad that they'd get to spend some time together in public.

Ares caught sight of our interaction and cleared his throat. "I need a beta, Marcel."

"What do you want me to do about it?" he said, voice tense, as he pulled his arm away from Charolette's. "There aren't too many people in this pack who know the ins and outs of it the way that Liam did."

I rolled my eyes at his cluelessness. "He means, you."

Charolette snorted. "You want Marcel to be your beta?"

"What's your fucking problem?" Marcel growled, whirling in his seat and glaring down at her with passion and anger, hurt and anguish in his eyes. He shook his head, sending pieces of his long white hair flying. "I'm never fucking good enough for you, huh?" he asked, voice raw and full of emotion.

While I understood why Charolette didn't want to get close to Marcel, seeing how much it affected him made my heart hurt too. He wanted to love her so fucking much, yet her cancer was holding her back.

"I never said that." She jutted out her chin. "All I'm saying is that you're no leader. You can't even finish your *duties* when they need to be finished, you never give your all, you never—"

"So, that's what this is about?" Marcel interrupted. "This morning."

They bickered back and forth, talking so cryptically, careful not to hint to Ares that they were mates, fated to be together for eternity.

Ares leaned closer to me, bumping my knee with his. *"Is something going on with them?"*

I pressed my lips together to hold back the biggest grin. *"Hmm, I don't know."*

"You're lying. Did he do something to her?"

Charolette hummed angrily and slammed her hands down on the table, making the torch-like candle flicker. She scooted off the couch, face red with rage, and yanked Marcel up. "We need to talk in private." She stormed out of the diner, leaving her purse and bagel.

Once they left the café, Ares pulled out his phone and texted Vulcan. There was no more time to waste. We needed as much information as possible because these hounds were now attacking us, killing us, and wandering onto our property without being caught.

Ares: We leave in two days.

I rested my head on Ares's shoulder and read the message coming through.

Vulcan: My warriors are ready. I believe Minerva and her warriors are coming too.

Good. The more warriors, the less likely we'd all die from a surprise attack.

Ares deposited the phone back into his pocket and sighed. "Don't you think they're taking a bit long?" Ares asked, glancing at the café door.

Marcel and Charolette had disappeared behind the building and out of view, probably doing the nasty.

And if they were, my plan to get them together had worked.

Two cats appeared at the glass door, Ruffles peering through at me. Someone opened the door for them, and Ruffles and Pringle walked in together. She jumped onto my lap and rubbed against me as Pringle hopped into Marcel's seat on the other side.

"Meow."

Ruffles sank her little teeth into my wrist and tugged gently. When I didn't budge, she bit down harder and nodded toward the door. *"Meow."* She gave me that look she always did whenever she saw Ares and me sleeping together—pure disgust. *"Meow."*

"Girl, stop," I scolded her because I knew she had probably seen Marcel and Charolette outside. I didn't want her giving out any information to Ares about his sister and now-beta. "It's not like you weren't just doing that with Pringle last night," I whisper-yelled when she bit me again.

"Doing what?" Ares asked.

"Meow."

I flared my nostrils down at her and placed a finger to her mouth to get her to shut up. But then she stared out the window and then at me. Looking back and forth, as if something was urgent and that something wasn't our two friends having sex in the forest.

"What is it?" I asked, stroking her soft fur.

"*Meow.*"

Urgency and fear lay heavily in her eyes.

"Did you see something?"

When the diner door reopened, Charolette and Marcel walked back into the room. Charolette was glowing, radiating with happiness, a grin stretched across her face. And Marcel looked a lot more relieved.

"Why the fuck is there a cat in my seat?" Marcel asked, staring down at Pringle, who was perched on the cushion, whiskers coated in some sort of salt. Marcel went to gently push him off when Ruffles put two paws on the table and hissed at him. After grumbling under his breath, Marcel sat next to him, Charolette following.

Ares gave Charolette a long, hard look.

"*It's my sister, isn't it?*" he asked me through the mind link. "*The girl dating Marcel.*"

I tensed and placed a hand on his thigh. "*I wouldn't say they're dating ...*"

"*MEOW!*"

Ruffles gnawed on my wrist again and bit down hard enough to draw blood. Suddenly, she pushed her ears back and turned her attention to the window, where we could see some warriors rushing to Moon's.

A man shifted and hurried into the diner, completely naked. "Alpha," he said, hands on his knees and gasping for breath. "We found Liam, the rogue, and the rogue's child, but you have to come quickly. It's—"

Ares slammed his fist down on the table and shot up from his seat. "You found them?"

"Yes, but—"

"Move, Aurora," Ares said, trying to get past me.

"Alpha, I wouldn't act rashly. Hounds were spotted close to the borders too."

Jaw clenched, muscles tense, eyes searching the surrounding area, Ares hurried toward the exit with Marcel hot on his heels. Although warriors had spotted hounds forty miles east of our property, Ares didn't listen to warnings and shifted into his wolf, running through the forest to Liam.

"Prepare," Marcel said through the mind link to our warriors, stepping into his beta position without a second thought. Scanning the town for any threats, he ran after his alpha.

I cursed at the men who didn't listen to reason and chased behind Marcel. If true danger lay in the forest, Ares wasn't going to fight them alone. I might be a cripple, but once I shifted, I was just as strong as he was.

The farther Marcel and Ares ran toward the borders, the quicker I lost them. Picking up their scent, I listened to the forest become quieter by the second. My stomach tightened at the thought of it being midday and nothing—not even birds—were making a sound.

And then I heard it.

A desperate howl. Something so raw and sorrowful. From Ares.

With Charolette close behind, I hurried to my mate. What if those hounds had taken his father or maybe some of the pups or—

When I saw it, I froze. Charolette let out a piercing scream and ran forward, but I caught her arm and held her back to me, so she couldn't move. She struggled. Hard. But I wrapped my arms around her and forced her to turn around, so she wouldn't see the blood because, Goddess, there was tons of it.

I turned my head to the side to glance back and shuddered in disgust. Hanging on ropes by their left ankles, Liam, the rogue, and the rogue's child swayed dead from a single tree branch, bodies covered in deep claw marks, skin decorated with bites, and heads on stakes underneath them.

CHAPTER 21

ARES

"Get them fucking down now," I said, staring at the three hanging corpses.

As warriors scrambled to remove them from the tree, I shifted my gaze to the pale faces and heads impaled on silver stakes. Blood leaked down the poles, the silver still sizzling against the wolves' brains.

All I felt was anger at the hounds for doing this and sadness for my pack members. Liam had been my best friend since childhood, helped Mars through Mom's death, and stuck around when Mars's personality split and I barreled into their lives.

And now, he was dead.

Glancing at the pup dangling by his ankle, I balled my hands into fists. At barely ten years old, that boy shouldn't have been brought into this mess at all. I should've invited him to the pack house the other night; I should've done something other than reject his mother, which in turn rejected him.

He had shown signs of superiority and ruthlessness.

I could've made him stronger.

I could've made him a warrior.

I could've protected him.

Marcel grabbed the boy, but I seized his wrist and pulled him back.

"I got him," I said quietly, untying the rope with shaky hands and taking the headless pup in my arms. I pulled the stake from the ground and walked into the woods, far away from my warriors so they wouldn't see me break down.

He hadn't deserved to live as a rogue, just because his mother subjected him to it. He hadn't deserved to witness the hounds rip off Liam's head and his mother's head. He hadn't deserved to die so horridly to beasts that should've stayed dead.

After fifteen minutes of wandering aimlessly through the entire forest, I found myself in the cave. Alone. Without backup, without Aurora, and without anyone to fight with me if something turned out bad. Once I found a place to bury the boy, I laid him on the ground and started digging with my bare hands. I could only imagine the fear, the helplessness, the sorrow, and the guilt rushing through his mind in his final moments. Unable to stop the hounds from hurting his mother.

It hit too close to home, felt too much like watching Mom get raped and not being able to stop it, thinking that I should, knowing that it was the right thing to do, but unable to move from the fucking spot in the closet as it happened.

Why couldn't I protect the people I loved? First Mom, and then an innocent pack member. Who was next? Aurora?

An inescapable hollow feeling lay heavily in my heart. Something told me that this pain wasn't going to pass quickly. I'd hold this pup's agony for as long as I lived, just like I boarded up the torment I felt with Mom and Charolette and even Dad.

My entire pack relied on me.

And I couldn't even protect them.

"Ares," Aurora said through the mind link, *"are you okay?"*

I pressed my lips together and cut the connection between us right now, knowing that if I responded to her, it'd only be with another painful howl. I hated feeling so helpless in front of her. I wanted to be her rock, like I was with Mars. But sometimes, holding the entire world on my shoulders hurt too fucking bad.

Once I dug a hole deep enough for him just outside the cave's entrance, I laid the boy to rest and covered him with dirt. I wanted to plant a moonflower over his grave, but nothing would grow this time of year, especially not with all this fog.

Pounding against the dirt until it solidified, I stood and walked to the back of the cave to stare down into the hole where Fenris had raised the dead. Against my better judgment, I jumped down into it, hitting the ground with a thud, and collapsed onto all fours.

Nobody was here.

It seemed like they hadn't been here for days now, yet my wolf snarled. I sprinted through the cave in my wolf form, wanting to find someone or something to kill to release all this anger and hurt. How could they have done this to innocent people? How could they have killed a pup? Was it all for Aurora, or was there more?

My heart pounded, another vicious growl exiting my throat.

I wanted blood. I wanted fur. I wanted to kill those fucking bastards.

I wasn't backing down. We weren't going to let this go. We would track Fenris down—even if we had to go to hell and back to catch him. Nobody would get away with torturing an innocent pup and murdering my friend and former beta. Liam might've deserved to be hurt but not dead.

Scratching the walls. Digging into the dirt. Howl, growl, snarl, and nip at the musty air. I couldn't stop myself, and I didn't want to stop myself. I fucking hated hounds with everything I had. They had destroyed my life, Aurora's life, everyone's fucking life.

After what seemed like hours, I walked back to the hole in the ceiling and leaped out of it, landing on all fours in the cave. Scrapes covered my fur from colliding into the cave walls over and over and over again.

I had wanted to feel pain today because I deserved it. I was a shit alpha and let my people die. So many bad memories haunted my mind, and I thought back to the times after Mom died. How terrible I'd felt. How I'd thought I deserved all the pain. How I'd wanted to hurt myself because it made me feel better. Even the thought of death had sounded ... it'd sounded ...

At the thought, agonizing physical pain shot through my body. I hung my head low and whimpered, suddenly only able to think about Aurora. It was my wolf, begging me not to think destructively anymore. We had someone who cared about us now. We always did, but we needed to be strong for her.

We couldn't think about doing what Mom had done to herself. We fucking couldn't.

But Aurora knew that she couldn't fix us. She knew that she couldn't heal us. But she would stay by my side if we slipped, right? She would be there for us. She would love us still for who we were.

My wolf let out another growl and demanded that I stop now. Denise had taught me to spot the early signs of when I started to slip into negative thoughts, to not feed that side of me, but it was fucking hard sometimes.

I thought about cutting myself again.

I wanted to do it again.

It would ease the pain even if it was only for a moment.

It was the only real thing I could control.

But I couldn't. I couldn't. I couldn't.

I shifted into my human and walked to the cave's exit, glancing at the pup's grave. "Run with the wolves," I whispered. "Run with the wolves."

CHAPTER 22

AURORA

*A*fter Ares disappeared with the boy's body, I ached to chase after him to ensure that he wouldn't do anything stupid. The god of war was a reckless mess, driven by his rage for war and his sorrow for his people. And I had never seen him so sullen.

"This is all my fault," Charolette sobbed before I could go after him. She shook uncontrollably with fat tears streaming down her cheeks and rolling down her neck. "My fault."

The warriors around us stared at me and waited for my orders, but I didn't know what to do. Mom had never once given me this much responsibility, nothing even close to this. While I was an alpha, I never had the blood of my pack members on my hands like this. Maybe during the second hound attack on my old pack, but I had desperately tried to warn everyone.

This time, I hadn't because I didn't think Fenris could wander onto our property, kill two guards, help Liam and his rogue girl-friend and child escape, and flee as if he had never even been here. Whatever magic he was using was more than just hound powers or necromancy sorcery.

Nobody here should've died. Nobody should've been taken. Nobody should've been on our property last night. After glancing around the gloomy and foggy forest to see if Ares was coming back, I gulped and rubbed Charolette's back.

"Bury them," I ordered a group of warriors.

"But he betrayed us," one said, hiking his thumb back at Liam.

"He betrayed us and paid with his life. Let the dead rest."

"Don't make your luna tell you again," Marcel said with a scowl, staring at the warriors carrying Liam's body. By the look on his face, I could tell he didn't want to bury Liam either, but he wasn't going to disagree with me, not when Ares would be on his ass about it later. "Bury them."

With the carcasses and heads, the warriors disappeared into the forest and headed west to the cemetery. I would've gone with them, but Ares had brought me there once to talk about his mother, and the thought of going back now that I knew the hounds were undead freaked me out.

"Someone, clean this up, please," I said, crouching by Charolette.

Doubled over onto her hands and knees, she let out a harrowing howl. Chest heaving up and down, nails lengthening into claws, she transformed into a small wolf and took off through the forest, sprinting faster than I had ever seen her.

Not wanting her to be alone, I ran after her in my human form and tried to maintain her increasing speed. With her condition, she'd slow down in a while, and I'd be able to catch up with her. But I hoped she stopped way before she darted off the property and onto Hound Territory.

If the hounds killed her, Ares would lose it. And I probably would too.

"Charolette!" I shouted, breathing hitched. While I came close in my human form, I could never keep up with a wolf's speed.

Their bodies were prime for sprinting far distances and for an extended period of time. "Charolette, please, slow down."

When we approached a stream, she stopped and lifted her snout to the air to howl, the sound so heartbreakingly that I nearly cried out with her. She shifted and curled into a ball, head bare without her wig, the stream water coasting through her toes.

"We always used to come here. Liam would take me here every Friday. I ... this was our spot." Her body trembled. "He wasn't my mate. I was using him the entire time. I ... I didn't want to be with Marcel. I thought I'd die before Liam did. I didn't think ... I didn't think I'd ever see him like that."

My chest tightened, and a lump formed in my throat. But I couldn't cry now. I had to hold myself together for my pack and for my family. So, I pulled her into my lap and stroked her head, hoping to calm her down.

"I hated Liam for what he had done, but I didn't want him to die because of it." She grasped on to me for dear life, her lips parted, as if she wanted to say more but couldn't physically get the words out.

"That doesn't make it your fault," I whispered to her.

She clutched onto my shoulders. "Yes, it does because he did this."

"Who did?"

"My dad," she whispered.

"Mr. Barrett?" I asked, furrowing my brows. "What does—"

"My *real* dad," she cried.

My eyes widened in realization. She was talking about Fenris.

"He told me that nobody hurts his daughter. I didn't believe him. This is all my fault."

She spoke about Fenris as if it were normal, and I sat there stunned.

Was she in contact with Fenris? *Why* was she in contact with Fenris? When the fuck was she talking to him?

She thought that it was all her fault that Fenris had killed Liam, and part of me thought it was too; I just didn't say it aloud.

Needing her to tell me everything, I held her tighter. No way in hell that she'd admit this to Ares, but once I told him, he'd flip the fuck out. Not only was Fenris the man he wanted to rip to pieces, but Charolette speaking with him also threatened our pack's security.

I loved Charolette to pieces, but she had made a grave mistake.

"What do you mean, he told you?" I asked quietly.

"A few weeks ago ..." She hiccuped. "During the hound attack at your mother's pack. I stayed back with Liam, and then went out for a walk by myself, needing some fresh air." She pulled away from me and threw her hands over her face. "I saw him out in the woods. He told me that he loved me, that he wanted me back, that he was trying to get Mom back for us to be a family ..."

"Charolette," I snapped, unable to hold back my anger. "Why didn't you tell us?"

She whimpered, "I just ... I want him to love me. And I want Mom back too."

Her words came from the heart, and I saw myself in her—wanting and needing to be loved by a father. I couldn't explain the feeling, but when I felt alone, I did stupid things to feel good again too.

After another few moments, she stood and wiped off dirt from her skin. "I should go back home."

I followed after her through the woods. "Was that the only time he contacted you?"

"Yes," she said.

Yet my stomach tightened. Something was terribly off and didn't feel right.

Stopping in the middle of the woods, she grabbed my hands. "Please, don't tell Ares."

I shook my head in refusal. "I have to tell him. He's the alpha, and he needs to protect this pack, Charolette. I know Fenris is your father, but he's causing all this trouble and killing your friends. Who will he take next? Ares and Mars?"

Marcel jogged up from behind Charolette with her blonde wig in his hands. "Where'd you go? You should've fuckin' stayed where we could watch you. If anything hap—"

"Shut up, Marcel." Charolette snatched her wig and stormed past him toward town.

"What happened?" Marcel asked, staring back at her. "What'd you say to her?"

"She's been in contact with Fenris," I whispered.

Marcel growled, "Are you fuckin' serious?"

Before he could hurry after her, I grasped his arm. "Don't be hard on her and don't tell anyone about this. We don't know who to trust. Either someone helped Fenris get onto our property or he has some kind of magical powers to be able to go unnoticed. And as for Charolette, it seems like it was once—not that it makes up for anything—and from what I could gather, he didn't hurt her."

After extending his canines, he snarled in her direction. "Ares is back at the pack house. I saw him walk by when we were digging the graves. He had left with the boy but didn't return with him."

I nodded. "Thank you. And, Marcel, don't let me down. I convinced Ares to make you beta. I need you to step up and be the best warrior and leader that you can be. Love Charolette with all your heart, but remember that Ares isn't stable. This is going to destroy him. I need you to be ready to make hard decisions."

Looking back at me, Marcel nodded. "I'll do anything to help this pack survive."

Not thrive. Not succeed. *Survive.*

"Good," I said, watching the wind blow strands of white hair behind his shoulders. "Prepare to leave for the mountain within the next two days. Now that Fenris has attacked, we need to act quickly."

Once I departed for the pack house, I laid a hand on my stomach to try to suppress the knots inside of it. No matter what happened, Ares would spiral out of control and kill Fenris. But I feared that once he did, Charolette would rebel. Though she didn't even know him, Charolette seemed to be fond of her father for some ungodly reason.

I didn't know what he had been trying to accomplish by speaking with her. Maybe he was trying to prove his love to her in some stupid way or get her to trust him. Maybe he had known that Ares wanted the stone for Charolette and he thought that he could steal it from her.

But he didn't know that the stone was mine.

When I reached the pack house, I grasped the door handle with a shaky hand. I needed to tell Ares about Fenris, but I was terrified of the consequences. What if Ares lost complete control and killed his sister?

No, that wouldn't happen.

Ares and Mars both adored Charolette, but this could cause strain.

I followed Ares's hazelnut scent up to our bedroom and opened the doors. Freshly showered, wearing only a towel, he stood tensely with his scarred back turned to me. Beads of water dripped from his hair and onto his shoulders. And Ares was a frightening kind of quiet.

"Ares," I whispered, stepping into the silent room.

"It's my fault," he said, gripping the bedsheets in his fists. "It's my fucking fault."

My wolf howled inside of me, feeling more pain than the night Ares had confessed to me that his mother had killed herself.

I moved closer and brushed my fingers against his back. "Ares, it's not your fault. You couldn't have stopped this from happening. Fenris is a monster who will stop at nothing to torture you."

While Ares was always so strong and so wrathful, I hated to see him so broken like this. It clawed me apart on the inside. After witnessing Fenris rape his mother and finding her dead in her bed, Ares had held in his hurt for so long, so damn long.

"How am I supposed to just let it go?" He pulled himself away and glared with his canines drawn, eyes glowing red and body visibly shaking. After a couple moments, he shook his head and looked between us with guilt. "I'm sorry. I didn't mean to yell at you."

I stepped closer to grasp his hands. "Don't apologize."

"That boy …" he whispered. "He didn't do anything. He was just a pup, and now, he's dead. I couldn't help him. I let this happen. I didn't have enough security. I didn't have anyone protecting him. It's my fault that he's gone, and he will probably be brought back as a hound."

Not knowing what to say, I pulled him up onto the bed with me and cradled his head to my chest. I didn't care how long it took to calm him down. I laid with him until he relaxed and slowly stroked his hair until he snored softly in my lap. When he woke up, I'd tell him everything about Charolette. But for now, he needed peace.

CHAPTER 23

AURORA

"*J*'m sorry about the deaths," Elijah said, looking over Ares's desk at me.

After Ares had fallen asleep, I'd hopped out of bed to work. Now that Fenris had attacked our pack and killed three members, we had so much more to do in such a little time. Who knew when the next attack would be? Who knew what they'd try to take? Charolette perhaps.

Sitting beside Elijah, Adrian rested his hand on Elijah's knee. "Ares is taking it bad, isn't he?"

Tears welled up in my eyes, but I held myself together. I needed to be strong for Ares because he had always been my rock; he'd always been as strong as a damn god. Yet nobody could just erase the sight of headless bodies, hanging and swaying in the fall breeze, from their minds.

Memories of the day I'd almost died in the hands of the hounds in a violent and gruesome attack played through my mind on repeat. A tear slid down my cheek, and I thrust my face into my hands, unable to hold back the tears anymore.

"What are we going to do?" I asked, voice trembling. "Even though it doesn't seem like it, he cares so much, almost *too* much. I'm so afraid one of these days, he's going to break, and I'll lose him for good. One day, the hounds are going to go too far, and I won't ever see Ares or Mars again."

Every day that went by was another day closer to war, a war that I feared would be worse than the War of the Lycans. And we weren't ready. We weren't even close. If Ares went blind with rage during war, who knew what the hounds would do to him?

What would life be without Mars if I only had Ares? Or without Ares if I only had Mars? What if I lost him the same way he'd lost his mother because he couldn't handle this anymore? Ares had cut himself before because of all his pain—all the scars on his arms proved it. Would he do it again? Could he hold any more hurt?

"Aurora," Elijah whispered, taking my hand. "We'll be here for you, no matter what."

"What if he"—my lips quivered even more, and I leaned against Ares's oak desk, unable to hold myself up at the thought. I squeezed my eyes closed—"hurts himself?" Speaking the words aloud made them real.

I didn't—I couldn't lose him. If I did, I'd lose part of myself. My wolf would never forgive me for not protecting him at all costs, for not sacrificing myself before he took his life or someone else did.

"You make him stronger, Aurora," Elijah said.

"But what if that's not strong enough?" I asked, staring down at the scuffed wooden floor.

Elijah frowned deeper. "It needs to be. We have problems bigger than him. I know it's fucked-up, but if he isn't strong enough, then *you* need to be. You're an alpha; you need to lead this pack if he spirals out of control."

But I didn't want to lead this pack alone. I wanted to lead this pack with Ares.

"Do you want some good news?" Adrian asked.

I nodded. Anything would be nice to know this wasn't for nothing.

"After the hound attack this morning, more people have volunteered to help cement the underground shelters. Pack members are beginning to take it more seriously, especially the older wolves. We should be finished by tonight."

"By tonight?" I asked with wide eyes. "Thank the Moon Goddess we have some way to protect our pups."

"Next are the tunnels, which will start when you return from the mountains. I want you to be here to oversee the project, and I don't want to start anything while we're unguarded." Adrian glanced over at Elijah, who looked uneasy.

Leafless branches struck the window, screeching against the screen outside, as rain pounded against the glass. I stared out into the gloomy afternoon sky and wondered what had caused such a great shift in the weather lately. Sanguine Wilds had never been this windy, foggy, and drab during the fall.

"Have you thought about the stone at all?" Elijah asked.

"Ares wants me to do it now, but it's too risky. I don't know how long it'll take me to heal."

After last time, I hadn't moved for days. If I put the stone inside of me now and we hiked all the way up to Syncome Mountains, I wouldn't make it. And I would not in a million years let Ares go alone. Not after what Dad had said was there.

Though I wanted to wait, I feared I was making the wrong decision. I should put it inside me now. I shouldn't wait any longer. War would come either way, and I needed to be prepared. Yet how could I prepare if I couldn't walk?

"I think that immediately following the Luna Ceremony would be best."

Out of nowhere, Adrian said, "It doesn't make sense." He

looked over at us and furrowed his brows. "Sorry, I've just been thinking about the hounds. I don't understand it. Hounds don't kill for reason, and they certainly *don't* make statements like this. They would've killed Liam and the other two and left them for dead, not hang them by their feet and stick stakes in their heads."

Elijah nodded. "No hound has ever had the ability to shift, never mind have their human mind completely intact. Jeremy was close, but he couldn't shift. But this hound is different from the rest."

"And so am I ..." I whispered.

"If the hound leader has the ability to bring normal wolves back from the dead and turn them into hounds ..."

My eyes grew wide. "Then, how does that explain me?"

Elijah sat further back in his chair and swiped a hand across his face. "To be absolutely honest with you, I have no idea. None of it makes sense at all. It's been over a decade since we put the stone in your back. Dr. Farral has done thousands of surgeries since then, and I'm not sure if he'd remember something different about you. I haven't gotten enough time to talk to him, but I'll make time when you leave for the mountains."

I swallowed hard, my heart pounding against my chest. "You don't think that I'm a—"

"No," Elijah said quickly. "You can think for yourself. You can shift—though it's quite difficult—into your wolf and your human. You are able to speak and be civilized. I don't think you're a hound. Hounds can't do that."

"But ..." My voice was barely above a whisper. "But Fenris can. He can think. He can lead. He can command an entire army of the dead and he must be undead too."

Both Elijah and Adrian became quiet, and I sank into Ares's comfy swivel chair, feeling anything but comfortable at this news. I should've learned more about the stone, like how it worked, its true powers, how and when the best time was to place it inside of me.

"Fenris is different," Elijah said. "I don't know how. We'll have to capture him when we find him, study him if we can." He stood up and glanced down at Adrian, the corner of his lips curling slightly. "It's getting late," he said, looking at me and smiling widely. "We're going out to dinner."

Though I was still worried about what was going on with me, I smiled at him, my heart feeling light. Elijah deserved this—whatever he and Adrian had.

"I'll be here to watch over your pack when you're gone this week." He pulled me into a hug. "Just come back home, safe and alive."

CHAPTER 24

ARES

"*Ares!*" *Aurora shouted from the kitchen window, the yellow curtains blowing out into the night. She leaned over it and stared down at me, brows furrowed. "Ares, have you seen the pups?"*

"Pups?" I asked, eyes flickering to the bonfire about a mile east.

Some pack members had invited us to an elder's eightieth birthday party. Aurora had been complaining all day about not wanting to go. Hell, I didn't want to fucking go either. It was the first time in ages we were alone.

"Yes, Ares. Our pups." She waved me off, disappearing for a moment, and then walking out of the back door, arching a brow at me. "Where are they? I told them to be back by seven, and it's"—she looked down at the glowing numbers on her phone—"eight forty-five p.m."

I wrapped my arms around her waist and pulled her closer. "They're out of our hair, which means I get to spend time with"—I grasped her jaw—"my mate. I hope that you're not trying to get out of that, are you?"

She rolled her blue eyes, strands of hair blowing into her face. "No, I—"

Suddenly, someone shrieked from deep within the forest. "The kids! The kids!"

With wide eyes, Aurora grabbed my hand and took off running toward the screeching woman. My heart pounded in my chest as we ran through dense fog that seemed to roll in front of us. The further we got, the air became thicker, making it harder to see.

"Someone get Alpha Ares and Luna Aurora! Quick!" the woman yelled.

When we approached the woman, Aurora doubled over and screamed, "No! My babies, no!"

I stopped dead in my tracks to see our four decapitated pups hanging by their ankles with their heads on stakes. I dropped to my knees and shook my head in disbelief. No. No. No. This couldn't be happening. This couldn't fucking be happening. Our pups. Our only pups were gone. Killed by those ruthless, sinister, piece-of-shit hounds.

Jerking awake, I lay in the bed in a puddle of sweat. I fucking hated nightmares, fucking loathed those shitty-ass dreams. I stared up emptily at the ceiling and thanked the Moon Goddess that I'd had it instead of Mars because to live through that would've shattered him. He might have short visions of it, but to fucking feel every emotion... I could barely do it.

CHAPTER 25

AURORA

"*M*ars," I whispered, glancing into the bedroom after Elijah and Adrian left.

Ruffles and Pringle ran by me through the hallway, batting at a toy mouse. I slipped into the room and shut the door behind me, unsure of who I spoke to now.

Face void of emotion as if he was trying to think hard or remember something that Ares had dreamt up, Mars lay on the bed and stared up at the ceiling, his breathing uneven. When I crawled onto the bed with him, he wrapped his arms around my waist, laid me on his chest, and relaxed. Gently brushing his thumbs across my hips, he asked, "Yes, Kitten?"

"I need to talk to you about something," I said, drawing circles across his scarred forearms. I hated—*loathed*—the conversation about to happen, but I had to have it before we left to visit the necromancer tomorrow. What Charolette had done was a threat to our security.

"What is it?" he asked.

"Luna, your father is gone from his cell," Marcel said through the mind link to me.

Pain split through my chest. I didn't have the heart to respond. Dad was gone for good. I'd never see him again.

I clutched Mars's hand. "I love you more than anything, Mars, and I'll always be here for you. Please know that."

Sitting up, he grasped my face and searched it with concern. "What's wrong?"

While I wanted to come out and say that Charolette had betrayed him, I didn't know if he'd close in on himself and disappear from me for a long time. Ares would do anything to protect Mars from not only the truth, but also pain and heartbreak.

I softly kissed his lips and frowned against him, tears pricking the corners of my eyes. If this was good-bye for a while, at least he knew I'd be here when he got back. I hoped he wouldn't be gone for long. I needed him.

Not knowing how to say it, I held his face still. "Charolette met with Fenris a few weeks ago."

He released me and straightened his back, unimaginable fury flooding his golden eyes. "She what?" he asked, voice tensing by the second.

All the sorrow, pain, and grief disappeared from his face, and Ares clawed his way to the forefront, claiming control.

I crawled on top of him and refused to let him move from the bed. "I know you're furious. I know you're angry. Give it to me. Not her. She just wanted to talk to her father. Take all that anger out on me, Ares. Take me. Fuck me. Until you feel better."

"Aurora, don't," he said through gritted teeth.

It was wrong to stand up for Charolette, but I understood how she'd felt. She wanted approval from her father. She wanted him to like her, even just a little bit. I didn't accept of it, but I understood it. And if Ares flipped out on her now, he might do or say something he'd later regret.

All he was right now was a man of muscle and rage. I'd seen

what he was capable of when he beat up Elijah. I had seen what he did to countless hounds. I didn't want him to hurt his only sister.

"Aurora," Ares growled, shoving me off him.

I toppled over but quickly regained my balance and placed my hands firmly on his chest. "Love me the only way you know how to love, Ares." I wrapped his hand around the front of my throat and vowed to take Charolette's *physical* punishment for her. With one hand on his chest, I moved my hips back and forth, feeling him tense. "Hard. Rough. Ruthlessly."

Since we would leave for Syncome Mountains tomorrow, tonight was the last night that I was sure I would have him all to myself. I didn't know what would happen tomorrow. I didn't know if we would find the necromancer. If we would end up killing her, especially if we found out that she took part in helping the hounds. If we could stop the hounds once and for all.

Ares growled and flipped me onto my stomach, his hand around my neck. "I'm not going to hurt you because of her mistakes," he growled into my ear, pulling me closer. "Don't you ever say or think something like that again."

He needed to release his anger somehow.

He pressed his hardness against my backside and roughly swiped his thumb across my lower lip before pushing it into my mouth. "But if you want me to be rough with you, then I'll be rough with you, Kitten."

I sucked his thumb between my lips and ground my hips back against his hard cock. Ares tugged down his pants, enough to pull out his dick, and pressed it against my panties. He hooked a finger inside them and drew them to the side, positioning his cock against my pussy lips.

When he thrust himself into me, he grunted. My pussy tightened around him as he squeezed my throat and gently choked me, pumping in and out of me. It wasn't slow, it wasn't sweet, and it surely wasn't soft.

Each thrust was merciless, hard, and cruel.

An alpha releasing his rage, proving his dominance, and proclaiming his worth.

One arm slipping around my waist, he rubbed my clit in tortuous little circles and slapped it twice, making me whimper. I dug my fingers into the bedsheets, the pleasure coursing through my body.

"Is this what you fucking wanted?" Ares asked, sucking on his mark. He pulled my hips into the air and pushed my head against the pillows. "Answer me, Kitten."

"Yes," I breathed out, relishing in every inch sliding into me. "This is what I wanted." I arched my back hard and let his balls slap against my clit each time. "Are you going to come inside your luna's pussy?" I asked, glancing back at him. "Get me pregnant with your pups?"

He grabbed a fistful of my hair and pulled me off the mattress until his lips pressed against my ear. He tenderly bit my neck. "Tell me that you know I wouldn't ever hurt you. Tell me you're not afraid of me."

"I'm not afraid of you," I whispered, the pressure building higher.

He thrust into me harder, and I came all over him.

"I love all of you. Every single bit."

After he filled me with his cum, he collapsed onto the bed next to me and brushed some hair off my forehead. "I still need to talk to Charolette. She should know better," he growled, canines lengthening. "I'll have someone watch her tomorrow and deal out her punishment when we return from Syncome Mountains."

CHAPTER 26

AURORA

*I*n a thick cloud of fog, warriors crowded in our backyard, prepared to run to Syncome Mountains. Since we couldn't take cars, I stretched out on the lawn to hopefully warm up my muscles and brace my wolf for a painful shift.

"Stay here," Ares ordered to Minerva. "Protect the packs."

"I'm not letting you go without me," she said.

"Why the fuck not?" Ares's nails lengthened into claws, his teeth extending into sharp canines.

Since I'd warned him about Charolette last night, he hadn't given control to Mars. Ares had been hostile, angry, and ready to rage in the blink of an eye.

"Because you're unstable," Minerva said, narrowing her eyes. From what I'd gathered about her so far, she excelled at war, but unlike Ares, she kept her cool and always had well-defined battle plans. "I will keep fifteen of my best warriors here at your pack since the hounds seem to be targeting you, but I am going with you."

I stepped forward. "We need all the help we can get. Thanks, Minerva." I pushed Ares toward our warriors, calmly rubbing his shoulder and eyeing the warriors roughhousing by the forest. "Please calm down. Half our warriors are staying here."

From the plans Minerva and I had organized earlier today, it seemed like we'd be leaving our packs for about a day. It would take six hours to run there and six to run back, and that wasn't taking into account what kind of trouble we might find as we sprinted through Hound Territory.

The maps from Sanguine Wilds to Syncome Mountains hadn't been reconstructed since the War of the Lycans over two hundred years ago. Nobody dared return there, not even Alpha Ares, who wasn't supposed to be afraid of anything. Hell, people —entire packs—had turned to stone on those mountains and never returned. Traveling there was beyond dangerous.

After I said my good-byes to Mr. Barrett and Charolette, Ares nodded to his father and refused to step foot anywhere near Charolette. They hadn't spoken, and for once, I was grateful. If he opened his mouth, Ares would explode on her. I didn't want him angry before we left; his mind needed to be clear in case we ran into hounds.

I pulled Ares behind a couple of trees to shift because I didn't want any of the other alphas to see just how much this hurt me. I collapsed onto all fours and imagined my arms and legs breaking, my legs extending into limbs, my nose and mouth lengthening into a snout.

Squeezing my eyes closed, I said, *"Please, shift,"* to my wolf.

She whimpered in my mind yet tried hard to push through the excruciating pain. My unwilling bones broke and snapped back together, refusing to shift. I dug my nails into the dirt until they extended into claws and whimpered softly to deal with all the pain inside of me.

Pain shot through my body, and I worried about being in my wolf form for six hours. I hadn't stayed shifted for that long in over a decade, as I hadn't needed to. Would I be able to shift back? Would my wolf want to stay in control?

Pushing my worries aside, I willed my wolf to shift fully. After five more minutes, I screamed out and stood on all fours in my transformed wolf. Ares shifted next to me, rubbing his snout against my neck. He howled to signal to run and nudged me to the front of the pack.

And so, we left our pack behind and ran off our property in a thunderous roar toward Syncome Mountains, our strongest navigator wolves leading us and our best trackers staying on alert for unfamiliar scents.

While we tried our hardest to avoid Hound Territory, we found ourselves running past their foggy borders three hours later. My stomach tightened at the thought of an entire pack of undead awakening and attacking because of how loud we moved. Yet we didn't even see one of them the two hours we passed through their property, which made me even more nervous.

If the hounds weren't in Hound Territory, where were they?

My fur stood up as I imagined that when we got home, all our packs would be slaughtered mercilessly. I didn't want another doomsday like I'd gone through once during Jeremy's death. Ares wouldn't be able to handle that kind of pain. He was strong, but that would break him even more than his mother's death.

After quickly shaking off the thought, I continued to run with the pack. At first, the run had been difficult for me, as I didn't run long distances anymore, but the closer we approached Syncome, the stronger my wolf felt. Power amplified from the stone in my back, wave after wave radiating down my limbs, pushing me to move faster.

It almost felt like I had been *born* to visit this place.

∿

Heavy mist draped the jagged Syncome Mountains range, the narrow peaks vanishing into the clouds. I slowed to a jog and stared around at the patches of land that didn't seem to hold any life—no bugs, no animals, no vegetation.

Biting my tongue, I prepared to shift back into my human form, like the others. And for once in over a decade, I shifted with ease and within moments, like I used to do before the attack. The stone in my back swelled even more, power surging through my body.

Ares, who lay by my side in wolf form until I finished shifting, transformed and stared down at me with panicked eyes. "You shifted so easily. Are you ... okay?"

I stared down at my hand in awe as I comfortably shifted back and forth between paw and hand. What made this mountain range so special? Was it the necromancer or something else entirely? If I lived here for eternity, would I be able to shift this freely all the time?

"I'm fine," I whispered, scared and startled myself. "That was ... fine."

Bare and naked, Vulcan walked ahead of us, following statues of gods and goddesses in what seemed to be a smooth stone path that slowly encircled the mountain. I walked next to Ares and admired how lifelike they seemed, as if the stone could break away at any moment and reveal a living, divine being.

Maybe when Dad had said people turned to stone, he'd meant someone had carved divinities into stone and decorated the mountain with them.

About a mile later, we stood on a plateau on the other side of the mountain that overlooked miles upon miles of uncharted forest that didn't seem to receive any sunlight, low yowling coming from the darkness. I paused and stared down at it, my stomach tightening.

Ahead of us, Vulcan disappeared around some rocks and

reappeared a few minutes later in a pair of loose beige pants. "There's a house. Clothes too!"

I winced at the thought of Vulcan just barging into someone's home, especially if that someone was a necromancer who could raise the dead. If we got on her bad side before we even met her, we might be in some murky waters.

"She's here," Ares said, grabbing my hand and guiding me toward the house.

Built into one jagged peak was a small centuries-old house with carved and misshapen windows and dirtied white curtains blowing around inside. I stepped into some clothes that Vulcan had thrown to me and walked into the empty house.

Simple, ancient tools and writings filled the insides. I trailed my fingers against the walls, an eerily familiar feeling coursing through my veins. While I had never stepped foot in here before, distant, seraphic memories drifted through me. But I must've just been thinking of the stories Dad used to tell Jeremy and me about this mountain.

Continuing through the house, I searched for any signs of witchcraft or necromancy, for powders or chemicals, anything. Yet other than the number of ancient ruins within this home, nothing about it screamed necromancing sorcerer.

I pulled open the closet to the master bedroom, my eyes widening slightly. Twenty sea-foam tunics hung in the closet with matching veils, the cloth so thick that I couldn't even see through it when I held it up to the light.

After sighing, I walked out of the house to the group of warriors. Maybe Vulcan's information was wrong, and we'd just barged in on a random person's home, not a necromancer's.

"There isn't anything unusual about this place," I said to the alphas, staring out into the endless abyss of gloom. "Except the—"

"Who trespasses in my home?" a woman said, stepping out of the darkness.

Covered from head to toe in a sea-foam tunic, she wore a veil over her face and carried a woven basket around her forearm. Thick strands of what must've been hair slithered around under her veil. But as she moved closer, I noticed that it wasn't hair, but snakelike creatures with wolf heads, razor-sharp canines, and glowing gold eyes peeking out from under the covering.

Ares stepped forward, and I yanked him back, my heart pounding inside my chest.

"Who is she?" Marcel asked through the mind link.

"Don't approach her," I ordered in my alpha tone to my wolves.

When nobody moved, I leaned forward. "Who are you?" I asked, but I had a feeling that I already knew exactly who she was.

Growing up, Mom had forced me to study books about ancient mythologies instead of books about wolf packs and leadership. There was one woman who resembled her, but she'd lived thousands of years ago. She couldn't have survived this long.

"You know who I am," she said, her face level with mine, letting me know that I had her full attention. "I'm sure you've heard the myths told down through the ages."

"Medusa?" I whispered.

"Medusa. Gorgo. All the horrid names warriors have called me over the years," she said, voice filled with dreadful sorrow, as if the years that had passed were filled with torment and suffering.

After releasing Ares's hand, I stepped toward her. Something drew me to her, pulled me in, and made me want to ask her thousands of questions about the world she had lived in for thousands of years now, about life, myths, and those monstrosities called hounds.

"What's your name—your real name?" I asked.

"That's a story for another day, my dear." She stepped back and surveyed the warriors around me. "And so, I am still waiting for my answer. Who is trespassing in my home? You shouldn't be here."

I gulped, not wanting to anger her. She held the power to rain misery upon whoever she pleased.

I gestured to each of the alphas. "This is Ares, Vulcan, and Minerva. And I'm—"

"Aurora," she said softly. "I already know who you are."

My eyes widened slightly. *How'd she know me?*

"We're looking for the necromancer who has aided *Fenris*," Ares said his name through clenched teeth, "in bringing wolves back from the dead as hounds. Or any necromancer who knows how to stop this fucking war."

Tensing, Medusa nodded. "Hella is the woman you seek. She has raised hounds for centuries. You will not find her here, and you will find nobody else who does what she does, except divinities in the underworld."

"Can you tell us about her? Where can we find her? Who is she? How could—" I started

"You ask a lot of questions, my dear. I cannot reply to many, as I don't have the answers. Hella and Fenris are siblings, but she lives in the underworld and rarely comes to earth. For your warriors, there are only two ways to travel to the underworld, and I will not allow you to go by either right now. It's not your time."

My brows furrowed. "Not our time?"

"You will know when it is," she said.

Ares grabbed my arm and snatched me away from her. "There will be no time to go to the underworld for Aurora. She is staying here with me."

"Whoever said she was going alone?" Medusa responded.

A deafening silence descended upon us, and I gnawed on the inside of my cheek. This felt bad. And when I said bad, I meant, really, really fucking terrible.

Both traveling to hell? Were we bound to die soon? Would we not be able to go to heaven with the Moon Goddess and run in the clouds with other fallen wolves? Would I never be able to see

Jeremy again? And Ares ... would Ares never get to see his mother?

"You have your hands full, especially because"—she tilted her head toward me—"you have the stone inside of you," she said without me even having to tell her. It was as if she could sense the power radiating from me or had read my mind.

I nodded and stared at the sea-foam green veil, which hid her face. How'd she know about me? How'd she know that I was the one with the stone? Was it that powerful? Were these immense waves radiating off me since I had come here some sort of ... message to her?

"But you hold on to something more." She walked around me, small snake-like wolf heads slithering out from her veil. "You are plagued by fear despite possessing power this strong. Why?"

My heart pounded in my chest. It definitely wasn't because a veiled woman was stalking around me as she looked me up and down and told all my secrets to the world. *Definitely not.*

She answered for me. "Because you don't have the complete stone, right? You only have half inside of you. You fear that it's not strong enough to protect you, your mate, and your pack, your ..." She stopped short and let out a harmonious laugh. "You must not even know about that yet."

"How do you know that?" I asked, stricken with fear right down to the bone.

While she sounded so young, something about her told me that she had seen men and women like me before, like she had sensed the stone from the moment I walked into her home, and that was why she had come back from the forest. After all, her basket was empty and not filled with the food she would've scavenged that forest to find.

"You have the other half of the stone but haven't used it yet. You fear that you'll be weakened while it's healing inside of you."

I balled my hands into fists. *How? How was this possible?*

"Come with me," she said, disappearing into her home.

Wanting answers, I marched in after her and into her living room. She ambled around the room and trailed her hand against the rock wall. Ancient letters, words, and symbols that hadn't been there before appeared on the stone in a glowing green.

"If you had put the stone into you earlier, you would've been weak. The hounds would've attacked. You would've died," she said with so much certainty, like she had seen it before. "The only way to ensure a quick and painless healing process is if you perform the ritual during a full moon. Your si—*your goddess* will help you through it."

A circle glowed brighter than the rest of the symbols. It looked like ancient Greek or Latin or a language that I thought I couldn't quite understand, but then ... then it all started to make sense somehow.

Dawn, the moon guides the stone from the dark to the light.

She walked back around me and pushed some hair behind my shoulders to see the scar and the stone in my back. I sucked in a breath when her fingers glided against my skin.

When I had my first stone surgery, it wasn't during a full moon. It was a random night when Elijah needed to save my life. At that time, I couldn't have waited a few days for a full moon. I'd needed it then and there.

"During your first stone surgery, it happened on a new moon," she said, fingers tracing the small scar on my back. "And it hurt, didn't it?"

"I couldn't control when it happened last time," I whispered. My chest tightened as the sharp pain from that night rushed through my body, making me ache. "I was dying, and my friend wanted to save me."

"I know he did, but"—she placed her hand on my shoulder and squeezed gently—"now, you don't need saving. Now, you need to place the stone in your back as soon as the next full moon."

"The Luna Ceremony," Ares said from behind me. "When we planned to do it."

After nodding in agreement, I frowned. "Who are you? How do you know all of this?"

"I've seen it many times before. Thousands of people have tried to wield the stone before you, my dear. Thousands of people have died within a couple of years from stupid, senseless mistakes such as not being able to wield the stone's power."

I shook my head. "But I've had it for over a decade."

While I couldn't see her face, I could sense she was smiling behind her veil. "You have because it was meant for you."

She tugged me to the side, turned her back toward the rest of the group, and pulled the veil over her head to look me directly in the eyes. The wolves on her head swayed in all sorts of directions, yet their faces stayed turned to me.

I wanted to look away, to be afraid. Myths warned never to look Medusa in her eyes, yet now that she had pulled her veil back for me and only for me to see ... I couldn't seem to look away.

Bloodshot eyes with piercing green irises, sharp cheekbones, and a striking smile. I hadn't expected her to be so beautiful yet look so ... so sad, as if she had been weeping for hundreds of years.

"Won't I ... I die if I continue looking at you?" I asked her.

"Only men turn to stone when I look at them, my dear," she said, brushing her fingers through my brown hair. "You're special, Aurora. Nothing like the men and women behind me. Something more. Something greater."

CHAPTER 27

AURORA

*M*edusa stared at me with both immense fear and great pride. Inside my back, the stone cast power down my spine and through every bone in my body, the sheer force fabricating the idea that I could both destroy and repair our lonely world with just one growl.

When she stepped closer to me, she smiled. "You have more power than you think you do, Aurora."

"It's the stone," I whispered. "The stone is giving me power."

"It's not the stone." She grasped my chin and stroked her thumb against my jaw. "It's you."

Surely, she had to be joking. I had never been strong or wielded any sort of power. If I had been truly powerful, I wouldn't have been treated so poorly as a child, right? Mom would've been ecstatic to make me alpha.

After she pulled the sea-foam veil over her face, she turned back to the other alphas. "The stone can be put into the back of any human, any creature, and any demon. But no creature knows how to wield it; they are taken by power, by strength, and by gods and goddesses of the darkness and dusk."

My stomach tightened, and I shuffled my bare feet against the stone floor. Did that mean that I wasn't a werewolf? Or maybe I really was an undead hound, one of the first who could control thoughts, feelings, and actions. I shook my head and shivered at the thought.

"You see"—she stalked around each of the alphas, the wolf-like snakes atop her head baring their small yet vicious canines at everyone, except me—"there are plenty of Malavite Stones in the world, but if wolves found them ... the underworld would rise. There would be no peace, just violence."

"More stones?" Ares asked, standing straighter. "Where are there more stones?"

"Did you not just hear her?" I grasped his hand and yanked him to me. "We can't give the stone to your sister, especially if she doesn't know how to wield it. If Charolette dies because she doesn't have the knowledge on how to wield the stone, she will have the same fate as if she didn't have the stone at all."

"She's my sister," Ares snapped, eyes shifting from brown to gold. "She's my sister. I'm going to do everything I can to save her. If the stone can give her a few years, then I'm going to get her another one and fucking hope she'll reconsider after she sees how it transforms you."

Medusa paused for a few moments to let us argue and then drew the white curtains closed. She trailed her fingers across the cloth until a glowing green illustration of an empty field toward the summit of the mountain appeared. "They call this place Stone Valley. It's promised to have hundreds of Malavite Stones, but no mortal has found them, and no mortal will."

Staring at the image, I knotted my brows. With hundreds of Malavite Stones there somewhere, shouldn't the field be guarded by some hellish fiend or a divinity or some sort of immortal creature? Why was it so empty and bare? If others knew about this place, thousands of people would flock there daily to search and vie for power comparable to the gods.

"We're going," Ares said, pulling me toward the door.

"What's there?" I asked Medusa, yanking him back.

After staying quiet for a few moments, Medusa tapped her finger against the curtains, the image rendering clearer. Stone Valley wasn't just an empty field; inside it lay a battlefield with hundreds, if not thousands, of warriors who all looked to be fighting invisible monsters.

Dad's warning.

"Blood. Death. And hell." She pulled her fingers from the curtain, the drawing disappearing. "You must never travel there."

"We have to go," Ares said.

"Then, I must warn you that some people who travel there don't come back. They turn to stone, die, and disappear from this world forever. Thousands of men and women just like your-selves. They all came to me and most disappeared into the darkness."

My heart thumped loud against my chest. *Dad ... all his stories ...*

If Medusa was telling the truth, those weren't old fables that Dad used to tell me. All those rumors about people becoming stone and hellish fiends walking this earth were real.

"What do you mean, they turn to stone?" I asked, brows furrowed. "Those are real people?"

"Yes, men, women, and immortals," she started, her voice cracking softly.

All the ancient myths warned people away from Medusa, as if she were nothing but a fury-ridden monster. But seeing her bloodshot eyes and listening to her speak with such sorrow made her seem so misunderstood and, dare I say, motherly.

"The entrance of the underworld lies northwest of and above the Stone Valley. As a wolf, it's a one-hour run."

Heart racing, I grasped onto Ares's hand and hoped that he

would reconsider. The entrance to the underworld lay so close to us. Monsters that we weren't ready to fight probably roamed around these mountains and the dark forest behind us. We should leave.

"We have to go," Ares said. "Now."

"One last thing before you go," Medusa said to us. "Killing the true leader of the undead is a feat that no mortal could accomplish alone, but when the leader of the hounds dies, so will the rest of them. That's the prophecy I spoke to your pack thousands of years ago, Ares and Aurora. Be careful out there."

Squeezing Ares's hand, I let her words sink in. This must've been that curse Ares had spoken about a couple days ago. If we killed Fenris, then the hounds would die. We wouldn't have to deal with this anymore and could live happy, healthy, and vibrant lives.

But it would be arduous.

Fenris was stronger and smarter and stealthier than we'd originally thought.

If we wanted to destroy the hounds for good, we had to throw all our best weapons and warriors at Fenris because I didn't want to lose any more family or pack members. I would fight to the end of time to make this world a better and safer place, and nobody would stop me.

Ares, Minerva, and Vulcan walked outside to prepare our warriors.

But before I could depart, Medusa grasped my wrist, pulled the veil back over her face, and smiled at me. "My dear, we will meet again. But when we do, it'll be one of the last times I see you for quite some time." She glanced down my body and then back up. "If you want a family, hold off the hounds for as long as you can, birth a pup, and love her with all that you have." She brushed her fingers against my cheekbone, as if she was reminiscing on her life, and stared into my eyes. "You never know when you'll have to give her up to keep her safe or to give her a better life."

Her words were filled with so much sorrow that I had to bite back my own whimper. My heart swelled, and I wanted to stay with her and talk, but I had more pressing matters, like a determined-to-die alpha mate who I needed to protect.

Instead, I hugged her and rested my head on her shoulder, breathing in her woodsy scent. The snake-like wolves on her head curled around my body and pulled me in even tighter, and I enjoyed this moment with a woman I had never met but seemed like I had known for millennia.

~

"Ares, I don't think this is a good idea," I said through the mind link as we ran up the mountain's edge toward Stone Valley and passed divine after divine captured in rock. With every statue we saw, Medusa's warning about traveling here repeated in my mind. People who came here didn't always come back.

If we didn't come back, we wouldn't be able to hold off the hounds for our people, wouldn't be able to have a family, and would be forever damned and memorialized in stone. I didn't ever want that to happen to me. Our lives might be shitty at the moment, but we had so much to live for.

Either way, Ares and the other alphas seemed set on finding more stones. Even Minerva, who always thought through battles and plans, had urged us to Stone Valley. I guessed the desire for power far outweighed a content life. It was an incredible force that would drive so many people to death someday.

Despite my pleas to leave, we continued to run up the rocky path that encircled the mountain. I cursed myself for following him, but I couldn't let anything happen to my mate. Overcome with need to help his sister, Ares wasn't thinking straight. Neither was anyone, apparently.

The farther we ran up the mountain, the more my wolf claimed control, pulling me forward and refusing to turn back now. Like some innate radar, we could both feel the immense energy radiating from the stone in my back and the Malavite Stones hidden in Stone Valley.

When we reached the foggy summit, the alphas halted, their paws grinding into the rocky terrain. While no life had grown anywhere else on the mountain, up here, trees had been uprooted, struck in half, burned almost to the ground, leaving nothing but stumps and ash.

Unable to stop myself, I led the group and walked through the woods. I paused at the entrance to a mile-long field of stone. "Stone Valley," I whispered, shifting into my human with ease and walking aimlessly onto the field while the others stayed behind.

Hundreds of ruthless warriors—both in human and wolf form—had been preserved in stone, mid-fight. Some were doubled over in pain and grasping open wounds in their abdomens. Others were mid-bite with nothing but air between their canines. I stared at them with wide eyes. These people were my ancestors.

With every step I took, more and more energy surge inside of me. I glanced around at the impeccably undamaged and unharmed statues and wondered how fog, rain, hail, and snow hadn't worn their bodies away at all. It had been hundreds of years since the War of the Lycans. Their fragile fingers should've been broken off by the winter's harsh winds, their bodies eroded by the rainfall. Not so perfectly preserved.

Suddenly, the statue of a human warrior with a spear crumbled into hundreds of pieces, the sound of falling rock echoing throughout Stone Valley. My eyes widened at the unexpected fall, and I nervously looked around at the other warriors to see if the same would happen to them. None did.

But one stone man caught my eye.

Naked, muscular, and made of white stone. Unlike most other statues, the man stood stoically in the center of the field. He looked even more divine than Ares did during a fight, and Ares reminded me of a god himself. What seemed even more majestic was that a single ray of sunlight shone through the thick fog and illuminated his chiseled face, giving the white stone a goldish tint.

Despite Ares calling my name, I found myself drawn to and walking toward the man. When I stood before him, what seemed to be thousands of years' worth of memories rushed through my mind. I tried to grasp onto any of them, but I couldn't quite seem to visualize them fully.

A thriving vine of small sunflowers wrapped around his leg and up his muscular thighs, the petals and seeds all facing toward the sky. I glanced back up at him, brushed my fingers against his shoulder, and immediately pulled my hand away, feeling power swell in my body. Whoever this man was, the stone had drawn me to him for some reason. I studied him to try to remember if I knew him from somewhere.

Yet … I was certain that I had never seen him before in my entire life.

But I could feel this odd connection to him.

"Don't ogle him," Ares growled at me, snatching my hand and pulling me away from the godlike man. Canines bared, he dragged me through the field of stone. "We're here to find the fucking stones, Aurora, not to stare at naked fucking men."

After shifting my gaze to other statues, I pulled my hand away. "I'm not here for the stones, Ares. You heard Medusa. It could kill Charolette, and I'm not willing to take that risk. But by all means, go find it for yourself."

He snarled and stormed away. Along with all the warriors, he searched the perimeter for the Malavite Stones. But while we stood in an entire field of stone, nobody could find the ones they searched for.

The Malavite Stone glowed a bright white color, was about a quarter in diameter, and looked almost gem-like. They would have to search for days just to find it, days that we couldn't dedicate to something so deadly.

Rolling my eyes at how foolish the desire for power made wolves, I glanced around at the other statues and locked eyes with ... *him*. Preserved in stone on the other side of the field, Dad stood in his wolf form with his head held high and his nose pointed into the air, as if he was howling to the moon.

Once I sprinted across the field, I collapsed beside him. "No," I whispered, shaking my head from side to side. "No ... please, Moon Goddess, no. Don't let it be."

I grasped his stone face in my hands and could almost feel the fur graze against my palms, but it wasn't really there. It was all my imagination. It was what I wanted to believe.

Dad was the only fucking family I had left, and now, he was really gone for eternity too.

Had he come here to spend the rest of his life with his family? Was that why he'd refused to stay with Ares and me and why he'd wanted to be a lone wolf? I had so many questions that would be left unanswered.

I rubbed my hands over his snout and pulled myself toward him, wrapping my arms around his wolf for the very last time. If he had chosen to live in Sanguine Wilds, I might have seen him again ... but this way, I wouldn't.

"It's not fucking here," Ares barked hours later, storming through the bodies of stone and toward the center of the valley, where I sat with my head in my hands, still trying to come to terms with Dad being gone for good.

We had been here for three hours, and everyone had searched every inch of this place themselves. Some had started digging around the statues, which I'd strongly advised against because this seemed like sacred land. Destroying anything here would have consequences, but they hadn't seemed to care.

"Medusa said it would be hard to find," I snapped.

"What's your problem today, Aurora?" Ares asked me, brows furrowed together in a ruthless glare.

With his big, muscular arms crossed over his chest and that divine aura radiating off him again, I would've let him intimidate me if I hadn't known better.

I stood to my feet. "One, we've been here for hours. Two, the stones shouldn't be tampered with because nobody knows how to use them. Three, we're close to the underworld's entrance. And four, we are surrounded by thousands of people who turned to stone in this very field! My problem is that I want to survive, Ares. I want to have a family with you. I want to live my life until I can't anymore. I don't want to be here."

He cursed under his breath and gazed off into the dark sky. "We have to leave to get you back to our pack for the Luna Ceremony and so Elijah can put the other half of the stone inside of you, but I'm coming back here with more warriors right after that."

Overcome with emotion, I shook my head and held back my tears. "And what if you never come back to me?" I whispered, voice cracking. "You're going to travel back here after seeing all of this." I gestured back toward the hundreds upon hundreds of stone people. "You're going to leave me and one day turn to stone too?"

"If all these people turned to stone here, why haven't we?" he asked.

"I don't fucking know, Ares! But there are people here who were in the middle of battle. My dad is here!"

"Your dad?" he asked.

"Yes, Ares. He's stuck in stone forever now. Not only him, but warriors and gods are here. If we survive today, it doesn't mean you'll survive the next time you come."

Ares growled and turned away from me, canines emerging from under his lips.

I grasped his wrist and stared at his profile. "Do you really never want to see me again? Do you not want a family with me?"

It was a selfish question to ask because he was doing this for Charolette. But we didn't even know if it would work, *and* Charolette didn't want the stone. No matter how hard Ares tried to convince her, she wouldn't even consider putting half of it inside of her.

"Aurora, you know that's not true," he said through clenched teeth. "I love you."

"Well then, think about the consequences of your actions," I said, pulling away from him as my chest tightened. "I know it's hard for you because all you feel is pain and heartbreak, but think about what you really want. If you want that stone for Charolette —even though you know she won't accept it—over me, then come back here."

I turned away from him, acting as if I didn't give a shit anymore. But I did.

I loved Ares and Mars too fucking much.

If he came back here, I'd stupidly accompany him to protect my mate.

"Kitten ..." Ares grasped my hand and pulled me back toward him. "I'm sorry. I just ..." For a moment, Mars flashed in his eyes, but then he was gone. "I need it for her, for Charolette." He paused and wiped a tear off my cheek. "But I need you more. I can't—"

Lightning flashed through the fog, accompanied with a thunderous roar, northwest of the mountaintop. Suddenly, the dark sky cracked open, a whirling fiery-orange portal with black flames expanding above it.

Heart hammering, I curled my hand around Ares's bicep in fear. *What the hell was that?*

The portal stayed ajar for a few moments, and then a wolf with two diagonal scars running across his face jumped out of it.

Fenris stood atop the mountain beside us and raised his snout to the gateway, howling.

And then hundreds of hounds flooded out of the portal, circling around Fenris and baring their teeth, as if ready for war. I stared wide-eyed at the scene, nails lengthening into claws and puncturing Ares's bicep.

My Goddess, my fucking Goddess. We're screwed.

When Ares saw Fenris, he lunged forward, about to shift into his wolf and destroy him with everything he had, but as the hounds continued to pour from the portal, I grasped his wrist tightly and pulled him back.

"No," I said sternly.

Even being three mighty packs strong, we didn't stand a chance.

We couldn't run to death. We needed to return home for the stone.

"We have to go," I pleaded with Ares.

While Ares nodded in agreement, Vulcan shifted and growled at Fenris, catching his attention. I didn't know what had possessed him to do such a thing, but I fucking cursed him out for it inside my head. This could kill us for good, for fucking good.

When Fenris looked over at me, I sucked in a deep breath. We needed to get out of here now. No more looking for the stone. No more fucking waiting. This was life or death, and some fucking wolves didn't understand that.

Instead of running after us, like I'd thought Fenris would, he stood atop the mountain like a god, mouth moving yet no words being spoken. Then, suddenly, he lifted his nose to the air again and howled.

A blanket of wind swept across Syncome Mountains. Bones that some warriors had dug up and even *broken* statue pieces formed back together, just as the hounds had done in the cave.

We were surrounded from all sides with hundreds of more hounds coming to life.

"We have to go. We can't kill them all. Not with the others on top of that mountain," I said, pleading to Ares. I shifted into my wolf quickly and easily, and nudged his thigh. *"Please, I don't want to die before we have a family."*

"This is how hounds are made?" Minerva asked, brows furrowed. She surveyed the area and nodded toward the man with sunflowers around his thigh. "To the east, there are less of them. If we hurry, we can lose them in the forest."

So, we fled off the field. Sprinting for our lives. Slaughtering as many hounds as we could. Trying to escape Fenris's wrath. And as soon as everyone ran off the field, I looked over my shoulder at the man, made of white stone and sunflowers, wanting to see him one last time.

I swore he'd turned his head toward me and whispered, "Go, Aurora. Live."

CHAPTER 28

AURORA

*W*e sprinted through the forest for hours, on a mission to lose those monstrosities before they killed us. Like earlier, Hound Territory was unusually quiet, but this time, we knew why—because the hounds were gathered on the mountain and preparing for the deadliest war yet.

I didn't know how much time we had before they attacked— maybe a day, if that.

All I knew was that we had to get home, quickly race through the Luna Ceremony, and complete the stone surgery, so we would have a chance at survival.

As we reached our property, I glanced back one more time and sniffed, trying to catch a whiff of the hounds' musty stench. Yet it didn't seem like they had followed us, which made me think that those beasts were waiting for something more, something worse to arrive before they attacked.

Pack members raced back and forth on the lawn, carrying sturdy white folding chairs and silver decorations, preparing for tonight's ceremony. The celebration had approached so quickly that I hadn't done anything I wanted to do. I wasn't ready to officially become the luna and for the biggest war of the century.

Slowing to a stop, I bit my tongue and shifted into my human with so much pain. Ares rubbed against me, his thick brown fur brushing against mine until I lay at his paws on my hands and knees. Part of me wished that this was over, that this pain would disappear like it had at the mountain, and I hoped that it would after Elijah's doctor performed surgery tonight.

Ares shifted into his human and retrieved some clothes for me from the pack house. Children playfully ran around us, and older wolves cleared out the woods where the ceremony would be held, everyone cheery and chatting with each other.

My heart ached for our pack because they didn't know the agony that lay ahead.

But at least, they'd be safe. We had underground shelters now, thanks to Adrian.

After Ares handed me clothes and left to talk to Vulcan, Minerva commanded her warriors to return home. "Have a good Luna Ceremony tonight, Aurora. I hope that you won't require my help soon, but I'm afraid that you might."

"You're not staying?" I asked, stupidly thinking that she and Vulcan would stay and rest for a bit before Sanguine Wilds turned into a sea of blood and fear.

"No, I need to secure my pack for when the hounds attack. I believe they'll come soon. I thought Ares would be the one to set them off today, but it was Vulcan." She rolled her eyes. "Men and their bruised egos."

"Will you contact other packs in the area? Tell the alphas what you saw. They don't trust Ares, but they'll trust you. Please, try to get them on board with aiding us in this war. I'm afraid that we won't be able to protect everyone without as much help as we can get."

Minerva nodded. "Of course." Then, she shifted back into her wolf, howled to her warriors, and disappeared into the forest with her pack.

I hoped we wouldn't have a need to see her again soon, but we would.

"Are you staying, Vulcan?" I asked after walking over to Vulcan, Ares, and Marcel.

"Yes …" He looked at the ground and then back at me. "Sorry for the drama I caused there with the other hounds. I just …" He took a deep breath, chest rising and falling. "Someone special to me was there. Caught in the stone. I'd always thought we were mates, but she disappeared right before my eighteenth birthday. I dreamed of having a Luna Ceremony with her, but now, I know that'll never happen."

"What was her name?" I asked, brows furrowed.

"Her name was Venus." He gave me a half-smile that didn't reach his eyes. After staring off into space for a moment, his jaw twitching, he forced out a laugh. "Well, I hope to live vicariously through you two tonight." He slapped his hand against Ares's back, congratulated him, and disappeared through the crowd.

"Should I prepare the warriors to leave for Syncome Mountains after the ceremony?" Marcel asked Ares, walking toward the pack house.

I grasped Ares's hand, hoping that he'd listened to my pleas earlier but I doubted it. Ares did what he wanted, no matter the consequences. He made decisions based on emotion and emotion alone and never once thought things through before he acted.

"No," Ares said. "We're not going back there unless we have to."

Marcel growled, "We have to go back. There are stones there for Charolette. She could—"

Ares snarled and snatched Marcel by the collar. "Charolette doesn't want it," he said, voice almost cracking.

My heart broke for him. He had tried everything, every-fucking-thing that he could to help her. Yet still, he knew that she would never accept it either.

"We can't give up on her. We have to do something, Ares," Marcel said. When he realized that Ares wouldn't budge on this, he stepped closer to him and blew out a desperate breath. "We have to do something. Anything. We can't let her die."

"Why do you care so much about her, Marcel?" Ares asked.

"Because she's my mate," Marcel said, defeated. "I can't give up on my own mate."

Ares pressed his lips together. "She's your mate, but you go out with girls every night."

Marcel shook his head, chin trembling ever so slightly. "I don't want to. They were all just to forget her. She didn't want me for the longest time. Told me to find someone else because she was accepting her death. She was with Liam, and he made her happy. But I want her, Ares. I want her so fucking bad, and I don't want anything to happen to her."

Ares swallowed and pushed him away. "You hurt her, and I'll fucking kill you."

Bowing his head, Marcel thanked Ares, as if his alpha's approval to date his sister meant everything to him. "I'll come up with a way to save her, one that doesn't require us to travel back to the mountains. I can't let her die." Marcel ran off to find Charolette in the swarm of people.

After ushering me into the house, Ares shut the door behind us and stood with his back turned toward me, tense. "You're right," he said suddenly.

"Right about what?" I asked, brows furrowed.

He turned around to face me and clenched his jaw. "I make decisions based on emotion alone. I don't think things through. I want to see Fenris dead and his hounds hurting … and it's all because I can't fucking deal with my sister's decision …" He scowled. "But how the fuck am I supposed to be okay with my sister dying, Aurora? How am I supposed to fucking accept that she doesn't want to be here anymore without trying to persuade her or trying to help her live?"

Not knowing how to respond, I moved closer to him and rubbed his back. I hadn't had to prepare for Jeremy's death; I'd just had to accept it. But if I could've gone back—knowing what I knew now—I would've fought like hell to make sure he wasn't taken by the hounds. I wanted to tell Ares that I knew how it felt, but I didn't.

"I know how she's fucking feeling. I've been there. I've been hurt. I've wanted to end my life, hoping that wherever I ended up would be better than this shithole," Ares admitted, upper lip twitching.

Tears welled up in my eyes. I didn't want to hear Ares say something like that ever. I couldn't bear the thought of losing him or Mars. I loved them more than myself.

I shook my head. "Stop, Ares," I whispered.

But when he looked over at me, he was back to being Mars.

Mars thought this. Mars hated his life. Mars wanted to end it.

"Mars," I whispered, hugging my arms around his waist and resting my head on his chest. "I can't even begin to imagine your pain. I'll never fully understand it, and I hate that I can't take it away from you."

He wrapped me up in his arms. "I didn't think I'd ever have to choose between you and Charolette," he whispered. "I wanted to *hate* you earlier when you gave Ares the ultimatum ... but I can't. I want to have a family with you. I want to have pups. We love you more than anyone ever will, and we'll do anything to keep you alive."

CHAPTER 29

MARS

*L*aying Aurora down on the bed, I crawled up beside her and peeled off her clothes. It had been a long day, and all I wanted to do was relax with her during the little time we had before the ceremony. We surely wouldn't be able to relax afterward during her surgery tonight.

"We don't have much time until the ceremony. We should get ready," she said, tilting her head and moaning softly as I nipped at my mark on her neck and drew my tongue against each of the large puncture holes.

I wrapped her in my arms and rolled us over, settling her on me. "How could I get ready without pleasing my mate first? I can smell you, Kitten. You need this just as badly as I do." I ground my hips up against her bare ones. "You know you do."

She bit her bottom lip and slipped a hand between us, stroking my bulge against my gray sweats. "You're right," she said, crawling down my torso and bending at the hip to capture the head of my cock between her lips. She moved her tongue across the gray material, wetting it with her saliva.

Leaning up on a forearm, I trailed my other hand down her back to her ass, grabbed a handful of it, and then slapped it hard. "Lift your ass higher for me," I said. When she lifted her hips into the air, I smacked it again and growled, feeling my wolf ache for control.

Aurora pulled my cock out of my pants and sucked it into her mouth. I slowly lifted my hips and thrust my cock deep into her throat, her spit and drool rolling down my shaft. She wrapped her small hands around the base and squeezed. "Please, Mars ..."

I moved her hips closer to me, laced one hand into her hair, and thrust my other fingers into her wet little hole. At first, she tightened around me and tensed, but then she moved her hips back and forth, desperately begging me for more.

"Do you like that, Kitten?" I asked, pulling some hair out of her face to see her mouth stuffed full with my cock.

She sucked on me harder, bobbing her head up and down. Her pussy tightened around my fingers, and she gagged.

Before she could start to willingly choke on my cock, I pulled her up, made her straddle my waist, and shoved myself into her sopping pussy. All I wanted was to please this woman. She stayed by my side through everything, even when Ares made life-threatening decisions for himself.

"Are you going to be a good girl during the Luna Ceremony?" I asked, grasping her hips and pounding up into her. "Because if you're not, I might have to take you like this right then and there."

Aurora clenched down hard on me, bounced on my dick, and moaned to the Moon Goddess. I curled my fingers around her ass and met her with my own ruthless thrusts. As her breasts bounced against my chest, I pulled her toward me, captured one of her nipples between my teeth, and tugged.

She stopped moving, her body tensing up, and whimpered for me.

But I didn't stop thrusting up into her until my cum was deep inside of her. I kissed the mark I'd left on her neck and grunted against it, making sure every last drop was inside before I pulled out.

She slowly lifted her hips off me and stared down with wide eyes. "Did you come?"

"Yes."

"None is coming out," she said, glancing down between her hips.

Goddess, she made me rock hard again.

"I pushed it too deep. It's not going to come out of you." I chuckled and pulled her to my chest, sucking her bottom lip between my teeth. "One day, Aurora, I'm going to put a pup inside of you. Maybe today's that day. Maybe you'll start growing my babies."

CHAPTER 30

AURORA

"Can you get your nasty-ass hands off Aurora?" Charolette asked Mars, standing at our bedroom door, which she'd opened. Dressed in a white sundress and a pair of pink sandals, she scrunched her nose and turned away from us. "I need to help prepare her for the ceremony, and you need to get ready too, Mars."

Picking me up off the bed, Mars placed me on the ground, grasped my face, and kissed me softly. "Go, get ready with her before she screams at me." He looked back over at her. "And you're not off the hook, Charolette. We'll talk tomorrow about what you did."

After tugging on my clothes, I hurried down the hall with Charolette.

"You shouldn't be doing that kind of stuff before the Luna Ceremony!" Charolette whisper-yelled at me. "It's supposed to be a sacred time. What if our Moon Goddess finds out about it? She'll rain down hell."

Wanting to keep the conversation light, I laughed and walked into Ruffles's spare bedroom. Ruffles sat on her yellow blankets with her head in a bag of potato chips and a thick layer of salt and grease covering her whiskers.

"No Pringle today?"

She cut her eyes to me and meowed, stuffing her face with chips again.

Charolette bumped her hip against mine and reached for my dress that hung in the closet. "Pringle will be at the ceremony. I had to drag Ruffles away from him today. She wouldn't leave his side."

Once I took a quick shower, Charolette wrapped me in a plush silver robe and sat me in the bathroom chair, pushing a comb through my hair. "Someone is in love," Charolette hummed at Ruffles, who lifted her nose into the air in a *so what* manner.

I smiled at Ruffles, and then gazed at Charolette through the mirror's reflection. "I know I can't persuade you to use the stone, and I know that even if we find another one, you won't want to use that either ... but please, talk to your brother. Make sure he knows that you love him and that you're doing this for yourself. Not because you feel like a burden. Not because you feel guilty about what happened to your mother. *Yourself.*" I hardened my stare. "And if you're not doing it for yourself, maybe you should reconsider it."

Charolette stopped the comb mid-brush and frowned at me, guilt washing through her expression. She glided her tongue across her front teeth. "I—"

Someone knocked on the bedroom door, and Charolette happily hurried over to it. By the look on her face and sadness in her eyes, I hoped that my words had struck a chord inside of her and changed her mind. We both knew that she wasn't doing this for herself, but because she felt guilty about her mother's death.

Dressed in a black suit, Elijah raced past Charolette and into the room with fearful, wide eyes. "You might not be able to put the stone inside of you tonight."

Charolette shut the door behind him. "Why can't she? Is your doctor okay?"

"It all makes sense. I didn't want it to make sense, but it does." He pushed his thick black frames up his nose and shook his head. "What you've told me so far is that wolves die and then are brought back to life by those white orbs that faintly resemble dust particles that you saw at the cave. It turned them into hounds, correct?"

Unsure about where he was going with this, I nodded.

"We didn't put two and two together until now." He placed a manila folder on Ruffles's bed and laid out a bunch of papers across the blanket. Ruffles stood to give him room and stared down at the strong cursive writing as if she understood what they meant. "You are a hound, Aurora, because you died and came back to life, using magic."

"What are you talking about? I never died ..."

"You died during the stone surgery," Elijah said, lowering his voice. "Your injuries from the hound attack were far too bad to treat. We revived you three times ..." He held three fingers up for emphasis. "Three times, your heart stopped beating. It must've been buried in the files somewhere, but we found it."

Charolette ushered me back to the bathroom to finish my hair.

"The last time you died, we thought we'd lost you for good. You were dead for a solid five minutes, and we were about to extract the stone from your back because we thought it was useless. But you opened your eyes. The stone must've brought you back from the dead, as fully functioning, unlike hounds."

"So, are you saying that this necromancer grinds up stones and uses the dust to bring the dead back to life?" I asked, watching Charolette work her magic on my hair.

But it did make sense. If Hella the necromancer and Fenris

the hound master used complete stones on each hound, then the stones would make them able to think freely and for themselves again. Maybe she only used stone dust, so she could control the beasts.

Maybe we didn't need to kill Fenris at all but Hella.

"I don't know if we'll be able to do the surgery because you might need to be dead in order for us to do it." Elijah frowned at me. "We can try, but there is no guarantee that it will work despite whatever you learned at Syncome Mountains today."

"We'll try it. Just don't tell Ares. I want this ceremony to be peaceful." I glanced at Charolette and frowned. "I'll tell him right before the surgery and hope that he won't freak out."

My stomach tightened at the thought. I needed to go through with this either way. The hounds were coming, and nothing could stop them, except maybe me, if I wielded both halves of the stone.

After Charolette finished my hair, I grabbed the stone from my dresser's silver safe, where I'd had it locked up for weeks now, and thrust it into Elijah's hand. "Take it and prepare. I want it done right after the after-party. I had someone set aside a place at the hospital."

Elijah stared down at the glistening stone through his glasses, gulped, and enclosed it in his hand. "Aurora, I don't want to hurt you. I want you to live. If we can't put it inside of you tonight, we can't kill you to try."

"This is the only way and the only time you'll be able to do it," I said. Medusa had said that it had to be done tonight during the full moon. If we waited any longer, we'd be dead. "I can't pass up this opportunity now. I've lost too much already. I need to do this. I need to save this pack."

~

Less than an hour later, I stood outside the pack house with Charolette and Elijah.

Charolette bounced on her toes and grinned at me, her blonde hair flowing in the fall breeze. She smoothed out some wrinkles on my colorful pastel dress and clapped her hands together. "It's time! I can't believe the Luna Ceremony is finally here. I've been waiting my entire life for Ares to find his partner and finally claim her. And I'm so happy that it's you!"

"Let's go sit." Elijah grasped her shoulders and guided her into the forest. He glanced over his shoulder. "If I don't get a chance to talk to you after the ceremony, I'll meet you at the hospital at midnight for the surgery."

After they disappeared, I took a deep breath and stared up at the moon. From the hounds to this ceremony, so many thoughts rushed through my mind. I wished so many people could've been here with me to witness this moment and help us fight, like Jeremy, Mom, Dad, and some of my old packmates.

But things changed, and I had to make the best out of this ceremony. It might not be the ceremony or timing of my dreams, but I was with the best, most loving man that I had ever met. Ares and Mars both had shown up to prove themselves to me, both had laid their lives on the line. I couldn't imagine being mated to anyone else.

As I stared up at the full moon that glowed extra bright this evening, I swore I heard a divine female's voice drift through the air. "*I wish I could be there with you,*" the woman whispered. "*You look stunning and are destined for great things.*"

Lips curling into a smile, I walked toward the ceremony with my dress swaying in the breeze. Silver ribbon was wrapped around a path of trees leading to our pack, who stood in a semi-circle around Mars. Pups sat in front, crisscrossed on the dirt, pulling dry grass out of the ground. Elders stood off to the sides and awed in admiration. Warriors stood behind Mars and watched as I moved up through the crowd.

I walked toward Mars, who stood under a wooden arch draped with silver ribbons and olive branches. Despite the hounds and the war approaching, I set my lips into a soft smile and vowed to cherish this moment forever.

When I reached him, I grabbed his hands and interlocked my fingers with his. *"I'm so excited!"* I said through the mind link.

Dressed in a tux with his dark hair parted at the side, Mars beamed at me. *"I'm just waiting until I can take you back home and ravish you,"* he said through the link.

My cheeks flushed, and I resisted the urge to playfully slap him across the chest. This was supposed to be a sacred ritual, not sexual. But I wouldn't trade his dirty mouth for the world. He could ravish me the whole night for all I cared. Hell, even tomorrow too.

Mr. Barrett stood before us and looked around the pack. "Welcome to the—"

"MEOW!"

Everyone stopped, looked back, and parted as Ruffles sauntered down the path with a silver ribbon wrapped around her, swaying her tail, with Pringle in tow. She stopped at our feet, and Mars leaned closer to me, reaching into his pocket.

"I didn't want Ruffles to feel left out, so I got her something."

He crouched, pulled a pair of circle sunglasses from his pocket, and placed them on her face, the frames the same color as my dress. "Charolette mentioned that you'd picked out a pastel dress instead of the traditional silver dress, so I thought it was only fair ..."

I playfully rolled my eyes at him and giggled, so grateful that he could make me laugh in dire times. Moonlight flooded through the trees and created patterns on his tanned face.

I couldn't love anyone more than I loved him. He was mine. All mine. And nobody would take him away from me. Ever.

"As I was saying," Mr. Barrett said after Ruffles lay on her stomach with those glasses, "I'm deeply saddened that my mate couldn't be here to watch this special day. I'm sure she would've loved to be here with everyone to celebrate our new luna."

Mars held my hands tighter, blinking a few times, as if not wanting any bad memories to rush to the surface. I brushed my thumb across his knuckles. I wished his mother could've been here too. There were so many things I wished I could've talked to her about.

"But we are here to celebrate the addition of a strong warrior luna and—Mars wanted me to add—*alpha* to our pack," Mr. Barrett said.

My heart warmed at Mars's *and* Ares's constant appreciation for my strengths as an alpha.

The pups from my old pack cheered and waved moonflowers in the air. "Yay! Alpha Aurora!"

After smiling at them, I glanced back up at Mars.

"I can't wait to have pups with you," he whispered, leaning into me.

Butterflies erupted through my stomach at the thought.

"Now"—Mr. Barrett looked around the crowd—"does anyone wish to reject our luna?"

I glared down at Ruffles, who gave me a mischievous smirk, daring her to try to claim Mars for herself. She waved her tail and had the damn audacity to stand. I narrowed my eyes even more and smiled when she cuddled next to Pringle.

When nobody stood, Mr. Barrett placed a hand on each of our shoulders. "I'm pleased to announce our new luna."

The pups tossed their moonflowers into the air, watching them glow brightly like snowflakes as they drifted back to the ground.

Mars wrapped his arms around my waist and pulled me closer for a big, wet, sloppy kiss. "My luna," he whispered against my lips. "All mine."

CHAPTER 31

MARS

"*I* want to sneak you away and have my way with you," I whispered into Aurora's ear an hour into the after-party, dragging my canines against her neck.

We had spent the last hour talking to nearly half the pack because most wolves hadn't even had a chance to introduce themselves to her yet.

She gave me a halfhearted smile. "Well, before we do any of that, I need to talk to you."

As she pulled me aside, the elders chuckled, gave us knowing looks, and dispersed into the forest to celebrate with everyone else.

She tugged me behind a couple of ribbon-decorated oak trees and slumped her shoulders forward, moonlight bouncing off her skin. "Don't freak out."

"What is it?" I asked, gripping her hands tighter and tighter. "What's wrong?"

After glancing up at the moon, she grimaced. "It's almost midnight, and the stone ..."

My eyes widened. "We need to get you to the hospital, don't we?"

"No." She shook her head and bit her lower lip. "Before the Luna Ceremony, Elijah said that I'm a hound, that I died during the first surgery, and that's how they were able to successfully place the stone inside of my spine. That's how it worked."

"You're a hound?" I whispered back at her, and then I shook my head. "You can't be. You have free will. You ... you are able to think for yourself. You're not vicious. You can shift. You're exactly like ... Fenris." His name soured my tongue.

She glanced at the dirt and then back up at me with tears in her eyes. "That's not all."

My heart stopped, everything around us seeming to slow. "Please, don't tell me that you have to die again for Elijah's doctor to perform the surgery?" I asked tensely, taking deep breaths so as not to startle Ares.

But deep inside of me, I felt him rumble.

"Aurora ..." I grasped her hands. "Please, tell me that you don't have to die because I won't allow it. I can't have you leave me. You can't die, especially if we don't know if the complete stone will certainly bring you back."

"I don't know what needs to happen," she whispered, gulping and tucking some hair behind my ear. "Neither does Elijah."

While she needed the damn stone to survive, she needed to die for it. It didn't make an ounce of sense.

I shook my head, refusing to accept this. "What if you don't come back to life? What if I lose you forever, all because of a stone?"

"This is the only way," she said, fingers curling into my chest. "You heard what Medusa said. Tonight is the only night I am able to do it. Those hounds are coming, and I can't risk not being strong enough to protect everyone."

"Aurora—"

She took my face in her hands. "Mars, I love you. Please, accept this. I know it's difficult, but it's the only way that we have a chance to survive this. If there is hope, it has to be this and nothing else."

Though I didn't want to admit it, she was right. I had to stop thinking about myself and had to start thinking about what this could do for my pack and the entire werewolf species. If the hounds easily destroyed my pack, they'd be able to demolish the entire world.

After I hesitantly nodded, she kissed me and gave me the most breathtaking smile. "I love you more than anything. Thank you for this. I promise to be strong for you when I wake up out of surgery. I will protect you, and I will protect this pack. As you said, I'm not only a luna, but an alpha too."

The corner of my lips twitched up into a smile. It wasn't a real one, but one that I faked. I didn't want her to do this. I didn't accept this. I didn't think that this was all right one damn bit. But I smiled for her because ... because I couldn't lose her, especially not to hounds.

"Can I break you two lovebirds apart?" Charolette interrupted, butting right into our conversation. She grabbed Aurora's hands and pulled her away from me. "I wanna dance with our luna! This is my favorite song!"

As Charolette pulled her onto the moonflower-decorated, leaf-carpeted dance floor, Dad walked up to me and placed a hand on my shoulder. "Son, there's something I've been meaning to tell you, but with everything going on ... I haven't found the time."

"What is it?" I asked, brows furrowed.

He parted his lips and then pressed them back together. It wasn't like him to ever be lost for words or nervous about what he had to say. The last time I had seen him like this was the night he invited Aurora and me over to his house to tell us that Fenris was Mom's mate.

"It's about the stone," he finally said. "I know you're thinking about putting it inside of Aurora right after the party, and while I think she'd be great with it, you must know—"

"I'm not thinking anymore about putting the stone inside of her. She'll have it in her tonight before dawn," I said.

There were no more ifs, ands, or buts about this. It was going to happen whether or not I liked it. Aurora had full autonomy over her body and could make her own choices as alpha and luna. She was by far stronger and smarter than me. And I had seen those hounds, the way they eyed her with hunger. They were coming. For her.

"Listen to me, son," he said sharply, gripping my shoulder harsher. "I'm not saying don't put it inside of her. I want you to know what you're getting into before you do." He paused as someone walked by and gave them his best forced smile. "There have been many occurrences of the stone being placed in the wrong person, but there has only been one confirmed person that the stone has been put inside of and worked for eternity."

"Eternity?" I asked, brows furrowed. "What do you mean? Who was it?"

He glanced up at the moon, and my eyes widened.

"The Moon God—"

Dad slapped a hand over my mouth to shut me up. "Don't say her name out loud. You don't know what people will do if they find out that the stone is capable of immortality. It is more than just strength and smarts. It's forever and then some."

Immortality? Did that mean that Aurora was going to live for as long as the stone was inside of her? She was—

"Selene, our Moon Goddess, was the last person known to have a similar stone inside of her. It's what's made her immortal all those years ago. Nobody knows if the stone was real or just a myth, but it's what is accepted among many of the elder wolves. The younger generation doesn't believe it, but I do. You've seen what it can do. You've felt its power in your hands after Aurora ripped it out of her brother. This will change both of your lives forever."

Before I could respond, a wolf howled in agony, and people screamed from all directions, running in haste. We didn't have any more time. The hounds were here, and they were out to find the stone and my Aurora.

CHAPTER 32

AURORA

 erocious snarls rumbled through the dark forest. Men, women, and children ran in every direction to safety. Warrior wolves and patrol guards alerted us of the hundreds of hounds sprinting toward our property, some of their voices cutting from our minds suddenly.

Death.

The hounds had come with one goal—to kill us.

"Get the pups!" I screamed, hurrying to gather as many as I could find to lead them to the underground homes, where they'd be safe. But everyone started to shift to protect themselves and their families from the fiends. "Someone, get the pups to safety!"

After rallying as many as I could, I designated an older woman as their caretaker for now and hurried with them to the pack house, ushering them into the underground fort. Once I secured the door, I ran back out into the chaos to find more.

There had to be others. That wasn't all of them. I needed to find—

A huge brown wolf latched its teeth into my wrist. I snatched myself away, about to kick him in the snout when I realized it was Ares. He grabbed my wrist in his sharp bite and dragged me toward the pack house.

"Someone, tell Elijah to get to the pack house now," Ares said through the mind link.

We didn't have time to get to the hospital for the surgery. It was too far.

Ares quickly shifted into his human, grabbed my hand, and pulled me through the groups of warriors. Most of them I didn't recognize. They weren't Minerva's warriors. They weren't Vulcan's. They weren't even ours. But they looked familiar, as if they were—

I inhaled deeply.

The stone people.

Some old, others young, they fought against the beasts with everything they had left. My gaze traveled across the battlefield as I tried desperately to find my father. He had to be here. He had to—

A hound sprinted right at us and knocked us onto the ground. He stalked toward me, bloodied saliva dripping from his teeth and black pits for eyes. Ares regained his balance, shielded me with his arm, and bared his colossal canines, his eyes endless, chaotic pits of red. *Red.*

When someone ripped the hound off us, Ares grabbed my hand and stood. With glowing bronze skin and golden eyes, the man who had once been a statue of white stone snapped the beast's jaw in a moment.

"Go," he said to us as the hounds leaped at him from all directions and piled on top. "I'll hold them off as long as I can."

"Who are you?" I asked, staring at him with wide eyes. "Why are you—"

Chucking the hounds off himself, he said, "Go! If you survive the night with the stone, we'll have eternity for questions."

Not wasting any more time, Ares grabbed my hand and pulled me toward the pack house, sprinting faster than he ever had. I sprinted right along with him, knowing that we should stay out here and help protect our people but needing to have the stone inside of me. If I did this, I could save so many lives.

So many people and so many pups wouldn't have to endure a life of pain like I had.

Just as we approached the pack house, Ares stopped and cursed.

"What is—"

I gasped and stared at the hounds entering and exiting the pack house through the windows, glass shattering everywhere, chewing on couches, ripping apart clothes, eating up food. Tears welled up in my eyes, and I bit back a scream.

Everything … everything was getting torn to shreds. Everything was …

"Ruffles," I said, heart dropping. "I need to find Ruffles."

Ares wrapped his arms around my waist to hold me back, dragging me away from the pack house. "Trust her to hide and to stay safe. We have to go find another place for the surgery."

But I needed her. She was the only family I had left. I loved her with all my damn heart. She couldn't be gone. I couldn't let the hounds have her. They had my entire family. Finding Ruffles dead would be the end of me.

After picking up my flailing body and throwing me over his shoulder, Ares rushed through the vicious creatures toward one of the other bunkers built into a hillside. With no pups here, we wouldn't have to risk the hounds killing them if they found us.

Opening the door, he forced me into the room and mind linked someone to find Elijah.

I shoved his chest, trying to push him away so I could get back out there to find my cat. "Ares, please, let me go. I need to find her. She can't die."

Snatching my chin in his hand, he stared at me with both rage *and* fear in his eyes. "No. You need to be strong for your pack. You'll get the stone inside of you. You'll fight, and you'll fight, and when you wake up from this surgery, you'll continue to fight, no matter what you see outside."

Lips quivering, I shakily nodded. I didn't want to. I wanted to fight now.

But I had been preparing for this time to come. I knew what I had to do.

Someone banged on the door, and Elijah shouted, "Let me in! I have the stone."

When Ares opened the door, Elijah and Dr. Farral hurried into the room.

Elijah scanned the room for a few moments, found a metal table, and threw all their supplies onto it. "Guard that door with your life, Ares. And I'll guard Aurora with mine." He ushered me to the table. "Lie down and pray to the Moon Goddess that this goes smoothly."

Lying down, I stared up at the stone ceiling and tried to even my breathing, but all I could do was focus on everyone's ragged and rapid heartbeats. Ares locked and bolted the door, standing with his hands flat on the metal and his back to me.

"Ares," I whimpered, reaching out for him.

He held out one hand for me, our fingertips mere inches from each other. Though my Ares was the god of war, I saw the fear in his eyes as his pack screamed just outside the door.

"Calm down, Aurora," Elijah instructed as the doctor prepared as quickly as he could.

Since we weren't near a hospital or even the pharmacy, this procedure was bound to be tougher than expected.

After pulling out a knife, bandages, and a bottle of pills, Dr. Farral took a deep breath. "Please, calm down, Aurora. You're hyperventilating. You need to breathe in order for me to do this correctly."

I furrowed my brows. Ares ... I wanted Ares over here with

me. I was terrified. What if they killed me and I didn't wake back up? I'd leave him on this earth with nothing but pain. I wouldn't get to see my Ruffles again. All I wanted was to hold her one last time, to let her know that I loved her.

"Ares, I—"

Outside, a hound slammed against the door. They must've known we were in here; they must've sensed it. My chest tightened. My throat closed up. Tears raced down my cheeks. I struggled to stand, my wolf forcing me to hug Ares one last time.

Elijah pushed me back down and clasped my wrists in his hands. "Stop it, Aurora."

"Kitten," Ares said, hands flat on the door to hold it closed. "I will do anything for you, anything to protect you from all this darkness. Don't worry about me. Don't worry if I'm not here when you wake up. You're strong enough to lead this pack yourself."

"No! Stop talking like that. Nothing's going to happen to you," I screamed as I struggled against Elijah, my body trembling. "Don't say that! Please, please, don't say that. It's not true."

But something deep in my heart told me that it was.

Something bad was going to happen. Something bad *was* happening.

Elijah climbed onto the table, straddled my waist, and pinned me down. "We need to do this, Aurora," he said, his eyes pleading with me from above. "Please, stay still."

Overcome with so many emotions, I twisted and turned and tried hard to get out of his hold, but Elijah just held me tighter.

"Ares! Ares, please, be strong. Please, don't go out there."

The hound slammed into the door again, leaving an indent the size of a human body in the door. The muscles in Ares's back flexed as he tried to hold it shut, but the hinges were starting to come undone. I wiggled some more, my chin trembling uncontrollably.

"Aurora." Dr. Farral moved beside me, a bottle filled with

purple liquid in his hand. "Aurora, listen to me. You have to drink this. It will calm you down and put you out for a while as we complete the surgery."

Not wanting to never see Ares again, I pressed my lips together and shook my head. By the way Ares had talked, it'd sounded like he was about to make the ultimate sacrifice for me. And I wouldn't let it happen. I needed him just as much as that man needed me. I couldn't let him just die. I … I couldn't.

Elijah tightened his grip on my wrists and growled down at me. "Aurora, stop," he said in his alpha command, trying to get me to calm down, but my heart wouldn't stop racing.

"Ares, tell Mars that I love him," I said through the mind link, but I wasn't sure he'd heard me. I struggled some more as the doctor shoved the bottle between my lips and clamped my lips closed around it.

Another hound hit the door, making an even deeper indent, slamming against it over and over and over. The door flew open, and Ares was thrust back and slammed against the table. Two hounds sprinted into the room, and I tried to struggle toward Ares to help him, but my vision became cloudy.

"He's going to die! Stop him. Sto … sto … hi … him …"

My eyes closed, but I struggled to stay conscious. I didn't know if I'd ever see him again.

All I could hear was inhuman growling, claws slashing against fur, canines digging into flesh, coming from both inside the shelter and outside in the forest.

But the very last thing I caught before I passed out was Mars's voice through the mind link. *"I love you too, Kitten."*

CHAPTER 33

ARES

*I*mmediately shifting into my wolf, I lurched at the hounds who had stormed into the room. All I could focus on was protecting my mate. I'd do whatever it fucking took to ensure she safely received the stone, so she could lead this pack and end this war.

If it was my time to go, then she would be strong enough.

After killing the three beasts, I stood in front of the open door and guarded it with my life. Behind me, Elijah and Dr. Farral turned Aurora onto her stomach to prep her for surgery. I turned around to face the outside, not wanting to know when they cut her open and certainly not when she died.

Mars fought for control, but I seized it. He had spoken his few words to Aurora before she passed out, and that was all I'd grant him. Warring wasn't his forte, and neither was loss. If I had to shield him from this heartbreak too, I'd do it.

"Oh Goddess," Dr. Farral said behind me in a hushed tone.

Two more hounds sprinted at me faster and harder than the

last had, nearly knocking me down again. But this time, I made sure to stand my ground and rip each of their throats out until blood pooled below them.

"Are you sure?" Elijah asked, sounding worried.

"Yes," Dr. Farral said.

Elijah hurried over to me and crouched by my side, next to the dead wolves. "Ares ..." He gulped. "Ares, she's pregnant."

Everything slowed down, the wolves outside seeming to move in without haste anymore.

Aurora was pregnant.

My mate was pregnant with my pup.

CHAPTER 34

MARS

*D*uring that shocking moment, I snatched control from Ares by the canines. My chest tightened. I knew what I had to do to protect my family. We had waited for this moment forever, and now, I would never get to experience it with her. And if we didn't protect her and this pack, Aurora would never be able to experience it either.

I shifted back into my human, my mouth drying up. "Boy or girl?" I whispered, wanting to know the kind of family she'd raise when I was gone. "Do you know?"

Elijah glanced back at Dr. Farral, who turned Aurora back over, lightly pressed his hand against Aurora's stomach, and closed his eyes.

He smiled for a fraction of a second, a sorrowful breath escaping him. "Boys tend to have a slower heart rate, but hers is quick."

Unable to hold back, I placed my hand on top of her stomach and felt the slightest heartbeat. A tear slid down my cheek. A pup

… a little girl … that I'd never meet. It was the most blissful moment of my life, and I hoped that Aurora could find happiness without me.

Behind me, a hound growled. I turned back to it, ready to give this everything I had, and shifted into my wolf. We were having a girl. *Aurora* was having a girl. And I'd make sure that they had a good, safe life.

"Ares," Elijah said, pushing his glasses up his nose and nodding to me. "You're a good guy. I'll protect Aurora at all costs. Go protect your pack."

After holding his gaze for a moment longer, I lunged at the hound and killed him before he could enter the room. Then, I stood by the door and scanned the forest for that cynical hound leader I called Fenris.

Standing at the base of a hill with a smug look on his face, he ripped one of my best warriors into two pieces. I needed to end this once and for all. This evil that had plagued my pack for years —the curse that the hounds would take my luna from me—could be broken by me.

"Sacrifice an alpha."

That was what Dad had said needed to be done.

If offering myself up could end this war, if it stopped innocents from being slaughtered in their own homes, if everyone could sleep peacefully at night from now on, then I would do it. I would sacrifice myself for her.

I lifted my nose and howled to the moon, my heart aching.

Ares and I knew that it had to be done. This was the only way. We just wished we'd had more time with Aurora. We wished we could've had pups with her and watched them grow, becoming alphas and lunas themselves. But this was the hand that the Moon Goddess had dealt us.

Taking one last look back at Aurora, I smiled. *"I'll forever be yours, Kitten."*

Shooting forward and into the chaos, I weaved through

wolves and hounds and surveyed the woods for the one man that I needed to find to end this war. Ash rained down from the dark gray sky, a layer covering my brown fur.

My family. My friends. My pack.

The hounds were destroying all of it.

And they would try to take my mate, too, if I didn't stop it now. I couldn't hold back any longer, couldn't put this off a second more. I might not have been able to say good-bye to everyone I'd ever loved and cared for, but this had to be done. The world would be a better place.

"Stop it, Mars." Ares seethed at me inside my mind. *"Give me fucking control."*

I ignored him and spotted Fenris about to split a pup into pieces. Lurching forward, I knocked into the side of him and sent him flying against the tree. The pup scrambled to his feet and ran off, crying into the forest.

"Don't fucking do this, Mars," Ares said. *"You can't do this. You can't fight him alone."*

Refusing to listen to Ares, I roared at the man who had ruined my life over and over again. Fenris stood up, shook off the ash and dirt from his body, and growled back, his soulless black eyes fixed on me. Thick strands of saliva dripped from his bloodied canines.

When he leaped at me, I collapsed onto my stomach and waited for his attack.

The world seemed to slow, and all the memories I'd made with Aurora flashed through my mind, all the times she'd made me smile and the late-night pretzel-and-cheese feasts we'd had as Ruffles lounged at the foot of our bed, when she'd shifted for the first time in front of me, and when she had held me in the tub when Ares and I confessed everything to her.

I dug my claws into the dirt and bit back a howl, eyes filling with tears.

Fenris landed on my back, teeth ripping up fur and talons

stabbing into any unmarked part of my flesh that he could find. Tearing, jerking, tugging, twisting, slashing, slitting, scratching, and lacerating. All of me.

Unmoving, I squeezed my eyes closed, ignored the pain, and imagined what life would've been like if the hounds had never attacked us. Three months from now, Aurora and I would've welcomed our first pup into the world. We would've taught her how to run and shift and kick a boy's ass. And later on, we'd have been rocking on our porch chairs, gray hairs and all, watching the grand-pups play tag in the forest and sharing stories of our carefree younger days.

Fenris pierced his claws right through my heart. Blood spurted from my mouth. I closed my eyes one last time. All this would forever be lost in my hopes and dreams, as I would never live another day on this earth.

CHAPTER 35

AURORA

*S*lowly blinking my eyes open, I stared up at the tilted, flickering ceiling light that now hung a foot above my face. Blood smeared against the dented metal door, broken off its hinges. Every bone in my body seemed too heavy to move.

Nearly immobile, especially my neck, I curled my fingers around the edges of the table and glanced at the harrowing sight around me. Dead hounds, ripped couch, and Elijah. Broken glasses smudged with blood and bottom lip swollen and bloody, Elijah paced around the room and held his hand against the giant gash in his bare abdomen.

Using all my strength, I sat up and nearly screamed when I saw Dr. Farral in a puddle of his own blood with his face torn off and multiple slashes in his body. All my mind could seem to think about was finding my mate like that.

"Ares?" I asked, stepping down from the table. "Where is Ares?"

With wide eyes, Elijah hurried over and gently pushed me

back down. "Lie back down, Aurora. It's not safe for you to be up this quickly after surgery."

I shoved his shoulder but only pushed him a few inches before my arm unwillingly fell by my side, hitting the metal table with a thud. "Where is Ares?" I asked again, this time stronger. I scanned the room once more, hoping that I didn't find him in the bodies.

Elijah glanced at the chaos outside, and then grimaced.

Realization hitting me, I shook my head. "No," I whispered, trying to rise to my feet again, only to be held down by Elijah. I grasped his wrist to push him away. "No. I need to go find him. I need to make sure he's safe."

"You can't go out there," Elijah said, blood from his wound staining my pastel Luna Ceremony dress. "You need to stay here."

"I'm going out to find my mate!" I shouted, my limbs becoming lighter by the second and strength reverberating through my entire being. It must've been the stone's power because it couldn't have been mine. I had never felt this strong before.

I swung my feet off the table and took off toward the door.

"Aurora, you can't," Elijah said, grasping my wrist to pull me back.

Overcome with emotion, I shoved him. Flying back with incredible speed and force, he slammed against the metal table twice as hard as Ares had earlier. Doubling over, he clutched his stomach, the gash opening up even more.

He rolled onto his hands and knees with his head hung. "Aurora…"

Not knowing what to do, I stared at him and then down at my hands with wide eyes. *What was that? Did I just … did I do that? That was from … me?*

Wolves howled outside, their cries of despair and fear drifting through the quiet bunker. The alpha and luna inside of me ached to run into battle to protect my people, but the human side of me desperately wanted to help Elijah.

"Aurora, don't. Please, help me," Elijah begged. "Think about yourself if I'm not enough."

"Mate," my wolf whispered. *"Find our mate."*

Physically unable to ignore my wolf's pleas, I turned to the door. I wanted to stay to help him, but she wouldn't let me. She ached to find Ares, just to see him so we knew that he was okay and hadn't sacrificed himself for us.

"Aurora, you're pregnant!" Elijah shouted before I could leave.

I stopped, my heart racing. "What did you say?" I whispered over my shoulder.

With the help of the table, he stumbled to his feet and held his wound. "You're pregnant with a baby girl. My doctor found out right before the surgery. As far as I know, the baby made it through your death and resurrection successfully."

When he stepped toward me again, he stumbled into the wall, brown face paling. I grasped his arm and helped him to the nearest chair, taking off his cracked glasses so I could see his face. I couldn't believe what I was hearing. I didn't want to be pregnant now, not when we were in the middle of a war.

"Stitches? Bandages? Do you have anything?" I asked, scrambling to find something that could heal him. All the bags, boxes, and medication that Dr. Farral had brought had been emptied, hundreds of used rags covered in blood, orange pill bottles, gauze torn apart.

My thoughts raced so fast that I couldn't latch on to just one. Blood poured out of Elijah's abdomen faster than I could even comprehend. He was going to die because of me, because I couldn't control my emotions or my wolf.

Elijah shook his head, slowly closing his eyes, as if they were too heavy. "No. Nothing. We used everything we had on you."

I placed my hands over his, desperate to stop the blood as it pooled between our fingers and stained them sanguine. *This can't be happening. This really can't be fucking happening. I can't lose everyone important to me.*

"Aurora," Elijah whispered, holding his eyes open for a fraction of a second. "You're strong, but don't be stupid. Don't blindly go out there, looking for your mate. You won't find him. It's been hours, and he hasn't come back."

"No," I whispered, doubling over Elijah and refusing to believe it. I shouted at Ares through the mind link, hoping he'd answer me, but I heard nothing but silence. "No."

When his hand slipped from his torso, I screamed as loud as I could, making everything in the entire room shake. Power surging inside of me, I covered Elijah's wound with my trembling hands and curled my fingers into his skin.

Ares couldn't be gone. I needed that man more than I needed anything in my entire fucking life. We were going to have a baby. My belly was full with his pup, and now ... now, Elijah was telling me that Ares was gone. *Gone?*

A few moments later, Elijah opened his eyes, glanced down at his waist, and then back up at me. "Goddess ... Goddess, Aurora, you're healing me," he whispered.

The skin under my fingers started repairing itself, stretching across his abdomen and sealing up his wound. My eyes widened, head swaying from side to side, and suddenly, I collapsed on top of him, totally out of breath and my vision blurry.

Oh my Goddess.

What the hell was that? Was this really the power of the stone?

Trying to regain my composure, I furrowed my brows. "What's happening to me?"

Elijah scooped me up into his arms and laid me back down on the table. "I need you to stay here a little longer," he whispered, grabbing the doctor's notebook and scribbling some notes in it. "You're probably going to be dizzy and weak for a bit. Your powers are going to take some time to get used to at first. You can't be using them on just anyone and everyone."

I stared out the door and into the chaos. Sometime during the surgery, the dawn had begun, streaks of pink and yellows stretching through the sky, the colors so soft and warm, contrasting with the cold, dark blood covering Sanguine Wilds like a sheet of snow.

"I need to find Ares. Come with me to find him. Please, Elijah."

After glancing between me and the outside, he placed the notebook down and helped me off the table. "Only because I know that you'll go anyway. But if I tell you that we need to come back, then we will. Don't try to stop me from protecting you. Think of Jeremy. He'd have wanted you to be smart about this."

Jeremy.

He'd died for me and for this.

Agreeing, I ran outside and into the chaos, Elijah right by my side in his human form. Hounds and wolves sprinted in front of us, leaping over dead bodies and attacking each other's necks. Elijah pulled me out of the way and into his chest, his hand over my stomach almost instinctively.

I gulped and leaned into him, inches from a hound's canines. As the hound found another wolf to attack, Elijah ushered me forward.

I enclosed my hand around his and squeezed. "Sorry about earlier. I was so overcome with emotion that I didn't think twice about hurting you."

Elijah shook his head. "It's okay. He's your mate."

"But you're one of my best friends."

Pausing, Elijah stared at me for a couple moments and gave me a soft smile, and then he shoved me to the ground and shielded me with his body as another hound hurtled toward us. He swiped his claws across the hound's neck.

Instead of waiting for him to die, Elijah continued forward. "Come on. We don't have much longer. We need to find him."

Bodies littered the forest, so many carcasses of pack members, the stone people, and the hounds. My heart ached for everyone because while the hounds were vicious, in their first lives, they had probably just been innocent people. They hadn't asked to become undead with a certain necromancer forcing them under his control.

"There are so many people," I whispered, chest tightening.

About half a mile east, Marcel fought two hounds by himself to protect a cowering Charolette. I started toward him, wondering if he knew where Ares or his body was, but before I could even make it three steps, a hound leaped into the air, slashed his teeth into my arm, and forced me to collapse.

Within a moment, I shifted into my wolf with ease—the feeling of being free again rushing through my veins like adrenaline—and ripped my claws into his underbelly until he went still underneath me.

When I glanced back, Marcel was gone. I shifted into my human again, the gashes in my arm healing almost instantly. Elijah snatched my shoulder and scolded me for not letting him handle that hound, but it'd felt so natural. It was my first instinct to protect myself and my friends.

As we hurried through more of the war, my eyes landed on Ruffles. With fur matted in blood and a small gash in her side, Ruffles looked stronger and calmer than even *I* felt. Like troopers, Ruffles and Pringle ran through the chaos to find pups that I hadn't, sank their little teeth into the kids' hands, and pulled them toward another hideout.

I sprinted to her and scooped her up in my arms. Though she turned around to hiss, she immediately saw me and wrapped her paws around my shoulders, burying her face into the crook of my neck.

After Elijah grabbed the stranded pups, we sprinted to another hideaway, where seven pups were already huddled together in the corner of the room. Some of them reached out for me, calling for Luna, but I told them that I had to go. I couldn't stay. We had to leave, and we had to leave now to protect them.

"Ruffles," I said, crouching down to her level.

She put her paws on my knees and looked up at me with wide black eyes, her pupils dilated.

I patted her back. "You have to stay here with everyone. Keep them safe. Don't let any hounds through that door." I pointed up the ladder and at the metal hatch. "Do you understand?"

She licked my nose and brushed her face against mine. "*Meow.*"

After tugging her to my chest again and promising her that I'd be back, I followed Elijah up the ladder and locked the hatch door. I hurried with Elijah through the hundreds of wolves, desperate to find Ares and Mars, dead or alive.

I would not hide in the bunkers, knowing that I didn't do everything in my power to help him. But I had to be careful because it was more than just me who I had to protect. I had a pup ... a freaking pup ... and Ares wouldn't forgive me if I put his life over our girl's.

To my left, fire raged from the pack house and spread through the forest and to the town, a thick layer of smoke settling over the woods. I surveyed my surroundings, catching The Flaming Chariot burning but without the horse statues out front. Someone must've knocked them down during the battle.

As we sprinted through the clash, I ached to help my pack. But every time I veered off course, Elijah would pull me back and remind me of the only reason we had come out here—to find Ares. And when I found him, I stopped.

Standing on the other side of the forest was a god. And not just any god.

The god of war.

Gore seeped down the side of his fur, coating and matting it to his body. Saliva dripped from his bloody red teeth. Those eyes were a dark agony, a furious gold, tinted with crimson-red fury.

My mate was alive and, somehow, looked stronger than ever, moving with the speed and agility of a god.

Fighting Fenris, Ares snatched him by the neck with his teeth. Fenris had always seemed a bit stronger and smarter than us but now looked rather weak. What was giving Ares this power? I'd seen him fight before, just not like this.

Ares ripped Fenris into two pieces, right down the center of his body, splitting his fur, his flesh, and his bones in almost symmetrical bits. My heart pounded so loud that I could hear it in my ears, and I gasped.

Holy Goddess ... when the fuck did he get so strong?

Grabbing one half of Fenris's body, Ares went to rip him into more tiny pieces when a whirling fiery-orange portal with black flames opened up behind him. A woman dressed in a skintight blood-red metallic suit with eight metal horns protruding from her head at all angles stepped out of it and stood behind Ares with such evil intent.

Certain that I had seen her face before, I sprinted toward them at lightning speed. She drew a sharp horn from her head like a sword and aimed it at Ares's back. My dawn-colored dress blew behind me in the wind, almost holding me back.

"Ares!" I screamed, but the world around us was so loud that he must not have heard me.

As she was about to slice the blade into his back, I thrust my hands into her side and sent her flying back against one of the trees. She hit it with a thud, the entire tree cracking and toppling over into the forest, hitting others.

Elijah called my name, telling me to come back to him as he ran toward me, but I couldn't let my mate be killed by whoever this was. Ares turned around, dropped Fenris on the ground, and shifted into his human, wrapping his arms around my waist.

"What the fuck are you doing here?" Ares said. "I love you, but ... you shouldn't be here."

"You ripped Fenris in two," I said in shock. "What happened to you?"

Guilt washed over his face, but he shook his head. "Now is not the time for that," he said, but the words sounded a bit too ... weak. Ares pushed me behind him. "We have bigger problems than that."

CHAPTER 36

AURORA

"*D*awn," the woman said to me, staring me down.

Why'd she think *I* was Dawn? And why the hell was she after Dawn?

She seethed with a scowl, stood up from the debris, and dusted the dirt off her red metallic bodysuit. She glared in our direction, fury raging in her haunting, dead eyes.

I stepped in front of Ares, but he harshly pulled me back. "Don't."

Pointing her fingers at Fenris, she whispered something to him in Latin or Greek or some ancient language that seemed distantly familiar. Though I couldn't understand it right now, my mind raced with a thousand different thoughts.

Like magic, Fenris's wolf body merged back together, his soulless black eyes similar to the other hounds. My heart pounded even harder in my chest.

Holy fuck. This was Hella, the necromancer who Medusa had

told us about, the woman who could bring someone back from the dead with a sway of her fingers.

How could we defeat someone this powerful?

I rested a hand over my tightening stomach, almost instinctively, my head spinning slightly. Elijah hurried to me and tugged on my hand, but I didn't budge. What was the point if we were all going to die anyway? I'd rather stay here and fight than surrender to or hide from evil like her.

Hella stepped forward, lips tucked in a grimace. "I thought we got rid of you over two hundred years ago," she said, flicking her forked tongue in my direction.

A second later, Hella sprang into the air, grasped two of her horns that turned into sharp blades, and lurched down toward us so quickly that we didn't have any time to react.

Just before she hit us, a man on a golden chariot, led by flaming horses, flew through the air and knocked her back down and into the woods, his body burning almost as brightly as the sun. Fenris leaped at him, but the man in gold dodged the attack and landed his chariot in front of us.

"Leave her, Hella," he ordered the woman, hopping off his chariot and standing in front of me. "You took her from me once. You won't take her twice."

Hella laughed lifelessly and met his glare. "You think this is over?"

Ares grabbed my hand and pulled me back a step. *"We have to get out of here."*

"This war is far from over," Hella said with a smirk. "But I'm sure you know that after what happened to Dawn centuries ago, by the one and only *Nyx*."

At the mention of the name Nyx, the golden man shot a ray of light through his fingers at Hella. She swiftly dodged the attack, the light burning through a row of trees behind her until they were incinerated.

"Nyx," I whispered.

Suddenly, in bits and pieces, almost-sharp fragments … the memories came flooding back to me. Nyx was the last name I had said before something terrible happened, but I'd never said that name before—at least, not in this lifetime. Maybe this stone belonged to someone else, or … Nyx had been in my dreams before.

So many new faces and names, I couldn't quite comprehend any of it. These were real gods, no doubt, who held extraordinary abilities. But what did any of this have to do with me? Who were these gods? And why the hell were they fighting on earth?

The golden man tilted his head toward me. "Sacrifices need to be made." After glancing back at Ares and Elijah behind me, he clenched his jaw. "Sometime soon, you will need to make the hardest decision of your life, just like I did. It's a fight between life and death. Now, go, Dawn."

"Why do people keep calling me that?" I asked.

I had too many questions that I needed answered. What was going on? Why was Hella after me? How the fuck hadn't the hounds died after Ares killed Fenris? How could we stop gods who could just rebuild their armies over and over again?

Ares snatched me in his arms and ran through the chaos, yelling at his warriors and Vulcan to retreat to the underground bunkers as soon as possible. Warriors ran away from the hounds and headed toward underground shelters, pushing through the smoke and fire, as the stone warriors continued to fight.

Ares and Elijah separated, deciding to each protect a shelter with pups.

Setting me down, Ares banged twice on the metal door and shouted, "It's Ares and Aurora. Let us in."

A few moments later, the door opened, and pups stared up at us with huge eyes. Sniffling and shaking, they cried out for us to come save them. Ruffles and Pringle stood in the middle of them all, rubbing against their legs.

Starting down the ladder, I stopped and glanced back into the mess, making eye contact with the golden man. He watched me intently as he held off the beasts, and then he shifted his gaze beside us.

"Go, my dear," someone said from beside me. Dressed in her green veil and tunic, Medusa stepped out of the smoky shadows and urged Ares to start his descent into the bunker. "He won't be able to hold the hounds in this forest much longer. If you don't go now, there is no saying what will happen."

Needing to keep my people safe, I hurried down the steps. Whatever the cost of protecting the pups, the warriors, and my mate, I would pay it. At least we'd be safe down here for a while as everything went to hell above.

Ares closed the door and locked it above us. When I made it down, I leaned against the side of the room and took deep, unsteady breaths. Tears welled up in my eyes from the sheer amount of commotion and anxiety running through me, but I refused to let any fall. I needed to be strong for the pups as they crowded around us, wrapping their arms around our legs and telling us how scared they were down here, all alone.

Hounds howled viciously from above, trees cracking and striking the ground in thunderous roars. I pressed my lips together and vowed to calm my own racing heart, so I could be sane for these pups. The entire time, I told myself to be strong, that they didn't deserve this misery, that hiding out here was all for them. I'd do whatever I could to keep them safe.

"Are you ready to have some more of those therapy sessions?" I whispered to Ares twenty minutes later, trying to lighten the mood. But I wasn't joking. "Because I think we're all going to need them after this."

The catastrophe would scar every one of us, and this was just the beginning. If Medusa and the golden man couldn't defeat the hounds, we'd be here without any protection. We'd be weak and vulnerable. Many of our warriors were injured or dead by now.

How were we supposed to survive?

A loud *whoosh* echoed through the earth above us, followed by a deafening silence. My chest tightened for a moment, and I inhaled deeply, trying to find solace in Ares's hazelnut scent. The world sounded too quiet, and I wondered if they had all died.

Was it safe to come out now?

"Did anyone hear that?" Marcel asked through the mind link from another underground hideout.

"Don't go out until we know that everything is safe. Wait at least an hour. If there isn't anything, then we'll go," Ares commanded.

After waiting for fifteen more minutes, Ares turned to me, jaw clenched. "Who is that golden man?"

"He seems familiar, but I don't know how I know him."

Ares rested his hand on my thigh and squeezed tightly. "He knows you. You seem ... *special* ... to him."

"This is not the time to be jealous, Ares. He means nothing to me. I don't know who he is," I snapped, my fingers tingling. I glanced down to see them glowing slightly and curled them into fists to stop whatever it was that was happening to me.

Knowing I shouldn't have snapped, I looked back toward him and inched closer. "Ares ..." I whispered. "I'm sorry. Just so much has happened within the past twenty-four hours. You killed the man you'd wanted to kill for years. I have this stone in my back. We—"

"For what?" Ares interrupted me, voice teetering in anger. "So many of my wolves died today."

"We lost a lot of wolves, but you killed Fenris... at least who he was. I don't know what happens now that Hella raised him from the dead."

"Nothing good comes of this," Ares whispered, voice fading into the blackness of the bunker. "I wasted my life on that fucking asshole, only to find out that the hounds don't die with him. Medusa lied to us."

"What are you talking about?" I asked, brows furrowed. "You're alive and well, Ares."

As the pups whimpered from beside us, Ares spoke up again, "I wasn't going after Fenris only for my mom." He took my hand and squeezed it. "My pack was cursed a long time ago. The leader of the hounds was to take a luna of this pack. My dad said that the only way to get rid of the threat and break the curse was to sacrifice an alpha."

"Sacrifice an alpha."

Why was this the first I was hearing about this? Was that why he was so powerful? Did he sacrifice someone? Maybe his father, who had once been an alpha?

But still, I didn't understand where he was going with this. He couldn't have sacrificed anyone or anything to kill Fenris. He'd killed him on his own with his two bare hands. Elijah and Vulcan were the only other alphas here, and they were still alive.

"You'll hate me for this," Ares whispered, words raw and full of regret.

I tucked bloody strands of hair behind his ear. "I couldn't hate you, Ares, ever."

While I had seen Mars as an emotional wreck, I had never seen Ares that way until now.

He stared at me with tears in his deep brown eyes, lips quivering. "I thought it would stop everything. I was doing it for you and for our little girl ..." He curled up next to me, placing his head into the crook of my neck, right near Mars's mark. "Mars sacrificed himself. I couldn't stop him, Aurora."

My throat closed up. "M-Mars?"

Ares curled into me even more, grasping my hips and trying to muffle his cries in front of the children. "I didn't want him to do it," he cried, body heaving back and forth. "I wanted to protect you. He thought it-it'd stop this. Now, he's gone. Forever."

CHAPTER 37

AURORA

*S*tupidly, I believed that after a couple moments, Ares would crack a smile and admit that this was all one big, terrible joke and that he could still feel Mars. But Ares always had been the serious, hotheaded, possessive alpha who didn't tell jokes for fun.

Mars was gone.

Mars was really gone.

Burying my face into my hands, I bit my lip and wept silently until I couldn't hold back. I hiccuped and trembled back and forth, not wanting to believe that part of me had departed from this earth. How was I going to live without Mars? How was *Ares* going to live without Mars? They had been together for over a decade, and while they'd hated each other, they'd also loved each other.

They'd lived in the same body after all.

After two hours of silence from above and muffling my cries

so the pups wouldn't get nervous, I grabbed Ares's face. "It's going to be okay," I murmured to him, stroking his blotchy, tearstained cheeks and praying that the emptiness in my heart would disappear.

But who really knew if anything would be okay after this?

"Be strong," I whispered, brushing my knuckles over his cheekbones and knowing that neither one of us could be strong at the moment. "We need to get through this for our pack. We can talk more about it later, but the pups and our pack need us."

He grasped my hand tightly and leaned into it. "Do you hate me?" he whispered, lips quivering. "I would hate me if I were you. I would fucking hate me for trading his life instead of my own. I give you so much pain, so much hurt. You'd rather be with him."

"You don't give me pain, Ares. I know who you are deep down," I said, resting my forehead against his. "But right now, I need you to be that strong man that you always are. We have a pack to lead, people to protect, and a pup to raise."

Running a hand over my stomach, he let out another heartbreaking sob. I rubbed his shoulders, his arms, his chest, and his thighs, hoping it'd calm him down. I was asking him to be strong after the closest person to him had just died.

After ten more minutes, he took a deep breath, wiped the tears from his cheeks, and nodded. *"Marcel,"* he said through the mind link, though his words shook slightly. *"You're with the warriors?"*

"Yes," Marcel said almost instantly.

"Go check the surrounding area. Make sure it's safe for the pups to come out. I'm not opening these doors until I know they're safe," Ares said strongly, yet I could feel the pain inside him, sinking its claws into his veins and dispersing through his body like wildfire.

The mind link silenced, footsteps sounding above us.

"Ares," Marcel said, *"everything is secure, but you need to see this. Now."*

Ares climbed the ladder and unlocked the bunker door, pushing it open. After promising the pups that we'd be back soon, I hopped out after him and closed the bunker door, following Ares. With raging fires, fallen trees, and thick smoke, our pack lay in ruins.

I covered my nose and waved some smoke from the air, gasping when I saw the stone people. Every single warrior from the mountain who had fought with us were frozen in rock again, the wolf warriors all in fighting stances.

But neither the hounds nor Hella and Fenris were here anymore.

Did that mean that they were in this forest with us? Or maybe they were just dead.

Walking farther onto the property, I frowned at the golden man standing with his flaming chariot, the horses captured in stone but their wings still ignited in fire. My fingers glided across the man's stony face, and I frowned at him.

Where was he? Why was he gone? And who was he to me?

"Fuck," Vulcan said, approaching me and Ares from behind. "I've never seen anything like this." He glanced around at our pack, who wept over fallen loved ones or had started healing each other with salvaged bandages and medicine from the pharmacy. "Whatever you two need, I can supply it. I'm here to fight for this for however long it takes. Warriors. Food. Housing. You got it."

After thanking Vulcan, I glanced at Ares and then at all the destroyed buildings. We needed all the help we could get because this war was just starting. And I couldn't see an end in sight.

Vulcan ordered his warriors to put out the fires and to burn the bodies, so the pups wouldn't see their dead parents. Before running off after them to help, Vulcan placed a hand on each of our shoulders. "I'll get more packs to join us. When they hear of what happened, they'll fight, no matter what. I'll make sure of it."

When he disappeared through the smoke, I turned to Ares,

who hid his hurt behind a stoic expression. I grasped his cheeks and turned him to face me. "We can't stay here, Ares. We should take Vulcan up on his offer, or we should go to my mother's. Her pack house is empty. There aren't nearly enough houses in her pack for us, and it might be a bit crammed, but it's the only place that isn't in ruins right now."

Ares stared at me with ferocity in his eyes, but then he wrapped his arms around me and pulled me into a hug. "I understand if you hate me for what I did. I take full responsibility for it. But I just want you to know that I'll never leave you. I'll always protect you. I'll always love you. We'll go to your mother's pack house and start over."

"Last box," Elijah said, plopping a moving box onto the kitchen table and slumping down in a seat. One week had passed since the hound attack, and we had slowly started to adjust to this new normal life. He blew out a sigh. "This sucks for you guys."

"Actually, *this* is the last one," Adrian said, setting another box next to his. He placed a hand on Elijah's shoulder and squeezed. "Why don't we get out of here and give Ares and Aurora some space and time to rest?"

"Adrian," I called before they left my old and now-new pack house. "We need to talk about rebuilding the pack and securing it soon. I know it's only been a week, but I don't know when those hounds will be back. We should focus our energy here and on reconstructing the underground tunnels, so they're more stable."

After Adrian nodded to me, they walked out of the pack house, hand in hand.

Sitting down on the couch beside Ares, I rested my head against his shoulder as Marcel and Charolette walked into the house next.

With his arms around her waist and his face buried into the

crook of her neck, Marcel whispered something into Charolette's ear and made her giggle like a crazy person.

When she saw us, she fanned her flushed cheeks and smiled. "We just finished getting the pups situated with everyone. On the bad side, about half of their parents had died, but thankfully, a lot of families were willing to take them in."

Marcel nodded to Ares. "Which room are we staying in?"

Grumbling to himself about not wanting Charolette and Marcel sleeping together, Ares stood. "Two doors down from us, in Aurora's old room." He eyed Marcel's hands on Charolette's waist and growled. "But don't push it with her, or you'll end up outside."

Once they disappeared down the hallway, I led Ares to my parents' old room to rest. Ruffles and Pringle sat on the comforter in a ray of sunlight, snuggled up close to each other, Pringle's head on Ruffles's growing tummy. I had a sneaky suspicion that she was pregnant with little kitties.

Kicking the door closed with his foot, Ares gripped my waist and set me on the other side of the bed. Ever since the hound attack, Ares had become much gentler with me. I didn't know if he was being cautious about our baby or was trying to make up for the fact that Mars was gone and that he blamed himself for it.

He pushed me back on the bed, his lips traveling down the column of my neck to my chest, and undid the buttons of my shirt to pull it apart. I stared up at him, watching his hot, soft mouth run over my breasts, as if he needed to prove himself.

I trailed my fingers down his back and moaned when he brushed his thumbs over my hardened nipples through my bra. "Ares," I whispered, back arching.

He pressed his hardness against my pussy, and I clenched.

"You don't have to be gentle. I know that's not who you are."

"Kitten, let me do this *for you.*"

He brushed his teeth against one of my nipples, delicately sucking on it and making me moan out loud again. Heat rushed to my core, and I swallowed hard as he slipped a finger into my pants and rubbed my clit through my underwear.

My toes curled, a wave of pleasure shooting through me. I reached down between my legs and stroked my hand against the bulge in his pants. He slipped his fingers into my pussy and thrust them in and out in a rougher, more rhythmic fashion.

"Goddess, please, Ares," I whispered, eyes rolling back in my head. "Please, don't be gentle with me right now. I want to feel pain. I want it to hurt—"

"You like this, Kitten," he said quietly, fingers nestled inside of me, hitting my G-spot and driving me closer to the edge.

He pressed his lips to mine and bent his fingers over and over until my body trembled under his. I grasped his wrist, my heels digging into the mattress, trying so hard to scramble to the head-board. But he held me in place as the pleasure hit me in waves.

My body tingled, and I stared up into his golden-brown eyes. The red had faded from them over a week ago, and I hadn't seen him that rageful since the attack. He slowly pulled his wet fingers out of me and stuck them into his mouth, groaning at the taste.

"Kitten," he murmured, lying back on the bed and pulling me on top.

I pulled his cock out of his pants, desperate to have it inside of me, and tugged up my skirt, positioning him at my entrance. Maybe this wasn't the best way to make things better, but it sure did make us feel good on the inside for a few moments.

Lowering myself onto him, I let him fill my pussy. He dug his fingers into my hips and smiled up at me. For a split second, I thought I saw Mars in his eyes, but I must've been seeing things because there was nothing but heartache, pain, and love for me within them.

He slowly pumped into me, though I knew he wanted to make it faster, make it rough, make it feel so good for him that he forgot about all of his agony for a few moments.

I grabbed his hand and snaked it around my neck. "Harder,

Ares," I said. "Take me. Really fucking take me. Let go of the pain for a couple minutes."

After hesitating, he wrapped his fingers tighter around my throat, strumming them, and started to pound into me hard from below. The pain faded from his face, the heartbreak gone. I dug my fingers into his chest and let him take me even harder, the heat gathering in my core.

"Yes," I whispered, about to tip over the edge. "Harder."

Ares pulled me back down to him, captured my nipple in his mouth, and sucked hard on it. Pleasure rushed out of me, and I relaxed into his arms, eyes rolling back. After he came inside of me, I moved off his chest and stared up at the ceiling.

So many thoughts rushed through my mind, but I could only seem to focus on the ones about the hounds. "We need to prepare for divine war," I whispered to him, brushing some dark brown hair from his face. "We need more packs to get on board with this. We need to create alliances."

He wrapped his strong arms around my body and pulled me closer to him. When he'd told me that Mars was gone, part of me hadn't wanted to believe him, but after a week of not even seeing a glimpse of him, reality slowly set in. Having Mars gone hurt him as much as it hurt me. They had spent years together, and while they might've not liked each other ... they were still closer than anyone could be with someone.

"How are you feeling?" I whispered, forgoing the hound conversation for now. "Are you okay?"

"Sometimes, I think he's coming back to me," Ares whispered. "... but I haven't felt him. I don't think he's coming back. He left before he could see our pup." He ran a hand over my stomach. "But I'm going to be there for you every step of the way, and I vow to protect you forever."

I rested my head on his chest and listened to his heartbeat.

Little did we know that this war was going to be bigger than we'd ever imagined, taking us to places we never thought we could go and forcing us to make decisions we'd sworn we'd never make.

Continued in Forever Yours, Kitten

Read Forever Yours, Kitten here: https://books2read. com/u/3LY7LJ

ALSO BY EMILIA ROSE

Forever Yours, Kitten: https://books2read.com/u/3LY7LJ

Submitting to the Alpha: https://books2read.com/u/4N9Bd6

Alpha Maddox: https://books2read.com/u/bPXP8l

Nyx: https://books2read.com/u/bzg58q

ABOUT THE AUTHOR

Emilia Rose is an international bestselling author of steamy paranormal romance. With over 3,000 monthly subscribers on Patreon and over 18 million story views online, Emilia loves creating the newest and sexiest paranormal romances for her fans.

ACKNOWLEDGMENTS

Credit to Barbara Russell for the suggestion of Pringles!